PINYON CREEK, CALIFORNIA

A Novel of the California Water Wars

by

ELSA PENDLETON

PINYON CREEK, CALIFORNIA

Chapter I - Entering Owens Valley

Spence Richardson, eighteen years old, too tall for the pony he was riding, entered the town of Pinyon Creek, California, on a brilliantly sunny, breezy May morning, looking for work.

The Owens Valley was rich in silver and somewhat less rich in gold, but also held quantities of other minerals including some for which nobody had yet figured a use. It had running streams, several lakes of various sizes, snow in the winter and the burning desert heat in the summer. To the West, the Eastern side of the Sierra rose almost vertically in ripples of peaks impassible to most travelers. On the Eastern side of the valley the White mountains looked deceptively smoother. The road North led to Reno and to the stage road to the rich Nevada gold and silver mines, then eventually to San Francisco. The road South – well, there was no road South, only the faint trails used by mule teams, trails which were brushed away by every passing dust storm or gullywasher. If you came to Pinyon Creek, chances were you stayed in Pinyon Creek.

The town was going great guns, mills pounding and mines on the hillsides resembling anthills or gopher holes. Pinyon Creek was a one-street town, the stores and offices lining both sides behind a rickety wooden sidewalk. Most of the businesses were open as Spence rode in, with men and occasionally a woman walking briskly from one place to another. Behind the hotel, a forest of bedsheets waved from clotheslines.

Spence headed for the offices of Nadeau Freighting. As he clopped down the street, he could see that one of the mule trains was preparing to depart. A dozen mules stood quietly in their harness as the last preparations were finished and the driver climbed aboard. Then, harness bells jingling, they trotted past Spence and headed South to the mule trails. Spence tied his pony to the rail and entered the office. A burly man, sleeves rolled up, sat behind a battered wooden desk sorting papers. He scraped the papers into a neat pile and closed the deep desk drawer.

"Yes?"

"Mr. Nadeau," Spence began, "I'm looking for a job."

"Sorry, son, Mr. Nadeau is retired. Hasn't been here for a year now. My name's Finch. How can I help you?"

"Uh, Mr. Finch, I came to Pinyon Creek to get a job with your mule company."

"You did, eh? What do you know about mules?"

"I know a fair amount, sir. When I was growing up, we had a mule, Betsy. She would do just about everything she could for us. Then when we had -- when times changed -- we had to sell her and we moved to Long Beach and then I saw the mule trains and..." Spence realized he was speaking faster and louder and tried to

4

make himself slow down. "I want to learn how to drive the big mule trains and work with mules."

Finch smiled. "Most people come to Pinyon Creek to mine gold, son. Or silver. They have in mind to make their fortunes. You don't make a fortune working mules, but you probably already figured that out. Why mules? Why not horses?"

"Well, horses, they, they don't seem to care. They'll do what you want, but it's like they're reall thinking about going back into the field to eat grass. Mules, now, mules let you know what they're thinking. You get to work with a mule, he'll work with you." Spence stopped, feeling foolish. "I guess that doesn't make much sense."

"Oh, it makes sense to me," Finch replied. "But then, I work with mules every day. Well, son, I hate to disappoint you, but we're not taking anybody on right now. If you're really interested, here's my advice. Get a job here in Pinyon Creek -- there are plenty of mines looking for workers. Check back, say, once a week. Next time we have an opening we'll consider you."

Spence felt his throat tighten. He had never considered that he wouldn't get this job. "But I don't know anything at all about mining."

Finch stood, suddenly tired of the conversation. "Go to any of the bigger mines -- Ophir, Aurora, Cascade -- and ask for work. Or check with the assay office. They'll know who is busy right now. Or just ask around. And don't worry about not knowing mining. You don't need to know anything. You just need to handle a rock pick or pull a wagon."

"Thank you, sir," Spence said, and closed the door softly behind him.

Outside on the street activity had picked up even more. A stage coach outside the general store was discharging passengers, packages and mail packets. Dusty miners were coming and going. The bedsheets had disappeared from the back of the hotel, reminding Spence that he needed a place to stay. He set about learning the town.

He started in the general store, dark and crowded with people and merchandise. The shopkeeper was so busy he seemed to be a blur, as he accepted mail and packages, wrapped purchases, called out instructions to his small helper who was gathering items for a tall woman holding a baby. Clearly, he was not to be interrupted.

Returning outside, Spence spied a couple of miners sitting on the edge of the sidewalk drinking something from dark glass bottles. They looked much more approachable.

"Excuse me," Spence said, "I'm new here and I'm looking for a job. Somebody suggested I try one of the mines. How do I do that?"

The two men glanced at each other, then turned to examine Spence. Under his broad-brimmed hat his face, freckled, with a feathering of beard, gave away his youth. His overalls, washed until most of the blue had faded to gray, met boots with worn-down heels.

The older miner looked from Spence to the pony. "You come here on that, that animal?"

"Yes."

"Pretty short horse."

"She's strong. We get along."

"You know, they don't allow horses up in the mines." The miner glanced sideways at his partner.

"That's right," the second man agreed solemnly. "Horses kick up too much dust. And they fall down mine shafts. And they make way too much noise. Can't take a horse like that into a mine works. Nope."

"First, you'll have to sell that horse," said the first miner. "Probably won't get much, seeing as horses aren't allowed in mines. Probably nobody would want an animal that short, anyway. If I was you, I wouldn't even look for a job until I got rid of that short horse."

"He's probably going to have to buy some tools, too, if he wants to work in the mines. Miners got to bring their own tools."

"But no horses. Just tools." The two men stared at Spence, assessing his reaction. Spence tried to look as impassive as possible. By now a few more men had joined the group.

"I wouldn't pay for that animal," said one of them. "But I would take him off your hands. Might give you a brightwick for him, even."

"Oh, come on, I'd go a brightwick and a touselhammer," another chimed in.

"He doesn't need a touselhammer, you dolt. He needs an ironfiddle and a cowpin."

"If he goes into the Aurora diggings, he's going to need a brightwick AND a touselhammer AND an ironfiddle."

Spence's head was spinning. He knew what he had to do but he was too tired and disappointed and confused to do anything except stand quietly.

"Now about that short horse," the first miner said, standing up from his perch to circle the pony, "I think I'll just take it along now. You surely won't need it any more."

The group pressed in, waiting for the action. Mr. Finch opened his door, stepped out and stood quietly, watching.

"Sorry, mister," Spence. "I'll be keeping my pony. But I thank you for all your advice."

For a minute he thought he had succeeded. The first miner backed up a step while Spence began to untie the halter. But then he stepped forward again.

"I don't think I made myself clear, young man. I told you I'm taking your horse."

Spence sighed, looped the halter around the rail, took off his hat and laid it on the pony's back, stepped forward and swung. He had just spent a year forking hay into ricks, working long hours on his family's failing farm, and he landed a blow which sent the miner flying back against the sidewalk and into the dirt. He replaced his hat, untied the pony and nodded to the silent group.

"I'll be saying good bye now, unless somebody can tell me which mines are hiring." He began to lead the pony through the group and up the street, wondering where, in fact, he was going to go. The miner had regained his feet, brushing himself off, muttering darkly. The rest of the group was dispersing. Spence walked as slowly as possible, hoping something would happen before he reached the edge of the town. Pinyon Creek's main street was only one long block, and he was within three shops of the end, when he heard quick footsteps and a man's voice.

"Hey, hold up there." It was one of the men who had been watching. "You did pretty well there. How about joining me? I'm going to get some lunch. You can tell me about yourself. I might just have some work for you."

The hotel dining room was noticeably cooler than outdoors, the chairs were well-worn but comfortable, and the tablecloths, though darned and stained, had originally been thickly woven and white.

"I'll have my usual steak and beans," the stranger told the waiter, "and the same for my new young friend here."

"Thank you, sir," Spence said. "I'm a bit short of cash right now..."

"Everybody who comes into Pinyon Creek is short of cash by the time they get here," the stranger laughed. "My name's Gilmartin, Roger Gilmartin, and I'm a shift manager at the New Coso mine, not far from here. Finch just told me you're interested in mules. Is that right?"

"Word travels fast, lucky for me," Spence replied. "Yes, that's how I got here. I saw the Nadeau teams and they are just... just remarkable. I've farmed with mules all my life. If I could learn how to drive a mule train..."

"If you love mules so much, how'd you end up on that pony?"

"Won her in a card game last week in Mojave. I'm planning to sell her here, but I want to pick my time and my buyer myself."

Gilmartin nodded. "Hazing the newcomer is expected, but Rolly went too far. He's a mean one."

The steaks were large and sizzling and the beans were soft and sweet. A dish of jalapeno peppers and a plate of bread accompanied the meat. Spence forced himself to eat slowly; it had been awhile since he had had a real meal.

Gilmartin continued. "We need a couple of hands at the mine, mostly mucking and trucking. You probably don't even know what that means, do you?"

"No, sir. But I'm ready for anything, just about."

"The best part for you is that we use mules at the mine. Not like Nadeau did, of course -- nobody ever matched him. But it's a place where you'll learn to handle mules for packing and hauling, different from pulling a plow. We pay normal wages and there's a bunkhouse where the crew eats and sleeps. Are you interested?"

"Yes, Sir," Spence responded enthusiastically.

"Good. Don't sell the pony yet. You'll get along ok up at the mine and payday isn't far away."

They packed their animals, Gilmartin stowing several sacks in his packsaddle and Spence tying three bags on top of his bedroll on the pony. In the hot late afternoon sun they walked their horses down Pinyon Creek's main street and south along the dirt road. Before long a dusty dirt trail turned off east and they followed it, climbing slowly through scrub grass and creosote bushes.

"Pony have a name?" Gilmartin asked idly.

"Nope." Spence thought for awhile. "What was the name of that guy? The one who was after her?"

"Rolly."

"Think that's what I'll call the pony."

Although the trail seemed to meander along a flat valley floor, they were reaching the hills. Spence turned around and was surprised to see Pinyon Creek below him. Ahead, the trail turned and began to climb more noticeably. After several switchbacks they were once again on level ground, where a small collection of tents and shacks had been erected.

"Welcome to New Coso, Spence. You'll bunk in that larger building, down at the end. Harry!" Gilmartin called.

A short, bearded man in faded plaid shirt and jeans gave a wave and hurried over.

"Harry, want you to meet Spence, our newest hire. He'll be mucking and packing some, plus whatever else you need. Spence, unpack the gear and help Harry stow everything and he'll show you the ropes."

Spence could hear activity from inside the mine, although the opening was only a wood-timbered hole, the size of a man, against the side of a hill. Pounding, hammering, and the occasional shout mixed with above-ground noises of animals and people. Spence saw to his relief that the corral held several mules in addition to a half dozen horses.

Early the next morning, Spence twisted cautiously in his bedroll, suddenly wide awake. It always took him awhile to feel his way around a new place, and this room, with a half-dozen men close together, was trickier than most. He could hear soft noises outdoors as Cook began to prepare breakfast. A horse nickered.

Spence considered what he had learned so far. Harry had been helpful, happy to have somebody to talk to, somebody to teach. New Coso had started with gold, Harry had said, then when the gold played out there was a lucky rich ledge of silver which was still going pretty strong. There were other minerals here, too, even some that nobody knew what to do with, or how to process. That, according to Harry, was the really interesting part of the job. He was learning to assay minerals and appreciated having a helper -- it would give him more time for his study.

Spence would be spending much of his time just carrying stuff from one place to another. Once you got the feel of the place, the mine site was fairly orderly, and part of his job was to keep it that way His back and leg muscles already reminded him how out of shape he had become.

Spence quickly settled into the work routine at the mine. Pushing a wheelbarrow, he moved mounds of rocks from the mine shaft to the ever-growing heaps of tailings at the outskirts of the settlement. He occasionally envied the miners who disappeared down the shaft, small lights glowing above the blunt caps of their helmets. He was curious about the noises, from rock pick blows to the occasional muffled explosion, but was happy enough not to try to compete for that work. He had enough to live on, a comfortable bed at night, and plenty of food.

He also had new associates. Harry was happy to teach him what he knew, about the area and the work and the animals. Soon he had Spence adept at hitching the mule Daisy to a rickety wagon so that they could practice hauling loads along the winding dirt trails. Daisy was one of the older mules, calm and patient and strong. She stood quietly while Spence adjusted her harness and climbed onto the bench at the front of the wagon.

"So, Daisy, so Daisy, now good Daisy," he said quietly as he settled next to Harry. He checked the cargo, several wheelbarrow loads of small rocks and dirt. "Up, now, girl."

The mule started walking and the wagon jerked into motion. Harry pointed out the trail ahead of them. "We'll head up here, over the ridge and down the other side. The tricky part is just over the top, when you head down. There's a quick right turn you'd better not miss."

The uphill route, along a narrow dirt trail, seemed easy. Daisy walked along, occasionally flicking an ear at a fly. All of the human activity at the mine site had worn away most of the scrub brush, but here and there a creosote bush or prickly pear made a spot of color. It seemed that the path was level but, as Spence was rapidly learning, the desert is never flat. Small dips and rises could be felt in the wagon's motion, even if not seen. Before long, the wagon had reached the crest of the hill.

Suddenly in front of Spence and Harry the path disappeared. Looking straight ahead, they saw only air and the bottom of a shallow canyon. Spence pulled on the reins, but Daisy had already stopped. Spence looked toward his partner and found just beyond the wagon the trail which, as Harry had warned, made an abrupt turn to follow the ridgeline.

"Well, that's a relief," Spence grinned. "You had me going there. Good thing Daisy stopped."

"She always stops there. She's been doing this so long, she's got the habit. A couple of times I tried to make her turn and keep going, but she knows better. Just stops and waits for the new guy to figure it out."

The walk along the ridge line gave them a chance to see more of the land surrounding the mine. To Spence it seemed that just about every hillside was pocked with holes, with here and there a more elaborate entrance shored up with timbers. The hills rippled away on both sides, the ragged profile of the White Mountains to the east, the taller Sierra Nevada to the west. On this clear summer day they could see pockets of snow in sheltered corners of the Sierra peaks, which stood like an undulating curtain as far as they could see.

Harry pointed West. "See, that's Mount Whitney, way in the back. They say it's the tallest mountain here, but it doesn't look it, because it's so much farther away. We don't go across those mountains."

Spence frowned. "That must be why they carry the ore to the ocean, right? First to Mojave, then on train cars to Bakersfield, then South again, all the way to San Pedro? That's where I saw the Nadeau mules – San Pedro. Isn't there a better way?"

"They're supposed to be building a railroad train," Harry shrugged. "But who knows when it will get here, or if it will get here. If there was a river, we could float it down. Seen any rivers around here? Only the one, and it ends up in Owens Lake. Everything goes from here to San Pedro. They'll load it on boats there and sail it to San Francisco. You're right, it's crazy -- it's like going backwards to go forwards, to go south so you can go north.

But that's what these mountains will do for this country. And that's why San Pedro and Los Angeles came to be, anyway. No sensible man would build a city in the desert, and that's what all this land is. Desert."

Spence nodded. "We tried to farm inland from there. What a disaster! Couldn't get anything to grow. Now my pa and my brothers are building houses for some company, where we thought we were going to have a farm. I had to leave. That's why I'm here."

They dumped their rocks at the end of the trail, where another team of men was extending the dirt path. A log tied to the back of their wagon scraped along the dirt, carrying the larger rocks before it and smoothing some of the ruts from the surface. Two more men, farther ahead, loosened dirt and uprooted bushes. The larger rocks would find their way into sandy patches, sinking to an acceptable level. Eventually this road would lead from the mine to town, past other mine workings, making delivery of ore just a bit easier and faster. All of this activity involved a project which would take months yet to complete -- longer if winter started early. There were men working at the mining camp who would never see the inside of a mine tunnel, nor would want to. The owners lived now in Long Beach in expansive mansions and made their money from sales of ore and stock. The camp employees, − cooks and carpenters and general laborers -- would stay as long as the silver lasted, then move on to the next mine, as would the assayers and prospectors, muleskinners and engineers. Spence remembered his childhood hobbies of digging holes and tunnels, making designs of ever greater complexity until the dirt shifted or he became bored and flooded the landscape.

Did he want to make his life as a muleskinner, never knowing the electric thrill of finding the big nugget or the glinting shelf of silver or lead? All in all, he decided, driving mules was probably safer, the pay was regular, and being outdoors, even on this broiling day, beat living below ground with a candle in his hat.

Harry had no such emotions. As they headed back to the mine, he said,

"It's a good thing you know mules. You'll be able to take over this job now, far as I can see."

"Well..."

"See, I got hired on to the new mine they're opening, just past where we were right now. Silver and zinc, and it looks like it'll last a good while. I'm starting there on Monday, and you'll be on your own."

"Sorry to see you go." Spence was sincere, partly because Harry was the only man he'd spent time with. He had been looking forward to more conversations, learning about the mining life from someone in it.

"I'll be around, don't worry," Harry laughed. "Maybe I can find you a job, too, unless you're really serious about those mules. Tell you what, after we knock off this afternoon, let's go get a beer and I'll introduce you to some of the boys."

Chapter II – Hauling Water

Summer at New Coso Mine was HOT. Sunny, so dry that a wet shirt would dry lying on a rock in an hour, cloudless blue skies, the only advantage of summer was that the violent Spring winds had calmed down. Newcomers like Spence quickly learned to respect the barrels of drinking water arranged around the mine camp even though the task of refilling them from the water wagon was hard and boring work. Summer brought its own work schedule too: Cookie banged the pot he kept strung over his worktable as soon as the first light of dawn appeared. The men were up and working before six, so that by the hottest part of the afternoon they had finished most of the day's work. This was the part of the year when the surface workers envied the miners, because below-ground the air was cool and occasionally almost moist.

Spence's work station, the Lucky Seven, was farthest up the mountainside of all of the diggings in this group. It was one of the newest, with only a small work group of about a dozen men. Spence thought it was the best in his limited judgment (he had seen only one other), because from the level ground in front of the cookhouse he could see maybe a hundred miles north and south, and an unknown distance east and west where the ragged peaks of the White Mountains and the Sierra Nevada shimmered in the sun.

The mules weathered the heat by moving more slowly than usual. Spence alternated between worry that they had drunk too much water and worry that they weren't getting enough. He was confident of his ability to drive them, even on the tricky hilltop turn, but it seemed that in the summer the ground almost burned their feet. It certainly burned him. His skin had turned leathery, his hair was bleached by the constant sun despite his hat. In Pinyon Creek, the shopkeeper had hung a giant thermometer outside the door. Some days it registered above 100 degrees by late morning.

On these days, one of his most important jobs was to replace water barrels as they were emptied. He had worked out a scheme where he loaded empty barrels on the wagon, then filled them pail by pail, saving his back at the cost of taking extra time. When all was readied, he flicked the reins of his four-mule team and called them: "now, Daisy, now Pete, now Blanket, now Ted, up we go!"

The mules considered, then Daisy, always first, braced her feet and lunged against the harness, as the other three joined her. The wagon bounced forward, then settled into its rocking, creaking progress to its first stop.

Under the blazing sun Spence delivered his water, first to one mine entrance then to another, then to the clusters of above-ground workers examining rocks, preparing equipment, sharpening tools.   At the far end of his route he turned the team and began to head back, when he heard shouts ahead at the main diggings and saw men running.

One of the men stood and waved for Spence to hurry over. Others were crouched over a man on the ground who was moaning. One man, already covered in blood, was pressing a bunch of towels against the injured man's leg. Blood had pooled near him on the ground.

Spence stopped his wagon next to them. Men jumped up on the wagon, wrestling his water barrels to the ground. Others rushed up holding a wooden door wrenched from its hinges, lifting the injured man carefully onto it, tying him to it with ropes around his chest. The wound was now bandaged with many strips of material, but Spence could see that the leg was terribly damaged. Two men clambered into the wagon, receiving the door and placing it gently on the wagon floor. They braced themselves against the wagon sides.

"OK, kid, get started. We've got to get Jack down the mountain to Pinyon Creek to the doc."

Another man ran to the office, grabbed a saddled horse, and tore down the trail ahead of the wagon.

"He's going to get the doc, get him ready," a man behind Spence said. "Pick slipped, hit a brace sideways, went right into his leg."

Spence's wounded passenger was continuing to moan. He could hear the man's hands hit the wagon floor as his arms thrashed about. He flicked the reins, starting the mule team on what he hoped would be a careful but rapid walk down the trail.

The wagon creaked and swayed. Every now and then the wounded man wailed and the others talked urgently to him.

The trail was rocky and crooked. Occasionally a small sage or creosote bush bumped the wheels. The mules were edgy -- did they smell the blood? Spence wondered. Pinyon Creek looked far away, even though it was less than a mile from them. We should have brought at least one barrel of water, Spence thought. Or a tarp to block the sun. He urged the mules faster.

Down on the flat the road was better and Spence let the mules trot. The jingle of their harness bells and the creaking of the wagon sounded loud in the desert stillness. A buzzard circled above, then was joined by another. Probably just coincidence, Spence told himself. There were always buzzards here.

The doctor was waiting for them at the edge of town, sitting in his buggy with his medical bag at his side. He climbed out as soon as he saw the wagon and stood at the side of the road, climbing into the wagon almost before it had stopped.

Spence concentrated on keeping the wagon completely still despite the nervous mules. He listened to the doctor shouting orders.

"We've got to move him. Can he take it? Somebody give him some brandy. No, he's passed out now. He's almost done for, poor man. Wagon-master, move the wagon to my office."

Wagon-master. Spence felt the hair on his neck stand up. Wagon-master. He maneuvered the mules down the middle of the street to the doctor's office next to Lucky's saloon.

The door and its burden were gently lowered from the wagon and carried inside. One of the men who had ridden down in the wagon came over to Spence.

"You'll have to stick around for awhile, son," he said. "It'll take awhile for the doc to see what he can do, whether he'll be even able to save him." He shook his head. "Jack's a good man, this is just a terrible, terrible piece of bad luck. Anyway, while you're waiting you might check around, see what you can pick up to take back up to the mine. There'll be some mail anyway, maybe some other packages. We'll look for you when we're ready to head back up."

Spence wasn't about to admit that he had no idea what to pick up, or where to check. Since his arrival two months before, he had not left the mine. Pinyon Creek, however, was not hard to explore. Its single main street, a dusty, rutted trail just wide enough to hold two wagons abreast, was lined with businesses. He started at the near end, just past the doctor's office, and worked his way up one side of the street.

The general store proved to be his major stop. The storekeeper was happy to free the space taken up by boxes of canned goods and meat and sacks of vegetables, the mine's standing order. Reaching under his counter, the storekeeper handed Spence a collection of mail -- envelopes, catalogs, several newspapers -- tied together with twine. He wondered whether there might be a letter from home in that stack. He hadn't left under the best circumstances. His father, struggling to find work, accused Spence of running away. His brothers were partly envious about his chance for adventure but partly bitter about losing his help. Was his mother still sick? He almost hoped there would be no mail for him.

He bought an apple and stood on the porch watching the comings and goings. A woman with a small child walked into the store. Three dogs ambled down the street, sniffing the edges of the dusty road. A wagon pulled by two horses pulled up in front of the livery stable. He began to relax, enjoying the breeze which had just blown up and was riffling the leaves on a nearby poplar tree.

Suddenly he heard angry voices from inside the saloon next door. He could not make out the words but he could tell the shouts were getting louder. Something – a chair? A table? A body? – banged against the front wall. The door crashed open and a tangle of men fell out onto the sidewalk. There were only two but it looked like a crowd. They rolled on the ground, hitting each other wherever they could reach, pulling hair, scratching and biting. The dogs, interested, turned around to watch. A small group began to form, murmuring.

Suddenly the door swung open again. The bartender strode out onto the sidewalk, a pail of water in each hand. Swiftly he emptied them, one after the other, onto the two men, who gasped and rolled apart.

"Now get out! Get out and stay out! You're not welcome here any more! That's the third chair you busted this week alone, Homer Jenkins. Go home and sleep it off, both of you!" He turned and re-entered the saloon, slamming the door behind him.

The two men slowly rose, wiped their eyes and walked away from each other. The knot of bystanders dissolved until the street was quiet again.

Returning to the doctor's office, he found his group on the sidewalk, smoking and talking.

"How's it going?" Spence asked.

"Don't know yet. Hasn't anybody come out to tell us. Maybe that's good news. Oh, wait. Here's somebody now."

The young woman who stood in the open doorway ("doc's daughter Molly", somebody muttered) shaded her eyes, squinting into the July afternoon sun. She was of medium height, dressed in blue gingham with a blood-stained apron over her skirt. Her light brown hair was lifted into a thick braid which reached to the middle of her back. Her face looked tired. She was, Spence thought, a person who did not smile often.

"My father says that your man --Jack? -- will likely live. But it still looks like the leg will have to go. He says you all did a good job of work, bringing him that fast. Papa says that you might think about finding some work he can do with one leg, after. He'll be down here for awhile now. Next trip..." she looked directly at Spence, "...you could maybe bring some of his stuff down, clothes and that."

"Thanks, miss," one of the men said. "We'll be getting on back up the hill then. Can we come in and see him before we go?"

"No point. Between the brandy and the pain, there's not much left in him. See him next week, if he's still alive. Write and tell his family, or wait till we know for sure. Whatever you all think is right."

She turned and re-entered the office, shutting the door firmly behind her.

"Little Miss Happiness, I *don't* think."

23

"That's her. She's always like that. That's the most words I've heard from her at one time. She and her dad, they've been here maybe six months now, and she keeps to herself as much as she possibly can."

The dust from the dry street bed had floated onto their clothing. They brushed themselves off, stretched, gathered the door leaning against the hitching post, climbed back into the wagon. Spence clucked to the mules and turned the wagon back up the hill again.

By the end of July, it was, if anything, hotter than ever. Molly stood at the door of her father's office, watching the sandy wind billow down the street. It was still early in the morning, perhaps nine o'clock, but the temperature was already climbing. Catching a glimpse of the thermometer in front of the general store she could tell it would be one of the hottest days so far this summer. She could feel sweat beading on the back of her neck and beginning to trickle down between her breasts. This was so different from Cornwall. Nobody from home could possibly understand. For one thing, Cornwall was smaller. From town to town, across the hills, along the river, Cornish spaces seemed, in her memory at least, compact and usable. Here the mountains blocked you in on two sides, but the valley seemed to go on without ceasing. When you came to Pinyon Creek you either kept going, on North to the gold fields or the ocean, or you stopped. And if you stopped, you stopped for good.

But this was home now, she reminded herself. Pull yourself together, girl, she told herself. Her father had promised her that if she still hated this life after a year they would leave Pinyon Creek. She only had thirty-eight weeks left. She almost grinned at that thought -- I've already made up my mind, she told herself. I can be as patient as patient can be but I'll never like it here.

They had made several stops before landing in Pinyon Creek. The travel from Liverpool to Ohio was a blur of seasickness, hunger, dirt, noise and general squalor. Wood County, Ohio, was green but it was the green of moss and stagnant water and weeds, and it was a frightening place where Indians still made occasional raids, keeping settlers tied to their homes and fearful of exploring. And they already had all the doctors they wanted. Wisconsin, filled with miners and farmers who had come from Redruth and Truro and St. Austell, was welcoming and the rocky hills looked much like the land she remembered from home, but there was something about the concentration of Cornish folks that the doctor found stifling. And so they had continued their journey westward until reaching Pinyon Creek. Pinyon Creek, with its rocks and dust, Pinyon Creek out here in the middle of nowhere.

Now she could see a trail of dust at the base of Pinyon Creek Hill. Spence and his mules were coming to town. She shaded her eyes with one hand and waved with the other. Spence pulled his team to a stop and threw the reins over the hitching post.

He had drawn the job of visiting Jack who was recovering slowly. Every five or six days, Spence would hitch Daisy or Flora to the big wagon to make the trip to Pinyon Creek for mail, groceries and a visit to the wounded miner. More and more often, he included a visit to Molly as well. On her part, she learned that Jack and Spence were both fond of sugar cookies and gingerbread; it made her happy to cook for these eager eaters. Sometimes Spence brought meat: jackrabbits, chukar and quail, occasionally a deer. Molly found that learning how to dress and cure the meat kept her busy and introduced her to some of the other Pinyon Creek residents. She was happy to trade the meat for cooking lessons.

Today, Spence lifted out a heavy basket. It must be deer, Molly decided. Or a whole lot of rabbits. She hoped it would not be rabbit.

Proudly, he walked over to her and put the basket on the ground. It clattered. She lifted the cover and peeked inside. The basket was filled with rocks. She looked questioningly at Spence who grinned.

"I know it's not food. And I hope you've made some cookies for me because I've been thinking about cookies all week."

Molly smiled and handed him her basket, in which she had placed a dozen large sugar cookies, newly baked. "But why did you bring me these rocks?"

"I've been talking to your father sometimes," Spence answered. "I know he's interested in the different kinds of rocks and why the mines are here. So I thought if he was not too busy, and if you're interested too, I can tell him what I've been learning."

"I'll find out." She disappeared into the doctor's office, returning almost at once with her father. "Let's take a picnic to the creek and you can teach us."

Spence had been busy since his arrival at the mines. His natural curiosity had led him to bedevil the miners with endless questions: why did they make a mine exactly where it was? How did they know what to look for? What did you have to do to a rock to make it useful? What did that streak of color mean, inside this or that rock? What is the best way to get rocks out of the ground if you just want to see whether they are any good?

Now, between mouthfuls of sandwich, he taught them what he had been learning. He showed them rocks with bands of different colors, with shining bits, with odd pointy shapes — "crystals" he said. They reached into the basket and explored its contents with fingers and eyes, occasionally wetting a rock to see the difference a little bit of water would make to its appearance. Finally he showed them his best treasure, a rock with Hank had lent him for the demonstration. It was wrapped in an old sock which he carefully unwrapped.

"Look first at the outside," he instructed. It was mostly round, gray and undistinguished- looking. "Now I'mgoing to show you the inside."

The gray shell protected a dazzling inner core of purple crystals, shining and complex. Molly and Dr. Capshaw leaned forward, amazed. Molly touched the crystals delicately, carefully, with her finger.

"Hank told me that a friend of his found this one. He says that there are many more in the hills. To get it open, you crack it with a hammer. I would like to go looking for more sometime. Would you like to go with me?"

They nodded in unison, still staring at the geode.

The first lesson on rocks led to many others, and by the end of summer the three had taken trips into the hills whenever Spence had time away from the mines. They found geodes and other mysterious rocks. Molly began to keep a journal of their discoveries, and claimed several of the prettiest stones for decoration in her kitchen.

Molly and Spence had begun a regular habit of eating picnic lunch. She found herself thinking about what she would cook, what she would wear, and what they would talk about. She realized with a start that she was thinking less and less frequently about Cornwall.

When Spence arrived this day, Molly picked up the picnic basket and joined him, giving his hand a quick squeeze. It was one thing to share a picnic, but another thing entirely to show affection in the street. Her father would be furious, since he would be hearing about it from most of his patients. Behind the stores on Main Street a creek made its meandering way through a thin collection of grasses and tamarisk trees, providing a softer-looking, though shadeless, picnic spot so favored by the town that a collection of logs and boulders allowed sitting room.

Spence dug into the picnic basket and pulled out a package of sandwiches wrapped in a checked towel. He grinned as he took his first bite.

"Pickle, there's plenty of pickle," he reported. "I think pickles are even better than meat when they're in a sandwich."

Molly smiled. "My grandma taught me to make pickles, back home in Cornwall. Wait till I get some cucumbers growing here, then you'll really taste pickles!"

Spence looked at her, admiring her sparkling eyes, the curl of her hair, the way her long fingers arranged the foods neatly on a nearby rock. "You said, 'back home in Cornwall.' Surely you don't mean you would be going back there?"

"I wish I could go home. I hated leaving. But they're all dead, back there. My mother, my grandma, my baby sister. There's nothing, really, to go home for. But I haven't found home here. Papa loves it. He loves doctoring and he knows miners and all the things they can do to themselves. And especially here he loves it because of the air and the altitude. He has everything he wants. He's doing studies on how this climate is healthy."

Spence grunted. "Healthy, maybe, if you can understand that the heat just burns the germs right out of a man's lungs."

"Maybe that's part of it. He thinks if he can find enough folks with lung trouble, and treat them, he can start a kind of hospital here." She stood, folding the towel. "Come and see my garden."

Behind the doctor's office, Molly had planted a kitchen garden where lettuce, beans, tomatoes, cucumbers and melons were growing. A row of clay pots arranged along the side of the garden held small saplings. Molly pointed them out to Spence.

"There's two kinds of apples, some apricots and some peach trees here," she said proudly. "If I'm still here when they get big enough, I'll make them permanent. If we move away I can put them in a wagon right in their pots."

Spence was impressed. She had to have been working hard ever since her arrival, or perhaps her father was a dedicated gardener as well. The plants looked healthy -- he could almost taste the tomatoes.

"Well, I hope you'll stay on -- just for the gardening, of course," he joked. But he hoped she heard the seriousness of his words.

"But what about you, Spence? Do you really like it here? Will you be going into the mines?"

"I don't think about it much," he admitted. "I needed to find work, and so I was happy to get this job -- any job. I've always liked working with the mules. It's been something I wanted to do for a long time. I don't think too much about where I do it -- I just like driving the mules."

It was the most personal conversation they had had. Spence, not one for talking much, found himself composing sentences in his head as he maneuvered the mules from pit head to mine shaft. Molly wrote more pages in her diary than she was accustomed to write, and still had more questions that wandered away out of her head into the air. Now they sat silently, each thinking about the words the other had said.

Becoming aware that he had eaten everything in the basket, Spence rose. Molly gathered the basket and they separated there, by the river.

Chapter III – Stocking Fish

The mines were beginning to slow down. The veins of silver which had seemed never-ending were looking thinner, and the miners had to open longer passages to reach anything worthwhile. Some men, the ones who followed silver from state to territory to state, had already packed up and left Pinyon Creek. Others continued to work, either exploring nearby hillsides or learning how to recognize some of the other minerals which had not earlier seemed interesting.

Spence took his savings and bought a pair of the mules he had been driving. With Daisy and Flora and a wagon he'd found which was battered but still sturdy, he set out in business for himself, hauling dry goods from Mojave to the general store in Pinyon Creek, hauling apples from Manzanar and Bishop and crops from any farms willing to sell, hauling ore -- dolomite, copper, low-grade silver, whatever the prospectors found -- to the assay office in Bishop,. He found himself interested in the discovery of the different metals he was given. He tried to spend time with the prospectors, learning their methods for deciding where to stake a claim. He learned that there were dozens, possibly hundreds, of different materials in the mountains and even on the desert floor, but that most of them had no apparent commercial use.

He sometimes took Molly with him on his shorter trips, showing her the places which produced his various cargoes. They found borax crystals blooming on the desert floor. They were intrigued by the many colors of quartz which they sometimes found spilling from piles of pebbles near the road. They listened to the stories of the beautiful white marble found in the Marble Mountains, marble which was being shipped to San Francisco and Los Angeles to become floors and walls of office buildings. Gradually, Molly's father became interested as well; the three of them went exploring on nearby hillsides, poking into the dirt with trowels and hammers. They established collections of interesting rocks, carefully naming the locations where they had been found.

One morning Spence made an unexpected visit to Dr. Capshaw's office. He waited impatiently by the door, shifting from one foot to another, until Molly finished talking with a patient. Then he pulled her outside to a bench by the door.

"I just want to tell you that I'm going to be gone for a while now," he said. "Probably about a week. But if this works out I'll have a lot more work and I'll be making longer and longer trips. Two or three weeks anyway, might be as long as a month or six weeks. Nobody knows for sure."

"Whatever are you talking about?"

"I've got a job -- well, Daisy and Flora and I have a job and it's really Daisy that they want. Wally Pride, the ranger? at the fish hatchery? he is taking a string of mules up into the back country. They -- we -- we're going to dump fish into Big Tyler Lake."

"Well. That's something different." Molly tried to be enthusiastic. "But -- you'll be carrying fish?"

"Daisy and Flora have carried just about everything else," he said. "If this works, we'll be first in line for the next jobs. And it's for the government, so we know we'll get paid."

Dr. Capshaw had joined them. "You're carrying fish?" he asked. "Into the mountains? Whatever for?"

"There's no food fish to speak of in some of those back country lakes. The Fisheries folks want to start some golden trout, taking some of their fish up. Kind of an experiment, I guess, but they're paying me."

Molly had been sitting silently. Now she reached forward and put her hand on Spence's arm.

"There are lots of lakes in the mountains," she said. "Maybe hundreds. And some of them are near places where there are ranches and little towns. And some of them are on trails that connect with stagecoach routes. And some of them are in the forest land that Fisheries keeps talking about. People will want to come and fish. If this works, you'll be one of the first mule drivers! I think it is exciting."

Spence brightened.

"But is it dangerous?" Molly asked.

"Not any more than any other trip. At least as far as I know. What could be dangerous about carrying fish?"

33

"Well," Dr. Capshaw chuckled, "I've heard of shooting fish in a barrel, but carrying fish on a mule is new to me!"

When Spence, Daisy and Flora reached the Fishery center next morning, the other wranglers were already busy loading a string of three mules. Spence led his two up to the line and introduced them. First Daisy then Flora gazed at each mule, snuffled a few times, flicked their ears, and moved on slowly.

"We'll keep the two groups separate, just at first," Wally told Spence. "Until we see how they all get along. A couple of days should tell the tale."

He showed Spence how to pack the mules. First, they set saddle blankets on each mule's back to guard against rubbing. Then they lifted the packs and set them on both sides, insuring that the loads were level and that the cords binding them were secure.

Spence surveyed the stack of packs and gear. "Sure is a lot of fish."

Wally chuckled. "Only the packs for your mules have the fish. The rest is for us."

The packs designed for Flora and Daisy contained large jugs cushioned with blankets. Their narrow necks were covered with light cotton pads. Spence loaded the packs, double-checked all of the fittings, and led his team to the line.

"Let's let them go first," Wally said. "That will give my mules the chance to see them and get used to their pace. Maybe we'll change off as we go."

The first mile was an easy walk across the foothill meadow onto a trail which led gradually up the hillside. The animals walked confidently, while Spence and Wally walked along beside them. By late morning, however, the trail became steeper. Occasionally a muddy spot or puddle indicated a recent rain. Small rocks lay in the trail but the mules avoided stepping on their sharp edges.

They stopped for lunch and a rest break on the saddle of the mountain. Wally pulled out a sandwich for each of them. They dipped their canteens in a nearby stream. The mules grazed on the spring grasses and munched leaves of low-hanging branches. As they ate, Wally told Spence stories about his work with the Fisheries department.

The afternoon's walk was harder. The trail was steeper and harder to follow. Occasionally they had to walk almost touching the mountainside, with a sheer drop on the outer trail edge. Once Daisy stopped and would not step forward until Spence went ahead and cleared several large stones from the path. By the time Wally announced a stop, Spence was sweaty and sore; driving a wagon was child's play compared with this.

Their night's stop was in a small meadow almost surrounded by forest. They unpacked the mules and turned them out into a portion of the meadow in which Wally had made a kind of corral, pounding stakes into the soft earth and string rope from one to the next until he had a large circle. Spence noticed that the corral included a small stream, and the ground was covered with grass and wildflowers.

The two men quickly set up their tents. Wally opened one pack to reveal a small cook stove, which he lit with charcoal from a second pack. Soon meat and potatoes were frying briskly and a pot of water was boiling for coffee.

"Well, that was an easy day," Wally remarked. "Tomorrow's going to be a lot harder. The trail is pretty much gone in places and there are some pretty steep climbs."

Spence groaned, stretching one leg and then the other. "How far is the lake from here?"

"We have gone about a quarter of the way. I take it you haven't traveled much in the mountains."

"Not much. Doc Capshaw has some places he likes above Pinyon Creek, and he's taken me exploring around there. Most of the time I've been on the other side, up in the White Mountains. And most of the time I've been driving a wagon. This is pretty new to me."

"You're doing fine, so far. And Daisy and Flora look good. They look like they're enjoying it."

"They're born leaders. And show-offs."

"It's what we need. "

Morning came too early for Spence, who had tried without success to find a comfortable place for his body on the uneven ground. He decided he had pitched his tent over some tree roots; It hadn't been a problem in the desert and he had forgotten how the forest floor would feel. And it was cold, cold. His blanket roll, perfect for the desert trips, didn't begin to keep him warm. Finally he crawled out, re-lit the fire under the water kettle, and waited for it to boil. The sky was filled with stars. He thought he could see the eastern sky lighten just a little bit. He had no idea of the time. He poured a mugful of hot water and drank it slowly, warming up. He was ready to crawl back and try again to sleep, when Wally appeared, unshaven and shaggy.

Spence got breakfast under way, while Wally began collecting the mules, speaking quietly to each one. "Here Dawn, here Jackson, good morning, Tulip, there, Gus, so, Daisy, good, Cubby, so, Flora." The chant went on and and on as, one by one, the mules were harnessed and their loads re-packed. The men quickly finished eating and washed and stowed the cooking gear. They cooled the cook stove by emptying the coals and then dumping it in the stream where it sizzled a moment, causing the mules to move uneasily.

Daisy and Flora led again, with Spence by their side. He could hear the water in the fish cans sloshing gently. They moved steadily through the lightening skies to full sunshine and into midday, when they stopped to rest. Once again they found a meadow, but the only water was a muddy puddle. "We'll have to stop again so they'll have water," Wally said, trotting away to head off Gus who was heading determinedly into the forest. The short break allowed Spence to catch his breath and pull off the sweater that had seemed so necessary only a few hours before.

Heading along the trail again, Spence realized that the trail marks were becoming fainter. Whoever used this trail apparently only went part way. He realized that he had seen no signs that Wally had a map. He thought he could tell where they wanted to go. Ahead was another saddle between two Sierra peaks.

Soon Wally called a halt. He had found a small pond near the trail, at a point where the ground had leveled sufficiently to allow the mules to stop and gather to drink. Spence checked the packs on Daisy and Flora, re-tightening the cords and shoving

Daisy's packs to a more level arrangement. Then they were off again.

Lunch was sandwiches of cheese and some leftover meat from the previous supper. Spence was surprised at his hunger. He had, after all, eaten a large breakfast and although he was walking, he found it easier than many of his solo trips in the wagon. Wally finished first and began stacking away the utensils, a lump of chewing tobacco tucked in his cheek. He pointed ahead.

"See them?"

Spence followed Wally's finger. Three mountain goats stood on the trail. The largest had long curling horns. Suddenly they took fright and bounded ahead, disappearing into the trees almost at once.

"That's something I've never seen before!"

"One of the best parts of making this kind of trip. We may be the first humans that they've ever seen."

The mules were becoming more comfortable with each other. For the afternoon Wally took the lead, walking ahead of Daisy, while Spence brought up the rear, checking the trail, watching for laggards or problems. When they stopped for the night, he strung the corral, to Wally's approval, and for the following breakfast made his own specialty, flapjacks.

For the next day, the weather was good, the pace was reasonable, the mules gave no trouble and suddenly, shortly after lunch, they could see their destination, Big Tyler Lake, in the valley below them.

The temptation to keep going was overwhelming. The lake glistened in the afternoon sun, the adjoining meadow was golden with wild mustard, the sky was almost cloudless. Even the mules seemed to catch the spirit. Daisy tossed her head and moved along briskly.

The trail down the mountainside was no better, but they were on the inside curve of the hillsides, which made the mules more confident. The party moved along at a good walking speed, always coming down, and every glimpse of the water below seemed to bring them closer. The mules, loosely tied together, now stretched their lead rope as they picked up speed. However, as they continued to descend with the valley still far below them, Wally began to show some concern.

"I may decide to stop before we reach the lake," he called to Spence, "because we can't afford to overtire the mules at this late date, and we want to camp before dark."

Spence was torn. He had no desire to pitch his tent in the dark, and he knew how much time and effort were involved in end-of-day activities. But he was enjoying the descent, feeling how much stronger his legs felt, proud of his animals, not wanting this beautiful afternoon to end. Finally, they reached the valley floor and began to cross the meadow. Suddenly Wally stopped and waved his arms to Spence.

"This is no good! Help me get them back to the trail!"

The mules were not willing to stop when Spence called them. He whistled and kept calling until they reluctantly turned and began to walk toward him. He noticed that they seemed to have trouble picking up their feet. Their hooves looked bigger than normal. Great clots of mud fell off each time they lifted a leg.

Spence encouraged them. As the leaders moved faster, the rest of the mules were quicker to change direction, and finally the party was reassembled on the trail.

"It was like quicksand," Wally exclaimed. "That whole meadow is just soaked." He showed Spence his pants glued to his calves with mud speckled with yellow flowers. "I started to sink in until I really got scared."

Now they must find a camp for the night away from the meadow. Wally looked around, distrusting any of the area near them. The trail had intersected a path at the foot of the mountain which turned left into a forested area and right into the meadow.

"We can go back up, or we can try the woods," Wally said worriedly. The sun was getting low in the sky and it was getting colder. Spence put his sweater back on. "Let's try a little way toward the forest and stop at the first likely place."

Cautiously they walked along the edge of the hillside until, rounding a bend, they found a clear meadow. It was slightly higher than the ground near the lake, and apparently mostly dry, with a small stream running long one edge. The two men set up camp, taking more care with the corral in case the mules decided to look for more water. Then they loosely hobbled each mule to discourage wandering. Finally they set up the cook stove and prepared some food for themselves.

Over coffee, they discussed plans for approaching the lake. They would explore it again tomorrow, on foot and without the mules. They would circle the boundary to see whether another kind of soil or drainage would allow them to get nearer. Maybe one man on foot could get across the mud, one fish-can at a time. Nothing seemed very promising. Disheartened, they sat quietly and watched the sunset.

"Kind of disappointing, huh?" Wally said.

"Well, yeah, a bit. Have you been here before?"

"No, not this lake. Like I said, we're just getting started with this. We found it on a map. It's actually one of the closer lakes. We're kind of spreading out, see what works."

"How's your wife feel about you being gone so long? Does she fret?"

"Oh, I'm not married. Too restless, I guess. You?"

"No. I guess I just never thought much about it. I've just been going along, from one thing to another. But there is this.... Molly Capshaw, do you know her? Doc Capshaw's daughter?"

"I sure do. She has patched me up more than once. Nice woman. Do you...?

"I don't know. I think I'd better get some better jobs before I try to take care of a family."

"Well, this is a start. You work your mules well. If you can handle the back country there'll be plenty more work to come. Did you hear about the park? They're talking about taking land for a national forest or something. Sounds like there'll be plenty of work."

"I'd like that."

Wally stood and stretched. "G'night."

Spence sat by the fire until the last coals burned down, thinking about the trip and Molly and the scenery he had seen for the first time, so different from the desert and the mines. Instead of rocks and sand, during the past days he had been surrounded by trees and brush and wildflowers, confronted by soaring granite peaks that seemed to go on and on in layers. The stars were just as bright here as in the desert, and just as far away. Would Molly be at all interested in him? Would she make her life with him in Pinyon Creek? Or was she determined to return to Cornwall?

In the makeshift corral, the mules shuffled and muttered. Wally thrashed in his blankets and said "Porridge" loudly, then resumed snoring lightly.

Spence thought he was happier this night than he had ever been.

Chapter IV – The Hills Above Pinyon Creek

The following morning they continued their walk around the lake, making sure to stay away from muddy places. The ground continued to show a slight rise which made walking easy. On the side opposite their first attempt, they found a collection of boulders, remains of a long-ago avalanche, which allowed Wally to clamber up to the edge of the lake. He surveyed the area for a few moments, then scrambled back down.

"I can get to a spot that is above the water," he reported. "We can take off the cover of the can, lower it down, and pull it around in the water till the fish are all out of it. Then we pull it up again. 'Kay?"

"OK. Here's the first can." They pulled the net cover from the spout of the can and peered in.

"We're hoping about half of them have survived so far," Wally said. "And I can see some of them moving around. Let's go."

One at a time, Spence carried the cans up to Wally, who tied a rope around it and lowered it carefully into the water. Then they both watched as he maneuvered it forward and back, finally raising it again, bouncing it to remove as much of the water as possible. Finally he shook the inverted can to empty it and returned it to Spence. As they improved with practice, the work went faster, until all sixteen cans were empty.

"Any idea how well we did?" Spence asked.

"Actually, we won't know for a year. We'll come back and check how many have survived and how much they have grown. But I think we did all right."

The return trip was easier. The route was familiar and the loads were lighter on the mules. Daisy and Flora now carried camping gear along with the empty fish cans. Spence and Wally occasionally caught a mule-back ride when the trail allowed.

Spence hoped that he would be asked back for fish stocking, but he was well aware that these trips took him far from Molly. Somehow going into the mountain country felt like more of a journey than the wagon trips, even though both lasted the same number of days. He would have some thinking to do if he were given a job offer.

Back in Pinyon Creek, Molly found herself imagining Spence's trip. Here was a man who was not afraid to try new jobs or travel to new places. He reminded her of her father, who was never satisfied with his current situation, no matter what that was. Would Spence want Molly to travel with him? Would he want her to make a home for him? What kind of a family would they be -- Spence and Molly and Dr. Capshaw? Because Molly couldn't imagine leaving her father, who clearly depended upon her to provide food and housekeeping and companionship.

She moved about the house doing her morning chores mindlessly, her thoughts completely occupied by these questions. After Dr. Capshaw asked her three times to find his favorite coffee cup, he gently drew her over to the kitchen table and pulled out her chair.

"Molly girl, he is just fine, up there in the mountains," he said. "Don't fret. He'll be back in a few days and eager to tell you about everything he has seen."

She shook her head impatiently. "No, papa, it's not that I'm worried about him. I'm just thinking about, well, about our life. I think he will ask me to marry him. I think that is why he took this job, to get some money for a house."

"You two have been talking about that?"

"Well, a bit. But papa, you and Spence love this valley and I still don't. It's too hot in the summer and too cold in the winter. The wind knocks me off my feet. My plants die even when I water them. Our house is leaky. It is so hard to find good food, like fruit. The miners are so large and noisy and there are fights all the time. And too much drinking...."

"Stop!" Dr. Capshaw held up his hand. "I know you're unhappy here, and I did promise that we could leave in a year. But you're quite right. I love this valley. I think I haven't worked hard enough to show you why. I think I can teach you to feel better about it. What do you think?"

"How?"

"I will take you exploring with me. There are places here like no others on earth. Actually, I'm thinking about a new project, and this is a good time to start working on it." He stood up suddenly and pushed his chair in. "Pack a lunch, Molly. We're going on a ride."

By the time she had put together a picnic basket with sandwiches and apples and jugs of water, he had brought his horse and wagon to the front of the house. The two of them set off down main street and up into the hills west of town.

"Now, this is probably the route Spence took, or one just like it. We're heading straight ahead, looks like we'll just run into a solid granite wall, right? Well, watch."

Molly held tightly to the picnic basket with one hand and the frame of the wagon with the other as they bounced along the trail. It was hard for her to see their path because there were only faint markings from previous wagons. The ground was stony with occasional prickly pear and agave cactus. Occasionally a small animal would scuttle out of the way. As they neared the wall, she could tell that the path turned sharply, snaking between two huge granite outcrops.

"Now look back," her father directed. Molly twisted in her seat. They had climbed enough so that the town was below them. She could see across the valley to the White mountains on the east, blurry in the summer haze.

They drove on into the granite maze. Molly began to look all around her, surprised by the mysterious shapes of the boulders. She hoped her father knew where he was going. They twisted and turned and suddenly found themselves at the edge of a meadow.

"Lunchtime," Dr. Capshaw announced.

They dropped the rear gate and spread a blanket across the wagon bed. Dr. Capshaw released Amber to graze on the dry meadow grass. Molly set out the sandwiches and water bottles, discovering that she was quite hungry. As they ate, her father pointed at some sights: the nest of a large bird, perhaps a turkey vulture, on the top of a nearby boulder; some drawings scratched on the side of another boulder; small yellow flowers, each no bigger than her thumbnail, growing among the grasses; a coyote, running like a dog across the opposite edge of the meadow; a small rock with a cup-shaped indentation. Ahead, she could see the direction of their trail, a faintly darker strip across the ground, heading ever upwards and leading to greener patches in the hills.

"Now let's take a little walk." He helped her down from the wagon. She discovered that up here a light breeze lifted her hair. The air seemed cooler and fresher than the air at home. She watched a pair of butterflies dance around each other. She found a bush bearing some fruit unfamiliar to her. Dr. Capshaw, striding ahead of her, stopped and looked to the west, then beckoned her. As she approached, she began to hear the sounds of water.

A narrow stream tumbled across stones at the meadow's edge. Even now, in late summer, the water looked cold and clear. She knelt down and cupped her hands, tasting the water.

"It's the same water that runs through Pinyon Creek," Dr. Capshaw told her, "only here it is clean and clear, before the cattle and the farmers have had a chance at it. These mountains are just full of these streams, and most of them are where nobody has found them yet."

They stood together, looking from one direction to the next, taking in the unfamiliar sights. Finally Dr. Capshaw turned back to the wagon.

"It's a beautiful place," Molly told him. "It's altogether different from anything I ever saw at home, but it's beautiful. I didn't know."

"I hope you will learn to call our valley home," her father answered. "There are more things to show you. This is one of my favorite places, though. When I have had a bad day doctoring, sometimes I just drive up here and sit awhile, till I see how small my problems really are. Now I will tell you my project."

They walked back to the meadow.

"There's a meadow much like this, only higher, too far to come today. It is almost in the high forest, with evergreens and some other trees, and the river is close by. I'm going to build a sanatorium there, for people with consumption and other maladies, where they can come and get medical care and good food and peaceful scenery as they recover."

Molly stood silently for several minutes, then took her father's hand.

"You promised me we could return to Cornwall if I was still unhappy after a year. But you can't keep that promise, can you?"

"Molly, I can't. I couldn't bear to leave the valley now that I know it. I have so many ideas, and I'm useful here. I can send you back if that is truly what you want, but no, I can't go with you. And I hope you will find it in your heart to stay here. I was grieving so deeply after Sallie and the baby died, I didn't know where I was going or what I was saying. I just grabbed you up and left the places where I had been so happy and now was so sad. It was a selfish thing for a father to do, but I did it and all I can say is that I'm sorry."

Molly sat down on a nearby rock. Ahead of her she could see the road they had traveled and Pinyon Creek far down the hill. On the hillsides in all directions she saw patches of granite spotted with small green areas of forest and meadow. The river continued to bubble along nearby.

"I guess I can understand, Papa, but I trusted you. The idea that we could leave in a year if I still didn't like it here, that idea made me happier. Now I don't know...."

"But maybe that same idea kept you from really feeling at home here, Molly. You have stayed pretty much close to home, and except for Spence I don't think you have made many friends."

"That's true," she answered slowly. "I feel lonely much of the time. I... I.... I miss mama so much!" She burst into tears.

Wallace Capshaw sat down beside here and folded her into his arms. "I miss her too, Molly girl. I miss her so much, I miss her every day." His voice thickened and tears began to roll down his cheeks. The two of them sat together weeping for some time. Finally Molly stirred. She stood, wiped her eyes, and stretched out her hand to her father.

"I feel better. This was a good idea, papa, to show me this place. I'll try harder to like the valley. Lord knows Spence is happy here, and he just found himself here by accident. Do you really think you can make a sanatorium work here?"

The ride back down into Pinyon Creek was filled by Wallace Capshaw's enthusiastic explanation of his plans, and as always when she heard about his projects, Molly began to see the possibilities for success.

Chapter V – Minerals and Vegetables

The fish stocking trips turned out to be a regular part of Spence's work. Even though it would be a year before the results could be known, the benefits of stocking the beautiful mountain lakes with trout seemed assured. He and Wally made at least one trip each month, fitting them into Spence's freight-hauling business. As they worked farther into the mountains, they found many lakes which had not appeared on any of their maps. Sometimes they found arrows and dishes and tools left by the Shoshone Indians. Spence continued to think that it was somehow unnatural to plant fish in lakes. Surely if they were supposed to be there, shouldn't they already be there? Wally attempted to reassure him, telling him about all the trout being raised in the local fish hatchery, but all that Spence could see was that the hatchery people had found a way to keep themselves in business. But he liked Wally and enjoyed his company and was happy for the regular paycheck. Never a fisherman, he couldn't see the point of standing in cold water with a stick, and having to keep pricking worms with a hook.

People were beginning to learn about the Sierra Nevada and about Pinyon Creek. The narrow gauge train which had been supporting the mines was now connected to the wider gauge train which ran from Carson City to Reno and up to San Francisco. Explorers and adventurers had long found Pinyon Creek to be a pleasant place to rest after a strenuous trip, and enjoyed the new hotel.

Dr. Capshaw lost no time in building his sanatorium. His enthusiasm and his reputation in the community made it surprisingly easy for him to raise enough funds from friends and patients and shopkeepers to build a central building and several cabins in the meadow he had found. He found a local couple to live at the sanatorium and tend to all of the non-medical work – after all, most of the care to be given was simple: healthy food in large quantities, fresh air including wagon rides and short walks, clean surroundings. His first patients began to arrive almost before the buildings were complete, giving him a week of urgent rushing about gathering supplies and furniture – just the kind of excitement the doctor enjoyed most.

Spence, encouraged by the success of the fish-stocking work, proposed to Molly and was surprised that she seemed already to have thought about marriage. When he gathered his courage and asked Dr. Capshaw for her hand in marriage, the doctor chuckled and gave him a hearty handshake.

"You're a bit slow, son. Molly has been planning her wedding for some time now." He sobered. "It's a bigger decision than you might think. She is making her mind up that she will never return to Cornwall. That's the hard part. Living with you, that's the easy part!"

Once the date had been set, Dr. Capshaw dug into the boxes and trunks that he had brought all the way across the country, and gave Molly a large box. "It's Sallie's wedding dress," he told her, his eyes glistening. "She always wanted you to be married in it, no matter who you picked for husband."

Molly opened the box and lifted out the dress. She had never seen it before, but, looking at it she imagined her mother standing in front of her. It was a light pearl gray, a soft wool with a lace collar and pearl buttons. Additional pearl buttons added to the decorations on the embroidered cuffs. She held it up, then took it into her bedroom, reappearing shortly with a big teary smile.

"Look, papa. It fits as though it had been made for me!"

The wedding was small, but the party grew to include much of the townsfolk. Molly felt that it was almost as much an adoption as a wedding, since Spence had become so friendly with her father that he often behaved like a son as well as a husband.

The newlyweds moved into a small frame house at the edge of Pinyon Creek. Spence quickly built a corral for Daisy and Flora. Molly planted her fruit trees in a line across the back edge of their property, near a small creek. She hoed and turned nearby ground for a kitchen garden, chopping up weeds and working them into the baked-hard soil. And at the same time, the three continued occasional prospecting, expanding their knowledge of the local minerals.

The winter was just as cold as the summer had been hot. The nights were bitterly cold. Spence and the doctor spent more time than they liked, chopping firewood in the forests above Pinyon Creek, until Spence realized that he could profitably use Flora and Daisy to carry the firewood in the wagon to supply a growing clientele in Pinyon Creek. Dr. Capshaw, learning how to use chemicals to identify minerals, found himself tempted into his laboratory when he could have been treating patients. Molly, searching for projects to occupy her time indoors during the short winter days, planted seeds of the herbs she had gathered.

As she worked, she conducted a silent conversation with herself: I wonder whether it's too early to plant any of these. I've put them in little sections of my boxes, and I have mixed the soil carefully. Did I remember to add sand? Maybe I needed to add more. Maybe it won't matter. I wonder where Spence is right now. In the forest? Will he be careful? There are lots of things that can happen. A branch could fall on him. Flora could -- or Daisy could -- fall. The work is too hard. There is no money. What are we doing here anyway? Why is Papa so interested in the minerals? Does he think he will find some kind of magic medicine? He never tells me anything any more. He and Spence just talk to each other and they only think about me when they are hungry. I really hate it here. I'm cold.

She worked away so industriously that Spence joked that he would have to build another shed, just for her seeds. She could tell that he didn't believe any of them would sprout. She huffed away and started a pot of soup.

The winter days in Pinyon Creek passed slowly but fairly pleasantly. Scattered attempts at mining continued, but a new business was becoming more noticeable: ranching. While cattle had always grazed in the high meadows north of town, now more land was being turned into ranch land, and occasional cattle sales, formerly held only in Bishop, were sometimes held in Pinyon Creek at the fairgrounds. Molly's plants adjusted to their boxes and formed the subject of most of her care. At Christmas, the entire town gathered at the Masonic Lodge for potluck dinner with carol singing and dancing. And several times Molly and Spence took the wagon up into the hills to play in the snow, brilliantly white, wet enough for snowballs almost unknown on the valley floor.

By the time Spring arrived, Molly knew two things: she was expecting a baby, and she would be staying in Pinyon Creek. Leaving the Valley was an idea which had died a permanent death. Here in Pinyon Creek were the jobs and people and interests which absorbed her father and husband.

Well, she was going to make the best of things. Her seedlings had survived the winter nicely, and the little trees in their pots were ready to be planted outdoors. The icy winter nights began to give way to softer weather, and the rains of the earliest Spring days diminished.

In boots and shawls and a wooly hat, she set out to plant her garden. She drew shallow trenches with her shovel; last Fall's hard work preparing the soil was paying off nicely now. By lunchtime she had planted peas and beans and lettuce, with nasturtiums at the end of each row.

By the afternoon, sweaty and with muscles aching from the bending and stretching, she had planted a dozen fruit tree saplings along the back of the garden. She stood, stretching, and surveyed her garden with great satisfaction. The rows of vegetables lay straight in soft green lines. She could imagine the lettuce. She would have to make supports for the tomatoes and the peas, she decided. The little trees would provide fruit and shade when they grew bigger. She was proud of her work.

She found Spence and her father sitting companionably on the front stoop, mugs of cool water in hand. They had laid out an array of rocks and were considering them, one after another.

"OK, here's some silver in here, and some quartz," Wallace Capshaw said. "I think they call it smoky quartz. Looks lovely, right? But I don't know what use it is, except for jewelry."

"How do you know what a mineral is good for, anyway?" Spence mused. "When the first person picked up some borax crystals, did he know it would be a good cleaner? And how did he find out?"

"Well, we know what the first people knew about gold," Molly laughed. "They knew it was surely pretty."

Wallace picked up a rock and turned it slowly in his hand, scraping the surface here and there with his thumbnail. "So what if we said, 'This is softer rock, here, inside, and maybe it would melt more easily, and if we heated it -- fire assay method -- we'd end up with melted something and granular something.'"

Spence chuckled. "You'd end up breaking the bigger rock, that's what, and who'd say it's not just mud inside? There's silver and lead mixed, and you know silver is worth more than lead."

"Depends what you want it for," Wallace rejoined. "If you want bullets, you'd rather have lead than silver. If you want coins, you want silver. That's what I mean. If you want cleaner, you'll want borax. If you want, oh, axles for your wagon you'll take iron. We need to talk to more prospectors, ask them what they look for. "

"They're not going to tell us," Spence objected. "If they think they're on to something, they'll keep it as secret as possible. We need to study up on the rocks the miners left behind. I hear there's still a fair amount of gold left if we're just patient looking for it."

They bickered amiably, imagining future wealth, trying to rig a fire hot enough to melt the rock without breaking the skillet they'd put it in. Wallace, remembering his time learning medicine, drew sketches of burners and beakers which they could build or buy. Molly, amused, went about her chores to the calm background noise of the men's voices.

The vegetables grew beautifully for almost a week. But one Saturday morning Molly came out to water them and found most of them eaten to the ground. She caught a glimpse of a jackrabbit scurrying away. She felt that it was just about the last straw. Spence, hearing her sobs, rushed out and took her in his arms.

"It's only peas," he started, then realized that he was making matters worse. "I mean, we need to make a better fence. And I'll shoot any jackrabbit who tries to get through it."

"No use," Molly murmured. "They're gone. And those were the only seeds I kept. There'll be nothing left."

Spence bent down and examined the chewed plant stalks. "They're not totally gone, Molly. See?" He held his finger carefully under a chewed stem. "I'll bet they'll grow back. I'm going right now to get some chicken wire and stuff."

The two men, aided by curious neighbor children, spent the rest of the day constructing an elaborate, deeply planted wire fence, fortified with sticks and odd pieces of lumber. Molly tied small pieces of rag here and there along the fence to make moving shadows. By supper she had almost decided that something, somehow, might survive.

The fruit trees were sturdier. During the Spring and Summer months, as her baby grew and began to move in her, Molly dug channels from the line of trees to the creek. Even in the heat of the summer, the creek had a small amount of water. She lined her tiny canals with small pebbles, and proudly watched them become wet. With the channels and the buckets of dishwater and wash-water she gave them, the small saplings grew noticeably. Spence and the doctor had built a rabbit fence around each tree.

But by August the salty desert winds were burning the leaves, which curled and turned brown at their edges. Molly watched sadly, trying to figure out how to manage to keep them alive. She piled brush around the base of the trees, to provide support and to keep out the worst of the sun's heat. She sprinkled the leaves with water from her bucket, and watered only in the evening so that the the water would have the longest possible time before evaporating. She consulted everybody she knew in the town, but most had no interest in gardening; they had left farms and gardens back east and did not wish to be reminded.

She began to feel superstitiously that the garden affected the embryo growing inside her. If the garden failed, the baby would be sickly... or worse. She redoubled her efforts until her father and Spence became worried.

"Enough with the water pail, Molly," Spence called out as, sweaty and panting, she climbed the faint rise between the creek and the garden. "You'll wear yourself out and then what?"

She only grunted in reply. She needed to keep the fruit tree leaves damp. Her biggest worry was the wind, the strong desert wind which seemed almost as strong as it had been in the Spring. How had she failed to notice it? Could she have planted the fruit trees in a different place? She persuaded Spence to install new clothes poles. Now she hung up shirts and sheets between the trees and the incessant wind. She tried hanging a quilt, but it was too heavy and bent the clothes poles; Spence complained at the chore of straightening them.

Finally the summer heat broke. The wind calmed at least a bit, and the salt air stopped stinging Molly's face. By October she could tell that some of the plants would survive, and if they didn't provide food they could at least be turned under to enrich the soil for next year. The fruit trees, as well, seemed to have survived the searing winds and heat of summer. She wondered at herself: I'm planning next year's garden already, she thought, like I'll be here next year and beyond. She found herself both glad and sorry.

Near dawn on November 14, 1890, Alfred Richardson, seven pounds of bawling energy, was born.

Chapter VI – The New Doctor

Alfred was a sturdy and loud baby, demanding food and attention with every breath. As he grew, Molly took him with her, first in his basket and then on her back in a sling she had learned from her Paiute neighbors. The winter winds were sharp. It was a year of snow that stayed on the ground for days, unusually for Pinyon Creek. As she worked in the doctor's office, Alfred in a crib in the corner by the front window, Molly could see older children making snowmen and snowballs and sliding in the icy slush; it wouldn't be long before Alf joined them. Molly now spent her days tending Alf, helping her father in his medical office, running the occasional errand for the sanatorium, and getting to know her neighbors. Now that she had begun to see herself as a permanent resident of Pinyon Creek, rather than as a person living temporarily in the desert, she was more willing to invest effort in learning the local customs.

The doctor's business kept growing, as more and more Midwesterners learned about the supposedly healthy air of the western mountains. He didn't miss the mining industry, he would tell people. He would rather treat these consumption patients because they stayed long enough for him to get to know them. His curious spirit and delight in meeting all new people made him a popular doctor, with a growing waiting list of patients.

Dr. Capshaw was in his element now. His practice, now that the mines were not so busy, had changed from treating the wounds of mining accidents and barroom brawls to include the long-term care of patients with diseased lungs. His natural curiosity led him to study these cases, hoping to find new treatments. He wrote unceasingly to friends and colleagues as far away as Cornwall, and the mail usually contained at least one long letter or scientific paper for him to study. He persuaded Molly to plant as many vegetables and fruits as she had strength for, and offered some recipes for soups and stews which even Spence wouldn't eat. He tried various regimes of healthy walking, hot and cold baths, compresses and leeches, building up an array of equipment and supplies which began to overflow the closets of the sanatorium.

Trying to continue his regular medical practice was next to impossible. He relied upon Molly for all of the office procedures and basic nursing care, even though she disliked cleaning wounds and bandaging limbs. He tried to involve Spence, but got nowhere: the freight business, and the continuing intrigue of prospecting, took all of his time -- he had to spend hours playing with Alfred, after all!

"We've got a new patient," Dr. Capshaw announced one evening at supper. "He's been an assayer and a prospector, and when I told him we wanted to learn about new minerals he got quite excited."

Spence, who had been trying to keep Alf from crying, set him back in his crib. Molly listened as well as she could while spooning out the chili and biscuits.

"Did you show him some of our rocks?" Spence asked.

"I had a couple with me today -- I wasn't expecting to do anything with them up on the hill. He looked at the one that has that sparkly part and said it was pyrite. Said it wouldn't be worth anything by itself but there might be some good minerals nearby where we found it."

"I'd like to meet him."

"That can be arranged," the doctor chuckled. "Will you carry up a wagon-load of stuff for me tomorrow? Do you have time?"

"I'll make time," Spence responded enthusiastically. "Suppose we bring up some of our real mystery rocks and see what he says?"

The rocks, which they had carefully labeled, turned out to be mostly worthless. They told each other that they had expected that result, but were clearly disappointed nonetheless. Their new consultant did, however, keep a half dozen for further study. He sent back a list of the supplies he needed, including chemicals and hammers and equipment to heat the rocks.

The sanatorium manager, Anamaria, had taken to the job with such eagerness that she and her family were now installed at the sanatorium in a small grounds-keeper's cottage. Raoul added gardening to his chores and between the two of them, the sanatorium seemed increasingly attractive. A traveling photographer made a set of postcards which Dr. Capshaw bought in quantity for advertising.

It was clearly time to find a partner for the doctor's office.

Dr. Capshaw did not foresee any difficulty filling the position. After all, Pinyon Creek was a prosperous and growing town in an exotic location, ideal for a man with a spirit of adventure. But as the weeks passed without any letters from applicants he was forced to increase his efforts. He sent out dozens of the postcards of the sanatorium, but then realized that he wanted to publicize the soon-to-be-vacant Pinyon Creek office, not the newer structure in the hills. He ordered half a hundred fliers from the printer and sent them to medical schools and hospitals in the Midwest and East. He wrote to physicians in San Francisco and Los Angeles. And still nothing happened.

Spring and summer passed peacefully. Alf grew, chubby and happy. Molly expected her second child after Christmas and began knitting. She devoted most of her spare time to her garden, happy and relieved to find that the trees had weathered last year's burning winds, and that enough of her vegetables had survived to give her seeds which she planted early, to begin harvesting before the hottest of the summer days. She learned from Anamaria and Raoul how to gather seeds from her plants after they had flowered, and gratefully accepted herb and vegetable plants which they had brought from Mexico.

With so many projects to occupy them, the family found their days passing quickly. By late Autumn the air was chill and snow threatened. There had still been no interest in Dr. Capshaw's offer and he was wearing out. Regretfully he gave up his trips into the desert with Spence, leaving the younger man to collect and label interesting rocks. Their consultant, Will Pettingill, was helpful but not a communicative man. Dr. Capshaw told Spence wryly that it was a good thing he had serious lung problems, because he didn't want to see him recover too quickly.

Because of all of the changes, Pinyon Creek was growing and thriving. The meadows near Owens River held herds of cattle. Fields of hay and alfalfa stretched out east toward the Panamints. In Pinyon Creek, the permanent residents had begun planting and expanding their own gardens, just as Molly was doing, maintaining and increasing the little canals they created leading from the small creek west of town. Farther south, speculators planted larger gardens and apple orchards. With the growth of the town, Pinyon Creek was becoming more civilized. The saloons were balanced by a market supplied by Spence's hauling business and by itinerant peddlers. Two churches had opened -- Methodist and Baptist -- and the Baptist minister's wife had started a school.

Watching the changes to Pinyon Creek, Molly was sometimes heartened, sometimes sad. There were more interesting things to do and see now than when she and her father had arrived, but Pinyon Creek would never be a city, like Redruth or St. Austell or Truro. And there was still only a handful of women.

Just before Christmas, Dr. Capshaw received a letter. A new medical graduate, Stuart Pershing, and his wife would be arriving after the New Year, to consider taking the medical practice. As Dr. Capshaw repeated to one and all, "This was the best Christmas gift I could imagine!"

On the morning of Twelfth Night, Molly was preparing a welcome dinner for the Pershing family. Stuart and his wife Velda were coming from Ohio, a long and difficult trip. They could reach San Francisco by train, but then they had the choice of buying their own wagon and horses or taking a series of short train trips, and still ending up with the requirement of their own transport, because passenger trains had not yet reached the valley. Fortunately, the stagecoach made fairly reliable and frequent runs.

Anamaria was also expecting a baby. She had come down into Pinyon Creek to wait for the birth, which was expected in just a few weeks. She was hoping for a boy. Raoul had picked the name: Philip Xavier after his father's name and his own saint names.

As they prepared vegetables for the stew, the two women compared notes. Anamaria continued to enjoy her life at the sanatorium, although it was hard work taking care of an increasing number of invalids, many of whom were depressed in addition to being ill.

"I can understand," Molly said with a wry smile. "I'm depressed myself sometimes. I never expected to be living here. Never. "

"But in the winter," Anamaria said persuasively, "the mountains are so beautiful. I love the way the snow comes down, first on the tops of the mountains and then further down, until there is a line across them, almost like somebody painted it."

"Um. Too cold for me. In Cornwall we didn't get much snow. I have to agree," she admitted grudgingly, "that the winter can be peaceful and pretty comfortable."

"We have started taking the patients for carriage rides in the snow," Anamaria said. "We pile all their coats on, and sweaters and mittens, and load them into the wagon and take them up into the hills for an hour or so. They love to see the little creeks all covered with ice."

The stew was beginning to bubble, the rich beef broth and vegetables sending up delicious aromas. Dr. Capshaw entered, looking for company and a bite of supper.

"I hope they will arrive soon," he said, looking out of the kitchen window. "The wind is rising and it looks as though we might have snow tonight."

Just then they began to hear the creaking and jingling of the stage coach. Dr. Capshaw threw open the door and welcomed his guests. Stuart Pershing was a tall thin balding young man, the kind whose clothes always appear too short for his arms and legs. His wife Velda was shorter than her husband but tall for a woman. She was wrapped in layers of coat and scarves and blankets, which made it difficult for her to step up onto the porch and into the house.

"I'm just frozen," she said, moving as quickly as possible inside. "I have never felt such a wind. Not even in Cleveland. And Cleveland has terrible winters, just terrible. I am absolutely frozen. I expected that the desert would be warm and dry and I am just sopping wet. And frozen. "

Stuart helped his wife unwrap herself from the various garments, which he, helped by Molly, folded and stacked on a bench by the door. "Velda," he said patiently, "we talked about the weather here. It won't be winter all the time."

"And then what?" Velda responded. "Sun, heat, wind, insects. I know I won't like it here."

"Come and eat. You'll feel better." Molly ushered them all to the table.

During supper, they got acquainted through the stories they told. Molly and Velda, together at one end of the long table, compared stories of their childhood. Cleveland, Molly decided, did not sound very much at all like Cornwall. She tried to get Velda to tell her about her own interests.

"Well, I do enjoy needlework. I do embroidery. I made all of the cases for our pillows. You'll see them when our luggage arrives. And I made a cut-work tablecloth which is quite handsome if I do say so myself. I wonder -- are there any needlework clubs? or reading circles? What do the women here do?"

Smiling, Molly shook her head. "You'll have a good opportunity here to start whatever club you would like," she said. "Besides the church and the school, there's not much that's organized. Tomorrow or after you are all settled we can go meet some of the other families. This is a very small town, you know."

The Pershing luggage arrived within the week. By that time, Stuart and Velda had found a house, a small but pleasant home not far from the doctor's office, because Velda was fearful of living out in the desert. It took almost no time at all for the Pershings to unpack. It took longer for Velda to arrange the furnishings and to feel comfortable in her new house.

Stuart was almost immediately overwhelmed by his patients. The gold mines may have closed, but other mines opened throughout the area, and Pinyon Creek was growing slowly and providing more patients with all sorts of accidents and illnesses. Despite the claims of good fresh air, the valley experienced fogs in the winter and burning winds carrying alkali salts in the summer.

"But it's the men who work with the alkali salts," Stuart complained to Dr. Capshaw. "They fill the sacks with alkali and it burns their chests and their throats. I imagine some of them die from it."

"I have to admit that I didn't pay much attention to it," Dr. Capshaw responded. "In the first place, it wasn't so big a business when the mines were going strong. And the men don't complain much anyway. They're happy to have steady work. When the mines were really failing, they wouldn't know from one week to another whether they would get paid."

Spence was drawing sketches on the back of an envelope. "I wonder whether we could make a sacking machine? If all of that could be done automatically, then they wouldn't get so badly dusted. It's like at the mines, we would water the dust to keep it down. Maybe we could do something like that?"

Dr. Capshaw shook his head. "The men need these jobs. We wouldn't be doing them any favors if we make the work go away. No, we'd have to think of something that would keep them usefully employed but not subject to alkali dust."

"And the company would have to agree," Stuart put in. "They won't go for anything that would raise their expenses."

Anamaria and baby Josefina (Philip Xavier was being saved for the next child) had returned to the sanatorium. Molly missed her cheerful friend. She was finding that entertaining Velda was becoming a steady job, and she was tired enough now, her own due date almost upon her. Velda had managed to irritate a growing number of Pinyon Creek women by her comparisons between Pinyon Creek and Cleveland.

But in late January Molly woke with the first labor pains. By nightfall on January 23 Barbara Richardson was born.

Chapter VII – Jock-the-Dog

Mollie and Velda rocked gently back and forth in the tall rocking chairs on Mollie's porch. On a June afternoon, a breeze had picked up and cooled the air. The sky was growing a deepening shade of blue, signaling a rainstorm. Molly was grateful for the chance to sit and rest. Charles Wallace Richardson, her third child, was now two months old. The pregnancy had been a difficult one, and Charles was a colicky, fussy, demanding infant. Even his older sister, Barbara, would storm away from his cradle after trying unsuccessfully to distract him from his wails. But at the moment he was peaceful, watching shadows playing across the porch ceiling over his cradle, sucking on his fingers. Mollie was patching children's overalls, while Velda held up first one skein, then another, of embroidery thread from her work box.

"I think this one, don't you?" Velda asked, centering a skein of violet thread against the floral border she had begin on a white pillowcase. "I just think it is perfect. It will be little violets."

"Um," Mollie agreed absently. "I might put some flowers on Barbara's nightdress. I think she would like that. Have you had any luck starting a sewing class?"

"My dear, I have. Can you imagine it? I am so very pleased." She gestured grandly. "Sarah White, you know, the wife of the Baptist minister, and her mother, think it would be a grand idea, and they are going to have a tea for me. They will be sending you an invitation soon, so please come!"

"I might have to bring the children," Mollie said. "Charles won't be a problem. He'll just sleep. But Barbara will probably want to sew, too!"

"Oh no!" then Velda realized Mollie was teasing her. "Of course you must bring them. Barbara can play with Pris White. She is the darlingest child. Not that Barbara isn't, of course. But there I was, yesterday, at the parsonage or the rectory or whatever Baptists call their minister's house -- "

" -- I think they call it the minister's house," Mollie murmured. Sometimes she just couldn't help herself.

" -- and that darling Pris came right over and climbed up into my lap. Of course, I was startled and pushed her off -- gently, of course -- and Sarah came right away and took her from me. But she seems like a happy and healthy child."

"What kind of class will this be? Will you teach sewing or embroidery or both?"

"As I told Sarah, I will be happy to teach basic stitching, even though my heart is really in embroidery. There is something so genteel, so refined, so, so artistic about embroidery, don't you think? I told Sarah that this class could raise the level of culture here, give these women something, well, higher, than just regular life. In the desert. After all."

"And what did Sarah say to that?"

"I don't remember that she actually said anything. But I'm sure she agrees with me. Sarah generally agrees with everything I tell her."

Mollie smiled, folding the last pair of little overalls and closing her sewing box.

The sky continued to darken and the breeze was growing stronger. It was becoming uncomfortable to sit on the porch. Mollie and Velda gather up their supplies and took them inside.

"Alf," Mollie called. "It's going to storm. Go get Jock-the-dog and bring him inside."

"Ok," came a cheerful voice from the kitchen. The door banged as Alf set off into the back yard.

The rain began almost at once, large heavy raindrops that spattered against the windows and exploded against the sandy ground. The wind kept rising. The sky grew dark with heavy clouds. Mollie closed the windows, gathered hurricane lanterns and set them ready on the kitchen table.

"Velda, stay here with me," she said. "It's already raining too hard for you to walk home. You'd be soaked."

"Oh, I'm not leaving," Velda responded. "I'm staying right here till it calms down. Stuart will be busy with his patients today. He won't even miss me.""

Together they looked out of the front window. Mollie's house was near Pinyon Creek's main street which was now almost empty of people. The rain was pelting down. A pair of horses at a hitching post stood despondently, their coats shiny with water. Tumbleweeds, leaves, branches and debris bounced past along the street. The packed dirt of the road could not absorb the water, which was rising toward the wooden sidewalk. Through the windows they could feel the temperature dropping. Across the street the horses lifted one foot, then another.

Velda shivered. "Did I just see lightning?"

A thunderclap, small and distant, answered her.

"I'm worried," Mollie said softly. "Spence and Papa went out toward Keeler this morning. We had no idea it would rain, and they have no rain gear with them. Or tarps or food or much of anything. We almost never get rain this time of year."

Charles in his cradle had started to cry, soon joined by Barbara. Mollie hurried to the back door.

"Alf, Alf!" she shouted. "Come in now!" She tried to make her voice strong, but she could see that the creek was already almost in flood. Her voice was lost against the noise of the rushing water. And Alf was nowhere to be seen.

She pulled on her boots and her coat, tying a scarf over her head.

"Velda, take care of the children. I have to get Alf." She didn't look back but ran through the garden, Alf's jacket in her hand. Frantically she called him but could not see him or the dog.

She was almost at the creek before she heard him.

"Ma, ma, come here." It was a scared, thin voice but it was Alf.

She could see his little body under the trunk of a tamarisk tree almost at the edge of the creek. The water was touching his feet.

"Ma, come get Jock-the-dog. He's stuck."

The dog's hind leg was trapped between a rock and a branch. To Mollie it looked as though they had been washed up against the grass where he had been lying.

"I called him and I called him and he wouldn't come so I found him but I can't get him loose." Alf was trying hard not to cry. Jock-the-dog whimpered quietly.

"Here, Alf, put on your jacket. I know it's soaked but we are, too. Now let's see what I can do." She knelt in the mud next to the dog. Pulling on the branch did no good. It was too large, and was wedged into the mud. Was the water rising too quickly? She decided not to look.

"Alf, run to the house. If Papa is here tell him to come. If Papa isn't here, bring my shovel quickly down here."

The boy was off like a rocket, slipping and sliding in the sandy mud. Where's Spence? Where is my father? What is happening? I've never seen a storm like this. She held out her hand and Jock-the-dog licked it. He was trembling.

Mollie looked around for a branch, anything to use for a lever. The rain was so strong that it was hard to see anything. She tried to scoop mud out from the other side of the dog, but the rain was too hard. It was getting colder. She thought she saw little white hail stones.

"Ma, ma!" Alf was running back, dragging the shovel behind him.

Mollie took the shovel and levered it against the rock. She could feel it give slightly. Jock-the-dog squirmed, trying to get free. Alf pulled at the dog. The creek was definitely flooding now. Her boots were sinking into the mud. We will all three die right here, she thought. We will drown in muddy sand in the middle of the desert because of a stupid dog.

"Alf, stay away from the water,!" she cried, knowing how foolish that sounded. Alf held his dog tighter and continued to try to pull him.

"All right, one more time. " Mollie grunted, throwing her whole body against the shovel handle. It moved just a bit, just enough for Alf to pull Jock-the-dog out of the hole.

The dog whined, shivering, holding his foot off the ground. Alf was crying now. Behind him, a chunk of mud and grass fell away, carrying the rock and the branch into the surging water.

"Now take off your jacket," Mollie commanded. "We'll use it to carry Jock-the-dog." Alf brightened up a bit.

Just then a flash of lightning lit the sky.

"Away from the tree," Mollie screamed, gathering the dog into the jacket and stumbling toward the house.

"Ma," Alf called from behind her. She turned, every muscle tense with need for him to run to her. "I'm bringing the shovel back."

"Just run, now, Alf. Leave the shovel. We have to get into the house. Run, run, run!"

She had always thought her garden was small, but it seemed to take forever to cross the ground to the back door. Alf reached it first and flung it open for her.

Muddy, drenched, they stopped just inside the house to catch their breath. Velda hurried to Alf, pulling off his clothing despite his objections. Mollie set Jock-the-dog on the kitchen table. Velda handed her a towel and Mollie dried the dog as well as she could. He was still trembling and panting, but lay quietly under her fingers.

"His leg is hurt," she reported. "But I think it's not very bad." She put him on the floor in the corner, keeping the towel wrapped around him. He rested his head on his paws and lay quietly, watching.

Velda had found a flannel shirt of Spence's and dressed Alf in it. He rubbed his arms, warming up. The long sleeves of the shirt dragged on the floor. Velda rolled them as far as they would go. Alf giggled.

"Now you," Velda told Mollie, who gratefully stepped out of her soaked clothing and into clean clothes Velda had found for her. They gathered all of the muddy clothes and pushed them into the laundry tub.

"I heated water for tea," Velda said, "and I think Alf could use some, too."

Outside, the lightning and thunder were continuing, although apparently diminishing in intensity. The rain, however, seemed to be getting stronger all the time. The wind was blowing rain and hail; they could hear the plink of the hailstones against the house. Charles woke, needing to be nursed. Barbara, hearing his cries, awoke as well, fussy.

"Well, here is our tea," Velda announced in a cheery voice to the children. She gave them each a slice of bread with butter and a tea cup with a small serving of milky tea. Mollie gratefully sipped her own mug of strong tea, feeling it warming her over her anxieties.

"When is papa coming?" Alf asked.

"Soon, honey." "Soon, Alf." Their voices collided.

They both were thinking about the stories they had heard about flash floods. Everybody sat quietly for a few minutes.

"I think the rain is letting up just a bit," Velda said. She pulled the back door open an inch or two. "Yes, it's less windy, and there's no more hail. I think the worst is over for now. And look, Alf! Come here quickly!"

She braced him against her and pointed. "The most beautiful rainbow!"

Mollie, watching out the front door as the rains continued, wondered, Where are papa and Spence?

Chapter VIII – Rain and Flood

The rain continued through the night. By suppertime Velda donned her coat and Mollie's boots and left for home, where she was sure Stuart was busy with storm casualties. Mollie fed the children and tried to make a normal evening for them, but she could not help listening for the sounds of the mules or the creak of the door. She finally forced herself to climb into bed and try to sleep. The next day was the same; rain, sometimes pelting down in force, sometimes diminishing but never stopping altogether. The children had stopped asking about their father and grandfather, but could not be distracted by stories or games. They wandered about the house, stopping every few minutes to stare out a window. For supper, Molly gave them a special treat of hot cocoa, but they scarcely noticed. At bedtime she brought them into her bed, where they all nestled together.

The morning brought a sky heavy with clouds, but the wind had died and the rain had stopped. The main street was still uncrossable on foot, flooded with debris-filled water -- tree branches and small plants, debris caught up from behind the saloon and the general store, here and there a small drowned animal. The horses were gone from the hitching post. The street was empty of people and, except for the unfamiliar noises of the rushing water, almost silent.

As she was finishing her morning chores, Velda appeared, carrying her boots. "See, I have mine now. And I wanted to come over right away because we need your help at Stuart's office. The rain has made the Owens River into a huge flood. People are stuck and some are hurt. Nobody has seen anything like this in years, they say. Bring the children and somebody will tend them."

Mollie nodded, wondering why Velda hadn't asked about Spence and her father. Did she already know bad news and wanted Stuart to be the one to tell her? Or was she, as usual, simply attacking the first problem first?

Velda bustled about, finding jackets and boots for Barbara and Alf, while Mollie finished nursing Charles. They walked carefully, trying to avoid the debris which had blown onto the wooden walkway. Alf, staring about, found a drowned cat. Mollie noticed that he didn't say a word but his eyes got large.

The doctor's office was indeed crowded with people. Mollie spotted the minister's wife and left the three children with her. She put on her apron, washed her hands, and got to work, cleaning and bandaging the cuts and bruises presented to her. She quickly realized that most of the patients were worried, sometimes frantic about relatives and friends and their property.

"This is the biggest flood I've seen, and I've been here since I was a pup," one grizzled miner told her as she stitched a long cut in his arm. "I don't want to know what's left of my digs up at the mine. I can't get up there anyway, so I might as well just wait and see. But I keep thinking about my animals."

"You can't get home?"

"Ouch! Hey!"

"Almost done."

"Most of the dirt roads are either washed out or blocked. Rocks, tree branches. Some fools are out there even now, panning for gold if you can believe it. They're sure all this water has dislodged some good stuff."

Stuart came by and approved the stitches. His eyes were tired, and his clothes rumpled, but he moved in his usual energetic way. "I understand you had quite an adventure yourself yesterday," he told Mollie.

"I was so glad Velda was there. She took care of all of us." Mollie smiled. "And even Jock-the-dog is better after a good night's sleep. Have you heard anything of Papa and Spence?"

"No, but I'm sure they are safe. They are such seasoned desert travelers, especially Spence. Even their mules are sensible. They are holed up safe and sound, I'm sure. Be prepared to wait, they tell me, because nobody can go anywhere. That is partly why we have such a big crowd here."

They watched Velda moving this way and that, with a large pot of coffee and a basket of biscuits. Alf followed her importantly, carrying a basket of coffee mugs. She stopped at each patient and chatted a moment, getting them to tell their stories about the flood.

The three of them worked busily all morning. Mollie took time out to check on the children, but found them well cared for by several women. Others had set up a system, using Alf and two other children, to collect used mugs and wash them, ready to hand out again. At midday more women came, with pots of soup and pie for all.

"Alf could get used to this," Mollie laughed as she and Velda enjoyed their soup. Alf was everywhere, it seemed, running errands, fetching spoons or mugs, removing the dogs who kept trying to nose into the room.

"How is Jock-the-dog?" Velda asked.

"I think he is much better today. I think he just had bruises and maybe a sprain, or whatever it is that dogs get. But he won't go outside. Alf pushed him outdoors for a few minutes this morning, but as soon as he finished, he wanted to get back inside. He just whimpered and whined. I almost felt like whimpering and whining myself."

"Well, you can't," Velda said firmly. "I can't stand even thinking that I have to keep you cheerful as well. All these poor people."

As the day wore on, the crowd in the office thinned. People who had come in for treatment were stitched, encouraged, and bandaged and left. Many of them joined others at the newspaper office, exchanging stories and making plans for repair projects.

Mollie had been noticing a small boy sitting by himself on a stool near the kitchen door. He was a stranger to her, about Alf's age. His clothes were worn but not ragged, and his shoes were sturdy, unlike some of the worn-out footwear of many of the children, all of whom preferred to go barefoot whenever possible. The boy sat patiently and silently, watching the comings and goings.

"Who's that?"

Velda shook her head. "I don't have any idea. I tried to get him to eat something but he wouldn't. I tried to get him to tell me his name, but he wouldn't do that either. Nobody else seems to know him either. I don't know how he got here, or where his family is, or anything."

Mollie waved to Alf, who was playing with one of the stray dogs in the doorway. "Alf, do you see that boy? Do you know him? Well, go and make friends with him, please. He looks lonely."

Alf gave his mother an unmistakeable put-upon scowl, but trotted over and squatted down next to the boy. Soon the two were busily talking, Alf making grand gestures toward the people he knew. Before long, he came trotting back.

"Is it all right if Tony helps me do my work? Can I give him a biscuit and some milk? Can we take more biscuits to people? What will we do with the dogs? Tony has a dog named Buster. Buster ran away. Can I have some milk? Can Barbara have some milk? can we go outdoors and see the water if we are very very very careful? Are there any apples here? I'm bored."

Mollie laughed. "Yes and also no. Aunty Velda will give you some milk. I have to go do my work now, but you and Tony can help me clean things up. Would that be good? Where does Tony live?"

"Sure. We will help you very hard. Tony is five, too. I don't know where Tony lives. He is waiting for his family to come get him. Can we go outside now?"

"Not just yet. There's still too much water. Let's see. Get a box or a bucket, something we can put garbage in. And one for Tony, too. What is Tony's last name?"

"Ok. But later, ok? When it stops raining for good? And we can take off our shoes and stomp in puddles? Tony says he is Tony DeMarco. Hey, Tony!" And Alf was off again, flying across the room, dodging adults.

Mollie and Velda exchanged glances. DeMarco was not a name familiar to either of them. They rose and returned to their work. In the time they had eaten their soup, a line had formed by Stuart's door. Mollie would have her hands full.

Her patients had, for the most part, simple wounds, often needing only a clean bandage. As she worked, she wondered whether the supplies would last. Her father had taken boxes of basic supplies up to the sanatorium a few months ago; she thought they could have used them here today (but maybe they had wound up at the sanatorium too? Maybe that was where Spence and Papa were?). Would they have enough good drinking water? They were using so much to wash everything, and make tea and soup. What would the flood do to the well water? Her father would know, but where was he? Were there people stranded up in the hills at the mines and cabins? Spence had told her how many little isolated communities he had seen. Where was Spence?

Charles was fussy, so Mollie nursed him as she spoke with her patients, separating them into two groups: people she could help and people who needed Stuart's skills. The door slammed open and two husky men appeared, carrying a third between them.

He was moaning faintly and moving his head from side to side. They gently set him down on a cot.

"He fell, we think. We found him just outside of town, right by the road. Good thing the water's not so high now. He could have been picked right up in it."

"Looks like he fell from his horse. See, his leg is all bruised up. Didn't find the horse, though. Could have drowned, I guess."

Mollie considered him, moving his arms and legs gently, trying to get him to look at her. His eyes were mostly closed and his face was now pale. She couldn't find any blood.

"Alf and Tony," she called. "Go carefully, carefully down to the church and get Doctor to come here. Carefully," she repeated as the two boys trotted out, returning quickly with the doctor.

The two boys were getting tired and fretful. Velda took them to the kitchen and fed them more milk and biscuits. Tony leaned against her, putting his arms around her quickly, then pulling back. Velda sank into a chair. "Come here, Tony." She patted her lap. He climbed up. Within just a moment, he was sound asleep.

Alf wandered back into the main room, watching as Dr. Pershing examined the fallen man. Unconsciously his hands mimicked the doctor's movements as arms and legs were moved, the head lifted from the table, the neck turned. Mollie watched her son from across the room, thinking that Alf might be a doctor himself one day.

She could see that the worst of the storm was over. Alf had found Barbara and they were playing together, quietly, near the minister's wife. Charles was making waking-up movements of fists and feet. Most of the patients had been seen; Stuart still had an evening's worth of more serious cases ahead of him. She was, as her father would say, bone-tired.

She gathered up the children and hunted Velda, finding her in the kitchen, stroking Tony's hair as he slept. She looked up at Mollie and grinned. "I'll take him home with us tonight. Poor mite. We'll all do better tomorrow."

The following morning saw the community gathered in the Baptist Church for a prayer service. The church was crowded. Almost everybody in Pinyon Creek knew or was related to a casualty of the flood. Now that the storm was over, the sun blazed down and the interior of the church turned steamy. There were chairs for only about half of the participants. Children sat on the floor, or squatted against the walls, still in their parents' sight. Alf, Barbara and Tony had found a spot near the front. Mollie, Velda and Stuart sat crammed together on one of the few benches.

After a short message, the minister passed out song sheets with one of the congregation's favorite hymns. "Oh God Our Help in Ages Past" was one of the longer hymns, but it sounded especially appropriate, with its references to "Our shelter from the stormy blast", and "Time like an ever rolling stream". They rose and began to sing.

As they reached the last verse, Mollie began to hear a loud, confident, slightly off-key voice that she knew well. Alf raced to the back door, crying, "Papa, papa." Dr. Capshaw continued singing as he and Spence entered the room, broad smiles on their faces.

A few days after the big flood, Velda came to visit, accompanied by Tony. She sent him off to find Alf, then collapsed into a chair by the kitchen table. Absently she picked up a basket of peas and began to shell them.

"I am now a mother," she said. "A mother of a five year old boy who still doesn't talk to me."

"What do you mean -- Mother?"

"Stuart and some men went up the canyons, checking to see if anybody was hurt and needed help. We think they found the DeMarco cabin." Velda stopped speaking, checked to make sure Alf and Tony were out of earshot. "They found two people, a man and a woman, both dead. But it wasn't the flood. They say it looks like he killed her and then himself."

"But how?"

"Well, he was pretty well known in town. A bully and a heavy drinker. He had hurt his wife before, and lately he had been particularly mean because he couldn't get work. Nobody wanted to hire him, they say. I think Tony ran away and came into town, maybe for help, and maybe the storm scared him so much he couldn't tell his story."

Molly nodded, watching the two boys. Alfred was trying to teach Tony to play checkers. Their two heads, blonde and dark, were bent together over the checkerboard, their legs tangled up together on the big bench.

"It does explain something," she said slowly. "Remember, he appeared in Stuart's office in the middle of the storm, but he was dry. Even his shoes were dry. He must have been hiding somewhere, and then came in when he saw all the people. Are you going to try to find other people in his family?"

"I'm leaving that up to Stuart. He is getting just as fond of Tony as I am. And Tony seems to need lots of attention and hugs. He can talk. He just doesn't want to say much, but he seems to be -- well, not happy exactly, but maybe content with us. So we aren't in very much of a hurry to find them."

The two boys had reached some kind of decision. Now they came running to the women. Tony climbed up into Velda's lap. She hugged him and smoothed his hair, smiling fondly. Alf pulled at Molly's apron.

"We want to go wait for Granddad outside. Can we, can we?"

Just then Dr. Capshaw appeared at the door, smiling widely and carrying a big basket of tomatoes from Anamaria at the sanatorium. Even though he had moved up to the mountains he came down frequently from his sanatorium for a visit with his grandchildren, and, he admitted, some meals cooked by Molly. Alf and Barbara loved playing with their grandfather who was happy to play the same games over and over, most of which required building towers with wooden blocks and then knocking them over, although Alf was now old enough to demand real games, with rules.

By midday Spence returned from a delivery to Keeler and the two men went out for a walk, while Molly and the children prepared the lunch.

Just as she was lifting the chicken from the oven, Molly heard the door bang shut as the two men entered, quickly washed their hands and came to the table.

"Tell me, Molly," her father said, pulling out his chair, "which sounds better -- Capshaw's Retreat or Sierra Winds?"

"And tell ME, Molly," said Spence, "which sounds better -- Sierra Exploring Company or Richardson's Mule-back Tours?"

Molly stared at them. Her father, looking sheepish, sighed and said, "Well, girl, I went and bought a camera. Now we can do our own advertising."

"And where did you get a camera? And how will you learn how to use it?"

Her father beamed. "I traded with John Fischer. He decided he wants to go back to ranching. He doesn't like trying to be a photographer -- keeps him indoors too much, too much paperwork. He wants to get back on a horse, run some cattle again."

"Huh. Can't make any money making photographs, I imagine. Not enough people in Pinyon Creek with the money or the desire to have a picture, not these days." Molly slammed the dish of potatoes onto the table. "And what did you trade for it?"

"Remember last Winter, when I took out his appendix? and his son Tom needs his tonsils taken out. So I cleared it with Stuart and I'll do that. Fischer will give me lessons, too. I think I'll practice by taking pictures of my grandchildren."

Alf grinned. Barbara looked frightened.

"And you, Spence," Molly glared at her husband. "Are you part of this scheme as well?"

"Well, honey, I figure we'll need some advertising for our new company. So, we'll learn this camera together."

"Honestly, you are as bad as Alf! Always wanting the newest things!"

"We'll have time in the winter, when everything calms down. By that time your dad's cabins will be finished, and my packing company will -- should -- be up and running."

"And what about all of the parts and things and where will we keep it and what if people don't like their pictures and what will you do with the pictures and..."

"Molly. Sit. Eat. It's going to be just fine."

Chapter IX – Visitors to the Mountains

During Autumn and Winter the various projects were developed. Dr. Capshaw added several spacious cabins to his property not far from the sanatorium, calling the new endeavor SIERRA WINDS RETREAT. By Spring, they were ready for their first guests. Located just below the snow line, they were designed for, and almost immediately used by, wealthy city families looking for a wilderness adventure which did not require wilderness skills. By providing housekeeping and meal service (in a large dining room near the center of the cabin group) the daily needs of the guests were met. The first Springtime guests came to play in the snow and look for the first wildflowers of the season. Later in the Summer they would enjoy short hikes and swimming in the little lake. Many of them chose to go farther into the mountains on mule-back, the mules supplied by the Sierra Exploring Company.

As he became more skillful with the camera, Dr. Capshaw began to offer photographic portraits of the guests, posing them in front of their cabin with a "SIERRA WINDS RETREAT" sign tucked into a corner of the picture.

Spence made additional fish-stocking trips with Wally during the late Summer and early Fall. He could tell, however, that Wally was losing interest in the project. The more Wally talked about moving on, the more Spence became determined to take on the leadership of the project, and the Fish and Wildlife rangers were happy to have him. He happily spent the winter months designing improved carrying cases for the little trout and fitting them onto Daisy or Flora. When he received his contract for the Spring and Summer fish-stocking trips, he realized he could afford more mules. After much discussion, Molly reluctantly agreed.

A three-week trip to Mojave, which he combined with a delivery of mixed ores, produced four new mules: Peter, Gert, Toojay, and Banjo.

Molly and the children were walking home from the creek when they heard Daisy's bells.

They ran to the road to see a six-mule team pulling a wagon so light it bounced. Spence grinned from his high seat and helped the children climb up into the wagon. The ten-day trip back from Mojave had melded the six animals into a comfortable team.

As he unharnessed them, he introduced each to his family.

"Peter, now, he's the tallest, you can see that. His legs are the longest. But he's not as old as Daisy. Gert likes people pretty good. You can see she's interested in all of you. Otherwise she'd just start eating." He waved in the direction of Flora and Daisy who had already found their favorite corners of the corral and were busily munching hay. "Toojay -- I never could find out what his name means but he knows it, don't you, Toojay?"

The children giggled as the mule nodded in response.

"And Banjo. That's kind of a sad story. He used to be owned by a miner, a prospector down by Cottonwood Creek. That miner really loved to sing and play the banjo and he did it all the time. Couldn't do either very well, according to the man who told me. Couldn't mine silver very well either, I guess. One night he was up too late, drinking and singing and thumping the banjo till he just fell right down asleep. In the morning we woke up to find his mule had stepped right on the banjo, broke it all to pieces, except for a little bit of the sound box that got stuck on his foot."

"I don't think he should have to keep that name," Molly objected. "He should have a fresh start."

"Well, keep your eye on him and see what you and the little ones think. But if we are going to change his name it needs to be soon. Otherwise he won't know it's him."

That night at supper the children were still talking about the new mules.

"That's the most mules we ever had," Barbara said. "That's the most mules in Pinyon Creek."

"Probably," her father answered. "But it's not the most mules that anybody ever had."

"Why would anybody want even more?" Charles asked sceptically.

"Back in the days of the big mines here," Spence started the story while Molly cut pieces of pie, "they had to take large wagon loads down to Mojave. I have seen the wagons. You could stand Alf on my shoulders, and Charles on Alf's shoulders and Charles's head would just reach to the top of the side of the wagon. "

The children regarded each other, mentally measuring.

"So the cargo in each wagon weighed tons and tons," Spence continued. "The only way to move it was to take several mule teams and put them together. The biggest I ever heard of was twenty mules. They worked out of the borax mine in Death Valley. It's quite a story. The team was so long that the driver couldn't see the front mules. He had a jerk chain that led all the way up from mule to mule, to the leading pair. Then he would jerk on it to make the leaders turn right, or make a steady pull to turn them left. He had a helper who kept a bucket with small rocks or stones. If he needed to, he could throw a stone at a mule way up front if that mule was disobeying or not pulling his load. That's what they said, anyway.

"But this is the best part. If they needed to make a sharp turn, say like the turn up the hill by Shepard's Gulch-- " the children nodded "-- they had those mules trained so that the three pair closest to the wagon would step over the long chain and pull to keep the wagon going straight, while the others pulled around the corner. That way the wagon wouldn't fall over the cliff. They called it the dance of the mules."

Everybody sat silently for a minute, picturing it.

"Did you ever see it, Pa?" Barbara asked.

"No. Actually not many people did. It was only that one teamster, as far as I know, who ran that long a train, and they only did it for about five years until they wore out that mine. So people

– muleskinners – they all talk about it and wish they could do that, but nobody else ever did. As far as I have heard."

"We could do it," Charles remarked.

His father smiled. "But we don't need to, and that's all right with me. We have our hands pretty full with just the animals we've got!"

They had finished the pie and the supper. The children disappeared into the back yard, where they assembled as many ropes and strings as they could find, making a model of the mule train and taking turns being the dancing mule, stepping carefully over the central chain as Spence watched from the house.

All over the mountains, it seemed, work was starting as the first National Parks were organized. Spence found more work than he could handle. The first job for his new team was a pack trip hauling supplies into the new Sequoia National Forest.

"Now where am I going to find somebody to work with?" he grumbled to Molly one evening over dinner. "Everybody seems to be already working, or else so useless I wouldn't want them."

"I may have an answer. Papa told me that a couple of the men who built his cabins are looking for work. He liked them pretty well, said they were reliable and worked hard."

Before long, Spence had hired two helpers. They quickly learned the basics of working with mules and by early June he was ready for his first trip to the Sequoia forest. All the mules were involved. Daisy led, as always, her bell jingling jauntily. Flora walked right behind her, with Peter, Gert, Banjo and Toojay behind. It turned out that Peter was only happy when he was near

Flora, while Toojay was restless unless he was at the end of the line. He seemed to feel that it was his responsibility to keep the train moving. Spence and his new helpers Tom and Hank walked along beside the mules. Peter, Gert, Banjo and Toojay were loaded with bags of food, lumber, lengths of pipe and collections of additional supplies. Daisy and Flora carried bundles of tarp-wrapped hay.

Spence remembered his first fish-stocking trip as the pack train left Pinyon Creek for the hills north of town. This time, the trail was easier to follow and the mules seemed sturdy and capable despite their heavy burdens. The ranger had given him a good map, marked with locations for watering the animals and camping. Best of all, Hank had made the trip before.

They climbed out of the valley and skirted the river which was still roaring with snow-melt water. Tom sang quietly to himself. The mules had adapted to a steady pace just right for the men to walk alongside. The first day was pleasant, warm with a soft breeze. By nightfall they had made camp in a forest of tall pines.

On the second day, they came across an area not marked on Spence's map. It was at the edge of a grove of pines, but it looked ruined and wasted. Collections of scorched branches and sticks indicated many days of campfires. Trash littered the ground. Small trees had been cut, some apparently for firewood, some for shelter; the remains of hastily-built structures looked ready to fall.

Hank walked through the clearing, returning with a disgusted look. "They just took whatever they wanted and didn't bother to clean up anything."

"Can you figure out what they were doing?"

"Nope. But I have some ideas. I think they were hunting deer and just didn't know how."

"What makes you think that?"

"Tracks. Their tracks and deer tracks. Worthless fools."

Grumbling, they cleaned up the worst of the mess and continued on. As they gained altitude the trail became narrower. They began to see small patches of snow in the shadow of trees or boulders. They stopped earlier for the night, allowing the mules to range more widely to graze over the rocky ground.

The next morning found them walking occasionally on icy spots. "Snow in June," Spence exclaimed. "Molly will never believe it."

Now there was more snow. The mules slowed and set their feet carefully, avoiding icy patches. The air was crisp despite the brilliant sunshine. Snow covered much of the ground now, mounded by winter winds from months past. It looked worn, covered with tracks of birds and small animals, dotted with pine-cones. Hank picked up a handful, made a quick snowball, lobbed it at Tom. It was harder to follow the trail because the snow blurred the edges. Daisy was unhappy. She shook her head and walked as slowly as Spence would allow. He kept his hand on her neck as they walked, which seemed to comfort her. Apart from the jingle of her bell and the occasional comments from the men, the call of a bird or the crack of a branch, the air seemed silent.

Suddenly, the mood was broken by a shout from ahead of them on the trail:

"You! Mule team! Come over here!"

Everybody stopped. They saw nobody on the trail. But ahead and up on a rock, two men were waving their arms.

Hank snorted. "What in glory name do they think they're doing?"

The men were dressed as if for church. In woolen suits, white shirts with starched collars, shiny leather boots, and broad-brimmed hats of an unfamiliar style, the men on the rock looked as though they had dropped from the sky.

Spence waved back. "Come down to the trail, we can talk better there."

They stomped down the trail swinging sturdy, shiny walking-sticks. They were wearing knapsacks which looked almost new.

"Now, just who is in charge here?" It was the man who had first called out. "My good man, we wish you to take us back to the valley. We are in somewhat of a hurry, so let us start at once."

Spence, Tom and Harry looked at them, puzzled.

"I say, sir, I have requested your services. I am willing to pay you what you demand. Now step along lively, here."

"I'm sorry," responded Spence slowly, "but I'm afraid we can't help you. We need to deliver these supplies at Mount Royal camp. It's about another day to get there. Then we turn around and start back. You can come with us or wait here. Or just go down the trail yourselves."

"You don't understand," the second man said. "We are cold and tired and hungry. We got lost in this godforsaken wilderness. We need to get back to San Francisco and we will pay you for your help."

"Right," the first man chimed in. "Now you can turn some of these animals around and continue on with the rest. Give us a guide -- that one will do nicely, I'm sure -- " he pointed at Tom who was trying to keep a serious expression -- "and we'll be on our way."

"No. We can give you a blanket and some food, but we have to finish our work first."

Hank stepped forward. He was taller and bulkier than the San Franciscans and now, angry, he looked even larger.

"I think we passed your camp on our way up. Was that you who left all the garbage near the creek?"

"I don't believe it is any of your concern, young man. We can use the forest just like anybody else. Anybody who doesn't like it can just walk around it. There's plenty of room for everything."

Tom was sputtering. "I can't begin to tell you all the ways that's wrong. It'll take years and years for the trees you hacked to grow back. You left food scraps out -- that would have attracted bears. Probably did. Your campfire was still smoldering. Could have started a wildfire except we had a wet Spring....."

"Now listen here, son. You have no right to speak to me like that. I will make sure to tell your superior about your behavior. Who is your employer anyway?"

"The United States Army, sir," Spence did not bother to hide his glee. "We're delivering supplies for a camp they are building near the mountain top. We need to be moving on, now. So you can follow our trail down till you get to your campsite and you'll probably find your way home from there. If you can't make it, wait at your camp and we'll pick you up on our way back. Shouldn't be more than, say, four or five days."

The two hikers turned their backs and strode off. Spence clucked to Daisy who got the pack train started once again. They walked silently for awhile.

"They might have paid us," Tom said mournfully. "I guess I wrecked that plan."

"I bet they'll be gone by the time we go back," Spence answered. "So we won't have to figure out what to do with them. Good thing we don't see many like that, or I'll think twice about running pack parties."

Molly, waiting for Spence in Pinyon Creek, was deeply involved in her garden. After a series of failures, she had discovered how to plant her vegetables so that they would not be burned by the desert winds. She had managed a system of narrow ditches from the creek behind her house, so that the soil was kept damp throughout the growing season. She had visited other Pinyon Creek gardeners and farmers and talked to them. Now she was introducing Velda to the subject.

"I swear, I could almost find myself back home in Cleveland," Velda remarked as she adjusted her sunbonnet and drew on a pair of gardening gloves. "It feels to good to see the same old plants we used to grow there. Now corn, for example. We used to have the best corn. You plant it during a full moon, did you know that? My grandfather told me. And your peas look so fresh and good. Is it too late for me to plant peas this year? Where would I get the seeds? What do you do with them during the

Winter? Do you start them in little pots inside the house? That's what we used to do in Cleveland..."

"Velda, hush," Molly laughed. "You are way ahead of me here. I just thought I would show you and then we can build your own garden."

"Building a garden. It sounds serious and like very hard work. Like building a house."

"Well, once you do it, it's done, just like a house. Alf, collect Tony and let's go to Aunty Velda's house."

They tucked Charles into his wagon and walked into town and down the boardwalk to the Pershing house, a sturdy white cottage just down the street from the doctor's office. Alf and Tony ran ahead, stopping every few minutes to examine the ground for treasures, Barbara trotting behind them.

Velda's back yard already contained a small flower garden, but much of it was bare dirt.

Molly gave each boy a short shovel and showed them how to scrape, then dig, the dirt to begin two ditches. They would be the most important elements of any garden in Pinyon Creek. Velda helped by filling a water bucket and wetting the ground as the boys dug. Soon they were happily crusted in mud. The digging became easier as they got closer to the little creek which was running freely with the last of the winter snow pack runoff. By lunchtime they had the outlines of two parallel ditches running from the edge of the creek to Velda's garden-to-be.

They rested a few minutes, chatting about how they would design the areas for the vegetables Velda wanted to grow. They planned an excursion to the apple orchards North of Pinyon Creek near Bishop, to talk with the apple growers. Molly noticed that Velda had grown quiet.

"What's wrong?"

"Nothing's wrong. I've just had the best plan!" Velda exclaimed. "Some of the women in my embroidery class like to garden, too. One of them is even making a garden apron, with little pockets for her trowel and seed packets and string and things. It is really quite stunning, and she plans to embroider her name on the bib front."

"And...?"

"Well," Velda announced enthusiastically, "since they like to garden, and since we already know we want to make gardens an important part of life in Pinyon Creek, let's start a Garden Club!"

Alf and Tony cheered.

"How would we do that?" Molly asked.

"We call a meeting. We can have announcements in the newspaper and make some signs for, I don't know, the post office and the general store, and collect as many women as we can get. Then we all meet at my house and we will explain to them that the Pinyon Creek Garden Club will study the most improved methods for gardening, and we can share the produce from our gardens. Luella can demonstrate her gardening apron. We can each make one. We can make matching sunbonnets, too, because we will be out of doors. We will talk about how healthy it is to be out in the fresh air, and each one of us can teach the group something. I'm sure almost everybody can teach something, like when to plant peas, or which seeds need to be planted right side up, or whatever else seems appropriate. I think everybody could do that, at least a little bit. Well, maybe not Patricia, she really doesn't seem to know anything at all...."

"I must say, Velda, you just tire me out! But I think this is an interesting idea. Maybe we can get Fred Ricks to come talk to us. He's raising the most amazing melons. And we can show them the ditches we have built. And how important it is to have the water handy."

The women were talking so quickly that they didn't notice the two men who had appeared around the corner of the house, until Alf trotted to his mother and pulled at her sleeve.

Molly rose and walked toward them.

"Good afternoon, ladies."   He was tall and fair and well-dressed. His shoes were shiny and new-looking, his suit a light tweed. His carefully-barbered hair seemed to catch the sun, and looked golden. Wire-rimmed glasses shaded his eyes which Molly thought must be light blue. He was wearing two rings and carried a pewter-headed walking stick. He waited for Velda to join them.

"I would like to introduce myself, and ask you just a few questions, because my friend and I are looking at land with an idea to settle here and raise cattle. My name is Eaton, Fred Eaton, and this is my friend J. B. Lippincott."

"Good afternoon Mr. Eaton, Mr. Lippincott. I am Mrs. Spencer Richardson and this is my friend Mrs. Stuart Pershing. Welcome to Pinyon Creek."

"Thank you. We are just here for a few days, looking around, but I have many questions about the area and the people and the resources. I hope you don't consider this too much of an imposition?"

"Oh my no," Velda exclaimed. "Molly, let's invite these gentlemen into my house, here, and we can have tea and you can just ask whatever you want."

To the children's delight, tea and cookies were swiftly produced. The adults sat at the kitchen table. Eaton produced a small notebook in a brown leather case.

"I hope you won't mind if I take some notes. Now, I saw you are building a garden. How is the soil in this area? Are there any actual farms around here?"

Velda leaned forward. "We have farming and ranching both, here in the valley, and mining too. We can introduce you to more people who can give you good information. We are so pleased to have new people thinking of moving here. Are you thinking of moving here?"

"Well, I may set up a system where my chief wrangler actually lives here, but I haven't decided yet. It is certainly a pleasant spot, so surrounded by mountains. The mountains, by the way, are the most dramatic I think I have ever seen. I am surprised that there is enough water to supply the town and the ranches and farms."

"Oh, water!" Velda laughed. "If you had been here earlier this Spring you would have seen water! We had such a torrent, we had a rainstorm that lasted for days. It flooded just about everywhere, although you couldn't tell that now."

The other man had been listening intently. "The Owens river is a broad flat river at least along here. Are you saying it is prone to flooding?"

"Well, I couldn't say, because I haven't been here long. Molly?"

Before Molly could answer, the boys and Barbara, in response to a noise only they could hear, ran to the front door and pulled it open.

"Granddad! Granddad!" Alf shouted.

"Dad," Barbara echoed. The three wrapped themselves around Dr. Capshaw's legs.

"Papa, please come and meet our guests, Mr. Fred Eaton and Mr. J. B. Lippincott. They are in town because they may wish to buy some land in the area to raise cattle."

Dr. Capshaw disentangled himself from the children and shook hands. "Dr. Wallace Capshaw at your service, Sir. And yours, Sir. We are always pleased to boast about our beautiful valley. And the mountains. Anything you would like to know, just ask."

He pulled up a chair, helped himself to cookies, and settled Barbara on his lap.

"Mr. Eaton was asking about flooding," Molly prompted.

Dr. Capshaw launched into a rhapsodic description of the meadows in Spring, then stopped abruptly. "Oh my stars, he said. "Are you the same Fred Eaton who was mayor of Los Angeles not so long ago?"

"Guilty," Eaton said with a smile. "But nowadays I'm just another former politician. I want to start a small herd of beef cattle and this valley looks like a good place for them."

"And you, Mr. Lippincott, what brings you to our valley?"

"Well, Fred and I have been friends a long time and we enjoy traveling together. This country is beautiful and dramatic and anybody would love to be able to see it."

Wallace Capshaw all but rubbed his hands together in delight. "Let me tell you about a little project I'm running. If you are going to want to spend some time up here, I can recommend Capshaw's Retreat. It's a set of cabins partway up Mount Royal, and an ideal base for exploring. You can even sign up for a back country trip with my son-in-law's mules."

"Papa," Molly said disapprovingly, "You don't need to keep selling things! I'm sure these men have already made all their arrangements."

But it was quickly agreed that Dr. Capshaw would take them up to see the cabins after lunch, which of course they would all share.

Molly wondered just how far she could stretch the beef stew, and whether the children had really eaten all the cookies.

Chapter X – Views of Pinyon Creek

For Dr. Capshaw, the best part of the Eaton and Lippincott visit was the opportunity to take photos. He escorted the two visitors to his cabins and photographed them in front of the biggest cabin. Answering their questions about lakes and rivers and the mountain scenery made him think about taking landscape photos as well -- surely others from far away would like to see some of the dramatic natural phenomena.

The same energy and love of adventure that had brought him from Cornwall to America was bubbling away now as he pursued his new photographic career. He had turned over most of his medical practice to Stuart Pershing, and while his sanatorium was a financial success Anamaria and Raoul were doing most of the work. His tourist cabins were already mostly reserved and soon he would have a waiting list. He was ready to concentrate on photography. He had a wealth of memories from his early life in Cornwall and regretted that he had not been able to make photographic records: his marriage, the beauty of his wife's face as she bent over her needlework, the births of his children, even the deaths of his wife and baby should, he thought, have been marked with a photograph. Wouldn't Alf and Barbara and Charles have been amazed if they had seen pictures of their grandmother?

Well, he could at least make sure that the children had some photos so that they would remember these times. He started by making many portrait studies of Alf, Barbara and baby Charles. The boys tended to ignore him, but Barbara was always startled and fearful when Grandpapa disappeared under the big hood. Spence and Molly cooperated, but clearly thought it was an expensive and useless hobby. Wallace Capshaw was getting discouraged.

But on the very morning of the Eaton-Lippincott visit, Dr. Capshaw happened to read in a magazine an article about America's scenic wonders, including hints and tips for taking photos of scenery. He decided once again that he was a pioneer in a new field and only had to wait for the general public to catch up to his ideas – after all, it had worked for his previous plans.

He showed the visitors some of the photos he had taken, including some shots of mountainsides and the Owens River in Spring flood. He had done several photos of the mules, too, and they enjoyed them as well, chuckling at the woeful expressions on their mule faces.

The visitors were full of questions, filling their notebooks with the doctor's comments. They were particularly interested in the Owens River, that turbulent, unpredictable broad slice of water cutting through the center of the valley. They wanted to know when it flooded, and whether there were droughts so severe that the river would dry up entirely. Dr. Capshaw was proud to tell them what he knew about the Ditches Association, the groups of businessmen and ranchers who had developed a series of irrigation ditches from the river to their properties.

"Coming up from Los Angeles," Fred Eaton remarked, "you don't realize that you're climbing higher and higher as you go north. But the really severe part of the desert is pretty far south of here, I'd say."

"South and east," Wallace Capshaw responded. "You couldn't tell from your wagon, but there are mines – silver and copper and many other kinds – buried out there. Sometimes you can see the mine openings like little brown spots on the sides of the foothills. But other than the mines, there's little enough to make it worthwhile out there. That's why we feel so fortunate here."

"So you feel that there's a good future here in the valley? For ranching, say?"

"Well, I know you're looking to set up a ranch, so I won't say no," the doctor chuckled. "But it's not just ranching that goes on here. You should see my Molly's garden, and there are others besides. And hayfields! You can support your cattle during the winter on the hay you grow here in the summer. And I'm sure there will be more development as more tourists find out about us. See, Molly's husband has been helping the National Parks people set up buildings for some parks they're thinking of opening. Ever been to Yosemite?"

"I know it's hard to get here!," Lippincott laughed. "Even the little train just kind of chugs along. Don't you feel locked in, up here? Do you ever leave the valley?"

"Speaking for myself," Dr. Capshaw answered, "I welcome the isolation. But I know others would appreciate more contact with the outside – " He stood on his front porch looking out over Pinyon Creek and the green valley floor, lost in thought. Then he grinned. "I guess I'd have to say I haven't given it much thought. I manage to keep myself busy, as you can see. Say --" he turned to the two men.

"What brings you up here from Los Angeles anyway?"

"Oh, just exploring some," Eaton answered vaguely.

"I told Fred about this place awhile back," Lippincott answered. "When I was working for the Bureau of Reclamation I came through here several times. Thought then it would be a good place to retire to, run some cattle, enjoy the peace and quiet, that sort of thing."

"What was the Reclamation Bureau wanting from you, anyway?"

"Oh just the usual. Reports. They ask for reports on just about everything, nowadays. Nothing in particular as far as Pinyon Creek is concerned. Now, shall we go back down? I think your daughter is waiting dinner on us."

Just as they were preparing to leave, Spence and his helpers arrived, so the entire company had to hear the story of their encounter with the unpleasant hikers. Fred Eaton sighed.

"I guess it's no good saying we outsiders are not all like that!"

"Oh, we know better than that," Spence replied. "But we all hope that the valley can stay pretty much the same even after we get more tourists. They really made a mess of their campground."

"See," his father-in-law responded, "that's why our businesses will be so important. If we get folks to stay in our cabins and ride on our mules, we'll be able to show them the wilderness without having them ruin it."

"You won't be able to keep people out," Lippincott responded. "They'll come from all over when they find out about the big trees and the mountains."

"And the fishing and the hiking and the snow, " Wallace Capshaw added enthusiastically. "That reminds me. Molly, I have had an idea."

Velda and Molly both laughed. The doctor produced ideas as fast as Molly's squash vines produced blossoms.

"I'm going to have a photography exhibit. It will be in the bank building. I'm going to show my photos of the scenery around here. And some pictures of the children, too, if you will agree to it."

Residents of Pinyon Creek had grown accustomed to seeing the good doctor hunkered over his tripod in many different parts of town. The reaction to his proposal for a photography exhibit was enthusiastic, and as the first Sunday in September drew closer, Molly heard more and more people discussing their attendance. She began to worry, first, that the guests would not like the photos and second, that there would be so many people that nobody could see the pictures.

Velda and the members of the new garden club had volunteered to bring refreshments.

On the morning of the show, Molly made a pot of coffee and a pot of tea and a punch bowl full of lemonade.

"Careful! Don't drip on my pictures," Dr. Capshaw warned, only half joking.

"Now, don't worry, Papa," Molly said. "We're going to keep all the food far away from the pictures. We are setting up tables on the back porch. "

"Well, all right, then. Which picture do you like the best?"

Molly knew better than to select one. The doctor was proud of all of his photos, and resented any criticism. In fact, he had a natural eye for framing his subjects and his medical training had helped him become adept with developing the negatives, so most viewers were happy with everything they saw. He had selected three dozen photographs and tacked them to boards which Molly had covered with fabric. They included portraits of his grandchildren and his friends and some of the visitors to his cabins who had given him permission. Most of the photos, though, were scenes of life in the Owens Valley. Mine shaft openings, the rocky trail heading from Pinyon Creek to the mountains, a bristlecone pine with its stubby pine needles and burnished trunks, the mules in harness, snow on the mountain -- they proved very popular with the guests at the show.

People were entering Dr. Pershing's office, carefully viewing the photos, then collecting on the front porch and in the street to discuss the pictures they had seen. For most of them, this was the first time they had seen photographs except for the family portraits taken by John Fischer or by a traveling photographer.

"They look like magazine pictures," a man commented, accepting a cup of lemonade from Molly. "Never thought I'd see our town in a magazine."

"I remember working at the old Bar Twelve mine," his friend said. "That photo makes it look, well, important. The old Bar Twelve was never important. Dirty, dangerous, dusty. Not important, not like that picture."

"Sure is a pretty picture, though."

"Yup. They are all pretty. But are they real? If they look so good, how come we aren't rich?" They laughed and moved on.

Velda came out to the table with fresh cookies. She pointed to Tony and Alf who were collecting stones along the sidewalk. "They don't seem so impressed with the big show, do they?"

"Once they saw that there were only two pictures of them, they lost interest. And they are cross because I won't let them eat all the cookies."

"Molly, slip inside and watch your father. He has been talking to the same person for almost a half hour. I wonder what is going on?" Velda smiled and took over the lemonade pitcher.

Indeed, Dr. Capshaw was in a corner of the office, leaning over a woman who was seated in Dr. Pershing's visitor chair. He was engaged in enthusiastic conversation but called to Molly as soon as he saw her.

"Come on over here, Molly, and meet Mrs. Howell. She lives south of town on that big cattle ranch, that road over toward Higgins Creek. She was born in Cornwall, too."

Mrs. Howell was slightly plump with a round face, her curly brown hair tucked into a little hat which was topped by a blue bird feather. As she leaned forward to talk, Molly could tell that she was quite short. Her small feet did not quite touch the floor.

"Oh, I did miss my Cornish friends," she said. "And I miss the food. And the water. We lived right near the water, and I would go out on the cliffs to watch the waves. When John wanted to move here, I was so angry. I'm sorry now, because I didn't appreciate this place while he was still alive. He kept saying that Cornwall was no place for a cattle ranch, and he did love his cattle. Now it's mine to watch over and I can tell you it's a burden."

"I've told Mrs. Howell that I will be happy to help her with her business records," Dr. Capshaw interjected. "It's almost impossible for a woman alone to run a business like that. I'm going to show her how I set up the records for the sanatorium..."

"Don't tell me! You're thinking that the cows are like your patients!" Everybody laughed.

Dr. Capshaw's ears turned red.

"It's not like that at all! I'm just being neighborly!"

Molly patted her father's arm. "Now go be neighborly with some of the other folks here. Everybody wants to talk about your photos!"

Interval

Pinyon Creek celebrated the new century as most other American towns did -- with parades, fireworks, picnics, and prayers for continuing peace and prosperity. In Pinyon Creek's case, it appeared to most that prosperity was changing their lives at an alarming rate.

Fred Eaton had bought land at the north end of the Owens Valley, and was establishing his cattle ranch. Mrs. Howell, with the support of her new friend Wallace Capshaw, was increasing the size of her herd. Several additional cattle and sheep ranches had been established, although the cattlemen, like cattlemen everywhere, despised the sheep ranchers, feeling that the littler wooly beasts overgrazed the territory and fouled the waterholes and generally acted stupid. Sheep ranchers, on the other hand, could not understand how anybody would expend so much effort for big dumb slow-moving slabs of steak. The battles were mostly verbal and semi-humorous and nobody paid much attention.

The Reclamation Bureau was proceeding with its plans to develop irrigation and water control systems for the upper Owens Valley. They had withdrawn much of the farm land near the Owens

River from farming and were purchasing water rights from other farmers. The Bureau explained that their plans to build a reservoir would reduce the danger of Spring floods. J. B. Lippincott, the local manager, was making maps and plans for the reservoir. He and Fred Eaton made periodic visits to the valley. Other agents, representing the Los Angeles Water and Power Department, purchased water rights from Bishop South to the Owens Lake.

On his visits to the Owens Valley Lippincott continued exploring the area, visiting ranches and farms, spending some time in the various shops in town. Most of his questions were centered on water issues: how often did the Owens River flood, and how disastrous were the floods when they came? How long did they last? He attended meetings of the Ditches Association, learning how the irrigation ditches were built and maintained, and whether they were sufficient for the alfalfa and wheat and corn farms. He, too, talked about buying some land some day, but made no specific efforts to start a farm.

The Watterson Brothers' bank, which had started as a small storefront establishment, now occupied an imposing brick building with a marble floor (the marble came, of course, from the nearby Marble Mountains and was shown to visiting businessmen who might want marble floors of their own some day). They held mortgages on most of the land in the valley now, and sponsored the town fireworks on holidays. The town also gained its own newspaper, the Pinyon Creek *Town Crier*.

The railroad did not quite reach Pinyon Creek, but it came close. Spence was pleased that he had expanded his mule team work into pack trips because regular freight was now mostly being carried by rail. Daisy became too old to work and stayed in the Richardson corral; Alf and Tony learned to ride her. Barbara mostly liked making chains of grass and hanging them around Daisy's neck.

Velda's garden club was a big success. Within its first year, almost every woman in town had attended at least one meeting, and so many became active members that the meetings were held in the Grange Hall, since none of the houses in town were large enough to hold them. She was now thinking about starting a library.

Tony, Alf and Barbara were now studying piano, although neither boy would admit liking it. Dr. Capshaw had surprised the family with a small upright piano, purchased from Bill's Saloon when it closed with the last of the silver mines. Molly took piano lessons, too, finding great pleasure in learning the music and figuring out songs by herself.

Dr. Capshaw found himself busier than ever. His cabins in the mountains were a great success, and visitors liked having their photographs taken in the outdoors. Sometimes he took Tony and Alf along on his working trips, to show them more of the valley and to introduce them to photography. That is what he said, but of course his real reason was to have the companionship of the two boys. He found he was spending as much time as possible at the Howell ranch, getting to know Mrs. Howell, whom he found charming. She was a good cook and fed him Cornish dishes which made him quite nostalgic.

By now, Dr. Capshaw thought of himself primarily as a photographer and real estate developer, especially proud of the fact that he had organized Mrs. Howell's business affairs, finding her some reliable buyers for her cattle and working out a plan for farming alfalfa hay on part of her land.

More people were coming into the Valley, many making repeat visits to Dr. Capshaw's cabins or taking tenting vacations in the new National Forest using Spence's mule trains. Spence was developing some expertise in logistics, figuring out how much food and equipment he needed for each trip, and then adding extra for contingencies. There were always contingencies.

Farms were growing all kinds of crops, now that the irrigation ditches were well developed. Hay, of course, was king, but potatoes, corn, many vegetables were grown. People in the Valley had their pick of the crop, which meant that the women spent more time than they wanted canning vegetables and fruit each Summer. Whatever was not sold in the Valley was shipped out on the train to Reno.

Molly had grown quite fond of Mildred Howell, and watched with approval as her father began a tentative courtship. For her part, Mildred enjoyed the Richardson family, with their three boisterous children and their earnest parents. They included her in their family celebrations, including the Twelfth night dinner with the thimble buried in the cake, a custom she hadn't seen since she left Cornwall. She was beginning to think that if Wallace Capshaw said anything about marriage, she would seriously consider it. Her ranch house was too big for one person but she could picture herself and Molly and Barbara making cookies together. It was a happy thought.

It seemed as though Pinyon Creek had grown into a full fledged town now. They had developed just about all of the services they wanted -- newspaper, bank, school, doctor -- and the local sheriff controlled crime pretty well, especially since the rowdier miners had moved on into Nevada and beyond. Life was pretty good in Pinyon Creek in the first years of the twentieth century.

Then, one July morning, folks picked up their copies of the *Town Crier* and learned that Los Angeles, the city so far away and next to impossible to reach from the Valley, wanted to take their water.

Chapter XI – To Camp in the Mountains

"There's just too much going on!" Dr. Capshaw stormed into the Richardson kitchen, waving the *Town Crier*. "First, the national forest gets going, so there are forest rangers and army soldiers all over the place, and now Los Angeles wants us to GIVE them our water!"

Spence looked up from the stack of papers he was sorting and grinned. "You know you love all the excitement. And seems to me that Los Angeles is pretty generous. They're offering a good price for water rights, and for folks like us, people in town who don't even ranch, we're going to get a good payment."

"Maybe you think so now," Capshaw said darkly. "But wait. These -- these politicians were born crooked and grew up crooked and will stay crooked till they die. If you take their money you'll find yourself in their pocket forever."

"And what are you telling Mrs. Howell about all of this?" Molly asked. "I hear that they are buying some entire ranches."

"They are only looking along the river, so far," her father answered. "And they're not necessarily buying farms. They just want the water rights because they're going to pipe some river water down to Los Angeles."

"Well, I'm all for it," Spence said. "They have already talked to me about some freight services. If I can find some good mules, I'm going to send Hank down toward Mojave where they're building more railroad track. Builders can always use good mule teams for hauling supplies and people."

"I suppose you're right," Molly said loyally. "But I can't help but feel there's something nasty behind all that work. I didn't like that Mr. Lippincott."

"We won't see much more of him," her father agreed. "He was playing two sides of the story. He didn't tell us, did he? that he was working for Los Angeles at the same time as he was being paid by the government. That Bureau of Reclamation. Sounds like it was just some kind of smoke screen to let the rich get richer. The only bright spot is that Mr. Eaton isn't involved. He is well out of the Los Angeles government these days, and his cattle ranch up at Long Valley is going great guns."

Even with all of his new projects, Dr. Capshaw remained at heart a prospector. Whenever he could, he convinced Spence to accompany him on rockhounding trips. Sometimes he took one or two of the grandchildren, or another friend from town. If asked, he would say that he found walking outdoors a healthy way to exercise, or he would point to a grandchild and say that he was teaching the techniques of map reading and geology, but he nourished a secret hope that he would someday find a vein of some precious mineral.

This bright July day, Dr. Capshaw and Mrs. Howell, accompanied by Barbara and Charles, were taking a morning buggy ride up into the mountains just above the Howell ranch. The heat on the desert floor was not so strong here on the side of the mountain, especially in the canyons where scrubby trees provided some shade and a few small creeks bubbled down the hill. Dr. Capshaw was in his element, providing natural history information to the children and the older woman, both of whom listened intently to his lectures.

"You make it sound so interesting," Mrs. Howell remarked. "I can't believe I lived here for years and never learned the names of these plants. I never even realized there are so many of them."

"Wait till next Spring, Mildred, when I show you the wildflowers. They come out around April and in good years, when we have had rain at the right times, they just cover the ground. Only for a few weeks, and then they just disappear, until the next time."

They had reached a site of interest to the doctor, so they stopped to take a walk up a narrow canyon. Charles clambered from rock to rock. "Oh, be careful, dear!" Mildred Howell called. Dr. Capshaw laughed. "He's like a mountain goat. All of Molly's children are. They'll be fine."

Dr. Capshaw and Mildred Howell sat in the wagon, admiring the view. They could see the Howell ranch from where they sat although it was too far away for them to make our the animals in the pastures.

"Have you ever thought of moving into town, Mildred?"

"No, not really. I'm so used to the ranch. I do rattle around some in the house but I know all of its creaks and crackles. I feel safe out there with my dogs, and of course the geese honk like crazy – you know, you've heard them – and I like seeing the stars and hearing the wind in the trees. I think I'm not a town person any more. How about you, Wallace? You moved away from town up into your cabins. Do you regret that?"

"Only when I want to see someone and it means I have to harness up and drive to town. Spence and Molly have a busy life and the children can be exhausting after a few hours. And I have so many projects I have a hard time keeping up with them."

"Do you think this Los Angeles pipeline will change Pinyon Creek much?"

"No. I can't imagine they'll be able to take enough water to change the river much. Owens lake and Owens river have been here forever, sometimes flooding, sometimes low and they always come back to their usual state. No, I think it is mostly amusing to watch the townsfolk try to figure out how much money they can grab out of Los Angeles. What I can't understand is why they have to go so far for their water. It just doesn't make sense to me. What have they been doing for water all these years? I can't see that there is any big change in the city."

"Well, at least we don't have to worry about it."

They heard Barbara and Charles then, calling to each other and to them. They came bouncing back down, jumping from rock to rock. Charles pulled some rocks from his pockets. "Granddad, I want you to see some of these rocks."

He chuckled. "Well sure enough. That's what we came for, after all. Let me grab my pick."

He pulled two rock picks from a burlap bag in the buggy, handed a second, empty bag to Barbara. "Now, show me!"

When Molly went to buy some groceries, it seemed to her that the entire town was talking about the Los Angeles water project. The rumors were flying, each one wilder than the one before: The city was going to pay everybody several hundred dollars to use their water, even the people who didn't own any land; The city had discovered a new vein of gold near Pinyon Creek and the water story was a false alarm, to keep people distracted while the big spenders sewed up the mines; the City was suffering from an epidemic and everybody in Los Angeles would probably die, and their water was poisoned and that was why they were buying water from the valley; The Southern Pacific wanted to expand up through the valley, and this story gave them the backing and the money to do it; there were small grains of gold and silver suspended in the Valley's water from all the mining and panning and Los Angeles planned to harvest the metal.

Surprisingly, Velda and Stuart Pershing seemed unaffected by the news. Stuart, of course, was so busy with his medical practice that he had time for scarcely anything else, but Velda simply was not interested. She found Molly leaving the store with her groceries.

"Well, my dear," Velda exclaimed. "I missed you at the Garden Club meeting last week. We had such a good turnout and we learned so much about potatoes. And there are people south of here growing berries, too. You would have been fascinated. Just fascinated. I declare, I never thought that dirt and bugs and mud would be as interesting as it is. Do you think that's because there's not that much to do here? In Cleveland I wouldn't have thought twice about making a garden. It was always something for somebody else to do. Don't you think? Did you grow berries back in Cornwall? Tony likes digging in the garden, probably not surprising, I guess. He and Alf are so busy together. Somebody told me you were up at the sanatorium. Did you like it? Is it a long trip? Is it a lot cooler up there than it is down here in the valley? Did you know that Tony caught his first fish on Sunday? He and Stuart went fishing up at the lake, and Stuart said the fish were just crowding each other, there were so many of them. Is Spence still taking fish up in the mountains on mule-back?"

"And hello to you, Velda," Molly smiled. "You must come up sometime with me to the sanatorium. The views are just wonderful. Actually, I was really visiting the tourist cabins Papa built. I like to keep them swept out and stocked with coffee and some groceries in case guests come."

Alf came running up to his mother and took the basket of groceries from her arm. "Papa wants to see you right now! There's some people here with a big plan for a camping trip, and we can't find Granddad."

They said a quick goodbye to Velda and hurried home, where Spence had settled a group of men around the kitchen table.

A set of maps had been unrolled on the table. Molly could see that the area included the sanatorium and the Capshaw cabins, with ink marking trails leading to the west and north. Spence looked up at her and grinned.

"Gentlemen, may I introduce my wife," he said. "Molly, these folks belong to a group we've met before. They started a series of what they call Outings, and they've been doing it for -- what? five summers now?"

"Almost. It started small, just a few of us who want to explore the wilderness and learn how to do it without either taking too much planning or leaving too much behind." The speaker was a tall bearded man in thick glasses. "We find that many people who come into the mountains for a first visit want to return year after year. We want to teach people how to study the mountains, the geology, the wildlife. The back country is so huge, and so -- well -- wild. It's like nothing else."

Spence was nodding. "Every time I take a load of fish into the back country I find a different trail, or I make one, or I see the same place from a different spot and it looks different."

"What do you mean, a load of fish?"

"We're stocking a lot of lakes up in the hills with trout. The fish seem to do well, mostly. We go back to the lakes we visited a year ago, and there's plenty of fish. Still pretty small, mostly. The fisheries department is running this, and soon they'll be able to open some of the lakes for fishing."

One of the men had been designated the note-taker, and he was busily writing. The others leaned forward, each ready to speak. Molly put the kettle on to boil some tea. Alf had found a spot in a corner and was intently listening to the conversations.

"Of course, it's a good long trip, first to get here from the city," another man commented. "By the time we get to Pinyon Creek. It's already a couple of days. And we aren't even in the mountains yet."

"That's why we need to organize all of this in advance," the leader said. "I propose we plan one outing before the end of the summer. Then next Spring we'll know what works and what doesn't, and we can work out a series of trips for next Summer."

"We can start by making base camp up at these cabins," the note-taker said, pointing to an advertising flyer illustrating Sierra Winds Retreat. "Our organizers can stay there while the equipment is moved up to a higher camp." He turned to Spence. "We are talking about bringing between sixty and one hundred people up into the high back country for a month. That would be next Summer. This Summer we need to learn where to go and how much equipment to bring."

"And how much food, and how often to re-stock," Spence said slowly. "And if anybody gets sick, what would you do? We could keep one wrangler and a couple of mules up with you, and bring people down if necessary."

"Good idea, that."

They turned again to the maps. Spence looked over at Molly who was setting out cookies, and slowly shook his head in wonder. "I think they came here because they saw Doc's photographs," he said quietly. "Can you believe it?"

"I don't know where Papa is. Do you? He should come and enjoy this. He'll have some opinions, too!"

Alf rose and slid out the door, running down the street. Shortly he returned, followed by Dr. Capshaw who was dusty and rumpled.

"Mom, I found him," Alf reported. "He was just getting out of his buggy."

Dr. Capshaw stood in the doorway and regarded the roomful, taking in the maps and his advertising flyer. His eyes twinkled.

"Well, gentlemen, you have come to the right place, no matter what you are planning to do. We're ready to take care of you. But first I just have to take a minute with my son-in-law. Spence," he pulled at the satchel he had brought from the buggy, "Just look what the kids found! They're turning into first-class prospectors, if I do say so myself. "

Chapter XII – Career Planning

Dr. Capshaw emptied his burlap bag on the kitchen table, and several hunks of silvery rocks spilled out. They glittered in the afternoon light, as the crystalline shards on each sample caught the sun streaming through the windows. Barbara and Charles, attempting nonchalance, happily watched the intent expressions on everyone's face. Alf reached out and picked one up, cradling it in his hand.

"Wow! It's dense! This is new, isn't it? We haven't seen any of this before."

"That's what I thought," his grandfather said. "We'll have to take these up to Will Pettingill at the sanatorium, see if he can identify them."

"I'll do it now," Alf said enthusiastically. "Can I take Banjo, Pop?"

They returned to their guests. Molly found a tablet and some pencils and soon everyone was busy making lists. Spence took one of the men to the corral to demonstrate some of the ideas he had developed for packing the mules.   Barbara helped her mother set out coffee and cookies, and soon the general plans for the first pack trip had been sketched to the satisfaction of all, especially Dr. Capshaw whose cabins would be fully occupied for some time to come.

After the visitors left, the family settled down to an early supper.

"This is another example of what's happening to Pinyon Creek," Dr. Capshaw remarked. "I hear there's talk of building a hotel here."

"We still don't get more than a handful of travelers at any one time," Spence objected.

"Yes, but they have to stay someplace. Mrs Duggan's boarding house is not exactly fitted out for city visitors." The doctor sat quietly for a while. "Molly," he said slowly. "Have you ever thought about opening a restaurant? You and Velda and Barbara could do it. Just think."

Molly did not know how to respond. She never thought of herself as a cook, just a wife and mother responsible for feeding a hungry family. If she thought about business it certainly wasn't a food business. She wasn't a servant. She was really more like.... The realization that she didn't have an alternative in mind kept her quietly resentful.

"I'll talk to Velda," she finally said.

"Oh, mama, let's do it!" Barbara exclaimed. Quiet Barbara, who seemed never to have an opinion, was sitting up tall, her eyes sparkling. "We can make stew and chicken, and we can make cookies every day, and we can use vegetables right from our garden."

"See, she is the businessman here," her grandfather chuckled.

"Well, suppose we just do it in the Summer time. We can plan it this year and start next Spring if we think it will still be a good idea," Molly responded. She hated to discourage this unusual enthusiasm of her quiet daughter.

Planning and executing the establishment of the Outings camp occupied the family throughout the summer, leaving little time for prospecting or career planning. Alf and Will Pettingill studied the new rocks without determining exactly what their composition might be. Spence spent his spare time building elaborate packing rigs for Blanket and Toojay, the strongest of the mules. Dr. Capshaw divided his time between his cabins and Mildred Howell's ranch.

And Molly gardened. She found that digging in the soil of her vegetable garden, now rich and black after years of preparation, was a calming activity when she had been around too many people. Even Velda, visiting with Tony, seemed quieter as they sat on the back porch shelling peas.

"So the first Outings folks are due tomorrow," Velda said. "I'm sure Spence is excited, but how about you?"

"I don't think it's excitement I feel, exactly," Molly responded. "I feel a little bit out of control. They want him to take another load of fish, and he has passed that on to Hank, and Hank feels kind of left out because he was hoping to go up with these camper people. So Spence is trying to deal with that as well as pack the mules, and you know that dealing with people isn't one of Spence's best loves."

"He does it well, though," Velda responded loyally. "Now Stuart, he just lets all that wash off his back. He doesn't even seem to notice when somebody isn't happy."

Molly looked carefully at her friend. Velda had stopped shelling peas and sat motionless, gazing across the garden at the mountains. Tony, Alf and Charles had built a dam across the little river at the foot of the property and were splashing about, sailing little boats they had made.

"What's wrong, Velda?"

"Oh, Molly, I just can't keep going." Tears came into Velda's eyes. She mopped at them with her apron corner. "I will never be happy here. I don't know how you can stand it. You've been here a lot longer than I have."

"I thought you were feeling better about things."

"I try. I keep trying things, but most of the women around here just aren't interested in anything I'm doing. We have only six people in the garden club -- everybody else just doesn't come, and only Alf and Tony are taking piano lessons. Tony really would rather learn to ride a horse than play the piano. And I can't blame him. This isn't piano country." She smiled apologetically. "And every time I hear about things happening here, like the new hotel for example, I think, but other towns have had hotels for years and years. And they have had electric lights. And trains stopping right in town. We don't even have a paved street that doesn't just turn to dust in the summer and mud in the winter.

"Stuart just loves it here, but I think that is because he is the only doctor here, so he sees all the kinds of things he hoped he'd see -- everything from broken legs and babies to that horrid acid lung disease that's killing those workers. "

"Have you talked to Stuart about how you feel?" Molly remembered Spence's patient attempts to soothe her when she was starting her garden.

"I don't think he knows how serious I am. He sees me playing with Tony or doing my projects and he thinks I'm happy. As long as he has clothes to wear and food to eat, he thinks everything is just, just -- hunky dory!"

She sniffed, picked up more peas, shook her head. "And Tony is growing up so fast. He'll be grown and gone before I know it. What have I done with my life?"

"Oh, Velda, you mustn't cry! Think how much Stuart and Tony need you to be strong! You'll find your place here. I used to be so homesick for Cornwall but there's parts of the valley that I do love. Anyway, we're here and that's all there is to it." She stood up and briskly gathered the vegetables to take into the kitchen. "Now let's see what the children are up to!"

Molly considered Velda's words. Certainly she had had little experience with large American cities with their variety of goods, and felt she had still been almost a child when she came to Pinyon Creek. Now she was raising her own children, wondering whether she should be encouraging them to travel outside the valley. She would miss them terribly, she knew.

But there was little time for musing because the Outing organizers had shifted into high speed. The cabins had been prepared for the first team. Spence now spent much of his time, aided by Hank, Alf and Charles, loading massive amounts of equipment on the mules and taking them up to the campsite now under construction. They planned to work until the first snowfalls, hoping that this year the storms would hold off till late. Some of the equipment was expected: long poles, coils of rope and wire and pipe, lumber of various dimensions. But some was new to them.

"Whatever is that big boiler for?" Alf asked as yet another crate was opened.

"It's a boiler, just like you said." The man unpacking the crates had had almost too much of the boy's questions.

"They can't heat water over a fire?" Alf clearly meant to add "...like normal people" but stopped himself in time.

"These campers aren't used to roughing it. You'll see. They want cots but they want soft cots, and open windows but with screens. Wait till you see the food we'll ship up there."

Clearly it was a new world taking shape up in the mountains.

The boys continued to study the silver crystalline rocks which they continued to find in Poison Canyon. Will Pettingill, convalescing slowly at the sanatorium, taught the boys how to make simple assay experiments and supplied them with beakers and other lab supplies. Tony and Charles were more interested in the hunt for the rocks, while Alf found himself dazzled by all of the different experiments he was learning to do.

"This business of separating one kind of rock from another, when they are all together in one big stone, it's really complicated, but it's so much fun!" He told his father as they finished another pack trip. "It's like you've been saying. You find part that's hard, and parts that are soft, and then when you heat the rock, the soft part just melts."

He and Tony had been talking, Alf reported. "Do you think we can file a claim? We think these might be antimony rocks and we think we could get some money for them. "

Spence swallowed his immediate strong objections. Alf and Tony both were missing more school than they should, Spence needed their help with the mules, they needed to help their mothers more and there was plenty of work to do everywhere, almost every mine anyone started came to nothing more than dust.

"I guess," he told his son slowly, "I'll go talk to Pettingill and see what he thinks. Then I'll tell you whether you can proceed."

Will Pettingill had begun his career as a chemical engineer working at the gold mines near Cerro Gordo but as the gold mining slowed he followed the fortunes of other mines – borax, lead, potash, zinc. Along the way he had fallen prey to lung problems common to miners working with acid minerals, but he was fortunate enough to have a family willing to pay for his recovery at the sanatorium. He was now healthy enough to be bored with the regimen of long naps, long walks and light reading, and welcomed the boys' interest in the rocks.

Spence found him one afternoon on the broad verandah of the sanatorium, enjoying the thin autumn sunlight and the light breeze. The two men sat over coffee as Spence brought his friend up to date on his own work.

"I find it hard to think of you and Doc giving up your prospecting," Pettingill remarked. "Of course, Doc is always looking for something new, but I had the feeling you really enjoyed rock hounding."

"Well, I did, and I do," Spence smiled. "But it doesn't bring me the kind of money that packing brings these days. I'm happy to see Alf and Tony picking up my old hobby."

"They're good boys. And if they want to file a claim, I'll happily help them, even though I'm sure it won't come to anything. But there's something else I want to talk to you about...."

When Spence returned home that evening he was even more silent than usual. When dinner was finished he sent the children outdoors with a list of extra chores and pulled Molly to a seat at the kitchen table.

"Molly, remember when your dad suggested the diner? Well, I think it might be a better idea than we had ever thought. See, I was talking to Will Pettingill this afternoon and he tells me he thinks Alf should go away to school. There's this Throop Institute not far from Los Angeles, where they teach science and mining – and medicine too for all I know. We know he's got a science turn of mind, and Will says with tutoring he would probably be accepted. Will says he will help with the tutoring, too. But it means thinking about college, and I'd just been putting that off."

"Oh Spence, I couldn't bear for him to leave us. He's not old enough, and he would be so far away."

"Not that far, Molly. It's not even all the way into Los Angeles. And anyway, it would be another year, easy, before he's even old enough to think about it. And I haven't talked to him at all about this. But it made me think. We have Barbara and Charles, too. If they need extra schooling, it's going to be more money than I can bring in."

Molly was silent for several minutes. Spence picked up a knife and sharpening stone and worked away quietly.

"Spence, it's more like I never thought I'd be feeding other people. Or working for other people. I wouldn't know how to do it. I'm not that good a cook. What if they didn't like my food? And I guess I just really don't like the idea of working like that."

"Now listen, honey. How many years have you been helping your father, and Stuart, with their doctoring? You've been running that office a lot, and you've put bandages on how many folks in town? If that's not working, I don't know what is. And running a restaurant is at least as respectable as helping the doctors. Maybe more. You wouldn't be all covered in blood at the end of the day!"

She had to smile in spite of herself. "Well, maybe I'll think about it. We have the winter to put our ideas together. And we don't need to tell the children why I'm doing it. We won't even tell papa why, either. We'll just let him think that we liked his idea."

Chapter XIII – Molly's Place

The Los Angeles aqueduct project continued to be the big story in Pinyon Creek throughout the Autumn. Ranchers and farmers speculated about the effects on their crops, while the businessmen and miners, who were not dependent on farming, talked excitedly about possible payments for water rights. What was a water right, anyway? they wondered. Surely the Owens river was part of the valley and didn't belong to anybody, so why would somebody want to pay just to use part of it? After all, everybody used the river, for everything from swimming to running ditches to fishing, and even to skate on when it got cold enough.

"It hasn't been cold enough to skate on since I was a kid here," one old-timer grumbled. "You want to skate, make yourself a skating pond. Doesn't have to be deep."

"Anyway, Owens Lake has got enough water for anything we need. And if they do take some water, maybe we won't be getting the floods every Spring. That would be pretty good."

"As long as I can grow enough hay, I'm happy. Let them come. Already, they're spending money in town."

Representatives of the Los Angeles Water and Power Company visited the valley regularly now, looking for information and offering to buy land and water rights. Valley residents who had been just scraping out a living – miners whose jobs had disappeared as mines had closed, the old, the widowed, farmers who had had a bad year or several – eagerly accepted payment. Many of them packed up and moved away from the valley, leaving empty houses and fields which were quickly overgrown with weeds. Others who had built profitable farms and ranches or who were dedicated miners and prospectors were not happy with the possibility of losing some of the water they counted on and turned the visitors away before an offer could be made.

At the same time, others were discovering the valley. The Outings campground was bustling with building activity, as slabs were poured for large tents and permanent structures were assembled. Spence's mules became so accustomed to the trails that he hardly needed to direct them. Despite Will Pettingill's skepticism, the bars found by Barbara and Charles were rich in antimony. A mineral company in Bakersfield, hearing about the discovery, paid the two to guide them to the spot, then arranged for them to have a small share in the mine, should it be developed. This made the children so proud that they were impossible to handle for almost a week.

Dr. Capshaw, noticing the increased flow of visitors, developed a collection of scenic postcards which could be bought in local stores for mailing home. They featured wildflowers, mules – the most popular subjects of his earlier work – and a special set showing Barbara and Charles in the meadow above Pinyon Creek playing ball, picking flowers and playing with Jock-the-dog.

By early December the winter snows began. Molly, hanging out her laundry early in the morning, felt them stiffen in the frosty air. The tops of the mountains west of town were beginning to turn white. She decided that the time had come to start working on the restaurant plan.

She sat at the kitchen table with pencils and paper, making lists of everything she could think of. It did not take long for her to fill several pages with ideas and questions:

Where? On Main Street, maybe in the old school room?

When? Lunch only? Dinner too? Coffee?

How much food to make?

Where to get furniture and what kind of furniture? Seeing her restaurant begin to take shape in her head, she wrote faster and faster. Take extra chairs from the sanatorium? Build tables? Curtains? Sign in front --- oh! What to call it?

Molly's Cafe? Molly's Place? The Diner? Pinyon Creek Restaurant?

Tablecloths? Napkins?

Where to buy the food? How to cook the food? Is there a stove in the schoolhouse? How to get the dish washing done? She shook her head decisively – she was not going to wash a single dish herself, if she was the cook.

Velda appeared at her front door, a plate of cookies in her hand. Molly lit the kettle for tea and the two settled by the table. Velda seemed happier these days, or perhaps just aware that her choices were limited. Today she wanted to gossip about the Los Angeles water men.

"Remember Mr. Lippincott?" she asked. "The man who came by and said he wanted to buy some land? And we none of us liked him? Did you know that he is now working for the Los Angeles Water Department? I think he was in cahoots with them from the beginning."

"I guess I wouldn't be surprised," Molly agreed. "I think everybody is getting excited about getting money from them. It just doesn't sound right to me."

"Stuart says it's going to be a real problem, might be a big problem already, because people are selling their water rights and they don't really understand what it means. And they're buying new tools and clothes and things just because they never had money like that before. Even the Watterson Bank is warning them not to do it. And when bankers tell you not to spend money, that's serious!"

Molly laughed. "Well, we're not spending any money, that's certain. We haven't even been approached. I guess that's because we live in town and don't have any water rights. How about you and Stuart?"

"No, apparently we don't have anything to sell, either. Probably just as well. I'd probably want to buy a piano or something."

"I know Spence would just buy another mule."

They sat companionably for a few minutes, enjoying the cookies.

"Tell me what you think about this, Velda," Molly said, pulling her stack of papers toward her friend. "Papa put this idea in my head awhile back and I can't get it out of my mind. Do you think it would be absolutely crazy for me to open a little restaurant?"

Velda quickly read Molly's list, and leaned forward. "Not only do I think it is NOT crazy, but I hope you'll do it and I hope you will ask me to help! And why are we going to do this anyway?"

"Money." Molly gestured to the stack of lists. "We've begun to realize that Alf, at least, needs to go to school outside the valley. Will Pettingill has suggested Throop Institute which would be wonderful for him. Even though it's pretty far from home. And then there will be Barbara and Charles, of course." Simply repeating the facts made them seem more real, and her plan more realistic. "We don't have any money that would come anywhere near paying for any of this. But this should help."

Velda nodded. "I don't think Tony wants any more schooling than he's getting. He already has started to talk to the construction company about working on the pipes next summer, and I think maybe Alf has, too. This is a sensible plan, Molly, and it would help me, too. Please say I can help."

"Well, of course." Molly realized that having Velda at her side would be a great relief, even with all of her non-stop chatter. "Help me make our plans, and then we can talk to papa and Spence and figure out how I can hire you and how much I can pay you. Just like a real business!"

Before Christmas they had talked with the owner of the schoolhouse and learned he was interested in selling at a price

Molly and Spence felt they could afford after borrowing a thousand dollars from the Watterson Bank. That would allow them to buy the building and add the stove and water heater they would need. They told the children of their plans. After an afternoon of shocked outcries, everyone was prepared to help.

By Easter they had arranged for the furniture; Spence and Alf would build the tables and they would use the old school benches for seats. Velda was in charge of curtains and decorations and had designed embroidery panels for tiebacks and napkins. Barbara traced Velda's patterns on papers and a blackboard which would hold the menu. Alf and Tony took charge of scrubbing, whitewashing, and repairing the walls and floors which had been worn by fifty years of small feet. Charles started preparing the soil for a vegetable garden for the restaurant.

"Now all we have to do is start cooking," Velda said with a smile. "I'm sure I know what you'll be cooking first – stew and biscuits."

"You know my specialties," Mollie answered. "I'm thinking that we can offer sandwiches and soup, and one main dish, probably stew as often as we can get away with it. And coffee and tea, and pie."

"We'll write that on the blackboard. Now. What will you call this place?"

Molly laughed. "I can't decide. What do you think?"

"I think Mollie's Place sounds good." Velda picked up the chalk and printed it in large letters across the top, then entered the other items. "Now, how much for each?"

"That I do know. I've been figuring costs for weeks now."
They quickly finished the blackboard.

"And we want to be able to open by the first of May. I've been talking to Susan and the Odd Fellows President and Mr. Watterson. There's going to be a community party and barbeque then, and we can be part of it. I've told them we will have coffee and pie and cookies to sell."

With everybody pitching in, Mollie's Place opened early, on the last weekend in April. Mollie, Velda and Barbara were kept busy all day Saturday greeting friends and visitors, serving coffee and pie, accepting congratulations from customers and teasing from Spence's friends who spied him washing dishes, a large apron wrapped around his waist. It was an auspicious beginning for their new endeavor. Dr. Capshaw took many photos of all the activities.

Spence and his mules were busy working on the aqueduct from the very beginning. With some serious doubts about its practicality, he arranged a schedule with the construction crew which would not interfere with his commitment to the Outings. At first his mule teams carried supplies and workers from Pinyon Creek to the construction site not far from town, but as summer progressed he made longer trips as construction camps were established along the route. Townspeople complained about the dust and ruts in the road as more and more heavy equipment was dragged to the intake camp, but their grumbling seemed to be only halfhearted; after all, more newcomers were discovering the valley and its scenery, and spending money in town. They began to acknowledge Dr. Capshaw's farsightedness in developing tourist opportunities.

Alf and Tony had won jobs helping on the construction at the intake location. They had made a pact to save most of their wages for a project they would work on in the Fall, refusing to tell anybody what they had in mind.

It was a beautiful summer. The tumultuous Spring winds had died down, most of the snow had melted from the tops of the Sierra, and the wildflower season had been one of the best in years. Dr. Capshaw maintained that the floods of previous years had produced this bumper crop of wildflowers, but others chuckled and said it was just a lucky year.

The first pack train passengers for the Mountain Outings arrived in mid April. As their baggage was being transferred to the mules for the trip to their first night's stop at the sanatorium, the Outings Club members strolled the main street and took photos. The majestic peaks of the Sierra to the West and the White and Inyo mountains to the east fascinated them and they talked excitedly of being up in the forest and the mountains.

They were significantly less fascinated by Pinyon Creek itself. "There's nothing to do here" was a frequently heard outburst. To Mollie's chagrin, one woman, nattily dressed in jodhpurs and a tailored shirt and polka-dot scarf, walked up to her on the street, scrutinized her for what seemed like several minutes, then turned to her friend. "I see we must take special care to always wear our big hats," she said.

The Spring Community Barbecue had been scheduled to entice the first visitors and the aqueduct workers, as well as the townspeople who were always eager participants. The Garden club provided a booth with seedlings and seeds for sale. The Baptist

Church held a book sale. A group of parents organized contests and games for children. Velda's sewing group displayed embroidered aprons and pillowcases and baby clothes, and accepted applications for membership. The Outings Club handed out maps and leaflets. The saloons stocked extra beer and cider.

Starting in mid morning, groups of people gathered in town, to meet friends and stroll along the sidewalk, watching the barbecue preparations and offering advice to the cooks.

"Looks like bigger pigs than last year, Tom."

"Watch you don't add too much spices. My stomach isn't as young as it used to be."

Mollie and her crew set out coffee and big pitchers of cold water. She had made Cornish pasties filled with meat and potatoes, as well as sliced apple pies. By afternoon, to her delight, she had sold most of her baked goods, and Velda was busy putting more pies into the oven.

By the end of the day, when everybody had eaten and drunk to satiation and the winners of the games had been congratulated, the first fireworks of the season were set off. Each burst of color was greeted by applause and sighs of a-h-h-h.

Spence, comfortable in his rocking chair on their front porch, surveyed his family with pleasure. They were all tired and grimy but happy. The town had concluded one of its favorite celebrations and had demonstrated to outsiders that it was a fine place. And Mollie's Place was off to a roaring start. It was going to be a good summer.

Chapter XIV – Field Trip

"C'mon! c'mon! c'mon! They're here!" Charles Richardson flew in the front door, nearly bumping into his father and grandfather who were entering from the kitchen.

Outside, a dusty truck filled with an assortment of tents, tools and dufflebags had pulled up in front of the house. It was followed by a second truck which disgorged several tall dusty young men. Molly came to the door, calling them all to come in for some food, ready to hug her son.

Alf had finished his first year at Throop Institute, thanks to vigorous behind-the-scenes work by Will Pettingill who had procured a scholarship for him. Now he entered, gave his mother a hug which lifted her off the floor, and greeted the rest of the family with a big grin.

"It's a long trip," she said. "You must have left very early this morning."

"Yes," an older man agreed. "Before sunup. You can't make good time on these dirt roads."

"They're talking about paving the highway all the way up, some day. But maybe not now that they have a train coming pretty close by, " another contributed.

They all settled down around the dining room table and tucked into platters of sandwiches, pitchers of lemonade and mugs of coffee. Alf introduced his family to his professor, Thomas Wentworth.

"Now, what are you going to be up to, this trip?" Spence asked the older man.

"There are so many possibilities for prospecting here that we can usefully spend our week in the hills above Pinyon Creek. Throop is developing quite a geology program. Our first geology majors will graduate next year. I'm eager to see what they can -- literally -- dig up for this field trip. Then we'll take samples back and analyze them. I want to follow up on some of the suggestions you folks sent me."

Dr. Capshaw pulled his chair closer to the professor. He pulled out a sheaf of papers and spread them on the table.

"See, here is where Spence and Alf and I spent a fair amount of time," Dr. Capshaw said, using the handle of a spoon as a pointer. "We'd go up high enough to get past the gold mines which are pretty much played out anyway, and we found some dolomite and some antimony and a lot of quartz -- all kinds of different colors. It got us wondering, do people think of the minerals they need first, and then go find them, or do they find some interesting minerals, say quartz, or lead, and then figure out what to do with them?"

Amid the chuckles, Wentworth smiled at Dr. Capshaw, nodding. "Don't you think it's usually a matter of both? You find an interesting rock outcrop and you study it awhile, and you decide there's maybe some silver or something else that you can imagine a use for, but there are other minerals there as well, and you don't know what they are. Doesn't it make that particular outcrop more interesting than the ones around it?"

A general discussion broke out, as the group made its plans to go into the hills and set up camp. Spence and Dr. Capshaw, with Charles eagerly joining them, volunteered to accompany the group, to help carry the baggage which had overwhelmed the truck and to suggest some possible sites.

Alf pulled himself aside from the group to talk with his mother. "Mom, I'm really happy here at school. I'm glad I can do this. I'm sure I can be a good geologist. But living in Pasadena, it's well, it's really different from living here in Pinyon Creek. For one thing, it never gets dark down there."

"What do you mean?"

"At night you look out the window and there's a kind of glow from all the street lights and the headlights and stuff. And it's never quiet because there are cars and people around all the time. It took me awhile before I could even sleep at night. I'm happy to be back here, even though it's only for a week."

Molly and Barbara began the post-luncheon cleanup. After the group left, Barbara told her mother that one of the students, David, had been interested in their apple trees and their garden.

"Dave's family runs an orchard somewhere south of Los Angeles," Barbara said. "He was surprised to see how much of our land we had in garden. He was telling me about the orchards they saw on the way up, at Manzanar. He had heard about their apples even down south. I was telling him about the aqueduct they're building. He said they could see the plant going up as they left Mojave. I said we didn't think it would bother us much, but he just shook his head."

Molly sighed. "I don't want to think about moving. I think that between mules and the restaurant and papa's photography, we'll be able to find enough to keep us going. But I wonder about you children. Will you want to stay here, with all of the changes?"

"If I stay here, it will be BECAUSE of the changes," Barbara laughed. "I don't want to just watch the world pass by. I want to be part of it. I want to keep trying to raise fruits and vegetables here. Mom, I've been thinking about getting a summer job at an orchard in Manzanar, if anybody is hiring at all, just to see how they do what they do."

"Well." Molly put a stack of plates on the counter a bit more firmly than necessary. "Don't you want to apply for college? I thought you wanted to go to nursing school."

"I've been surrounded by sickness and injuries forever. It's just not the way I want to spend my days -- I've been thinking a lot about it. I would so much rather be surrounded by plants and trees and fruit, and learning how to improve them. There are some people working on grafting trees down there. Maybe I can go work with them."

During the week the students occasionally came back into town, for supplies, for mail, or just for a chance to explore the town. They reported that they had found plenty of interesting rock samples as well as many abandoned mines. The contrast between Pinyon Creek, high and green, at the edge of the Sierra, and the desert conditions to the east fascinated them.

At the end of their week-long field trip, the Throop students returned to Pasadena, promising to return in the Spring. Alf tore himself away from the family with some reluctance, although his parents could tell that he was excited to return to the city and school.

Pinyon Creek was now a mature town, with a hotel, a bank and a very small library (thanks to Velda) to add to the original mining-era buildings. The residents had built houses both east and west of the main street. They had even constructed bleachers and stables for rodeos and fairs. The local baseball teams played there when no other event was taking place.

Tony's job with the aqueduct construction company continued into the Fall. To Velda's chagrin, he was not at all interested in more education, largely because the construction company was teaching him to use a variety of tools, and had begun teaching him the rudiments of surveying.

Despite the long hours and hard work, he had energy and time available to help Charles and Barbara with the secret project that he and Alf had begun. The three would leave early on a weekend morning, returning at dusk exhausted and muddy, refusing to tell anyone what they were doing.

Mollie's Place continued to attract customers. She and Velda, with occasional help from others, were now serving lunches and suppers. They were even giving some thought to creating a special Holiday Event, maybe even a Thanksgiving Dinner.

"If we're going to something this big, we'd better start planning it right away," Velda said as they worked on the weekly shopping list.

"I'm thinking that it might almost be easier than a regular day," Mollie replied. "We would just have one meal, one menu, and we would know how many people because they would have to sign up in advance. We'll have to get the children to agree to help. Do you have any idea at all what they are doing?"

"Tony absolutely won't talk. I know he and Alf have already spent money on whatever it is, but I don't know how much or what for. Whatever they bought, they have hidden it away somewhere."

"I suppose I shouldn't worry, but..."

"Let's concentrate on Thanksgiving," Velda said firmly.

They decided on ham and potatoes and the vegetables they had canned during the summer. Mollie would make pies, Velda would make her special chocolate cake (three cakes, in fact).

"Let's see if we can get some entertainment," Mollie suggested. "I think I heard that there's a group working on the aqueduct that likes to sing."

It was not surprising that Dr. Capshaw proved to be a master at organizing the Thanksgiving Day Dinner. He was delighted to become involved with the planning, and enlisted Matilda Howell as his assistant. Mollie and her team settled upon a price which would cover expenses, provide a small profit and leave some money to be given to the Methodist Church to help local needy families. Almost as soon as it was announced, the dinner was fully subscribed, with many of the construction workers looking forward to a treat on a holiday on which they would be far from home. Their chorus, the Water Warblers, declared themselves happy to provide a program of songs. Dr. Capshaw volunteered his services as photographer, to make postcard photos of diners for anyone who wished to buy them.

Pinyon Creek was not only growing, it was becoming a friendly, busy place where the residents took pride in making improvements to their lives. They formed clubs, established several churches, supported the library and painted the city hall building. On national holidays a giant flag flew from the staff attached to the volunteer fire department. At Christmas time a group of men would find a pine tree in the hills and bring it down to town, setting it up in the little lot where the road turned off to the east at the end of town.

It was an early winter. The peaks of the Sierra began to show a dusting of white by early December. Spence and Hank gathered extra stores of hay for the mules and added to the stable area which provided cover during storms. By the week before Christmas snow had fallen on Main Street, to the great delight of all the children.

Barbara, Tony and Charles decided that as soon as Alf got home it would be time to unveil their project.

Chapter XV – Ski Tow

Alf arrived home December 20, exhausted. The journey from Pasadena by train and stage had taken most of the day and the weather had been brutal. Wet snow blown by strong winds off the mountains had covered the train tracks causing the train to slow to about half its normal speed. At Keeler he had climbed into a wagon whose cover had become ripped on the previous trip, so snow drifted onto the benches and stuck to his hat and jacket. What he wanted was food, bed and sleep and he was in no mood to deal with anyone.

To the great disappointment of Barbara and Charles, he merely grunted when they told him the surprise was ready. Tony calmed them and assured them that by morning Alf would be back to his usual amiable self.

In the morning the snow had stopped and the sun glittered off the white walls and yards. Alf was visibly in a better mood after a long sleep in his own old bed. Tony was already waiting for him, feasting on eggs and coffee. After a quick breakfast of biscuits and jam and coffee, Alf was ready for his co-conspirators. They bundled themselves into their warmest clothes and headed out of town. Just before they reached the sanatorium's meadow, they stopped.

"Now close your eyes, Alf," Barbara demanded. They led him carefully to a point near the edge of the meadow. "Now open them."

It was better than Alf had even hoped. With the skills Tony had learned in his construction job they had managed to cut and trim long poles, sink them into the ground and anchor them with concrete, string heavy wire between them, and wind the wire around the discarded wheel from a farm wagon. Finally – the incredible finishing touch – Tony started an electric motor, the wheel turned, the rope moved, and Charles worked his way up the hill, demonstrating their machine.

"It's the first ski tow in the valley." Tony couldn't keep the grin from his face. "We were going to just smooth out some ski runs, but then I started reading about other places that have ski runs, and they talked about the place somewhere in Europe I think, or maybe New York, that made something like this. So why not? I asked myself."

Barbara and Charles dragged some boxes from their hiding places in the shrubbery. "And the skis you and Tony bought are right here. We tried them once – they're great! Want to put them on?"

Alf just stood motionless. It was better than anything he had imagined, better than the pictures he had had in his mind all during the Autumn when, dazed by hours of schoolwork, he let his mind wander home. He gave everybody a big hug, including Tony who clapped his friend ferociously on the back. This produced a laughing, tumbling jumble till they all were too breathless to continue.

"Well, let's try it out!" There were four pairs of skis, waxed and ready.

"The ski wax came from my friend Annie," Barbara reported. "Her family raises bees. I think you're supposed to rub it on the bottoms of the skis."

"You've all been studying," Alf said. "This is so great!"

Strapping on the skis was a complicated process. None of them had ever used real skis before, although they had slid downhill on a variety of objects, from kitchen trays to fence palings. Nobody wanted to be first, and nobody wanted to be last, to try the tow, but eventually they were all ready. Alf went first "Because you thought of it" and Tony went second "because you made all the plans" and Barbara went third "because you are a girl " and Charles went last "because".

The next task was to learn how to use the tow. The little motor moved the wire uphill but it was not very powerful. It simply gave enough support that a skier, walking uphill, could feel that he was making progress. Separately and silently each of them decided to work on increasing the motor's power.

When they reached the top of the hill they stopped and looked down. Barbara and Charles had worked many hours clearing brush and pushing rocks away from a broad path now covered in snow. It went straight downhill and, from the top, looked rather alarmingly steep.

"Who goes first?"

"I will." It was Tony, so eager to try it that nobody wanted to object. He wiggled his feet a bit on the skis as though to settle them more firmly, then pushed off. His skis were very long, his ski poles so short that he had to lean down to drive them into the ground. He shot off down the hill and got perhaps half-way down before his skis crossed and he fell over, rolling sideways till he caught his balance.

"OK, I'm next," said Alf. Watching his friend, he had decided it was better to turn his feet out, and so he only went a few yards before he, too, tipped over.

Barbara stepped up next. Her skis looked as though they were twice her height. She took a deep breath, pushed off, and slid slowly down the hill, bending left and right to keep her balance. She got almost all the way to the bottom.

They all stood and cheered for Charles, who stood for several minutes at the top before starting down. He had clearly been studying everybody's techniques, because he stayed upright. He lasted until he turned off the path right into a bush.

They gathered at the bottom of the hill, brushing the snow off their jackets and pants.

"Needs some work," Tony remarked.

"I think it's us who need work," Barbara said. "And maybe shorter skis. I'll bet we can make skis. "

"Well, we surely made us a ski run," Charles said proudly.

"This is granddad's land. Will he be angry about the cement?" Alf asked.

"No. I hope you don't mind. We thought we needed to ask him, so we told him what we wanted to do and brought him up here and showed him. He thinks it's a great idea."

Alf smiled. "I'll bet he does! I can see him now, telling everybody about it, getting the whole town up here and then taking everybody's picture!"

Everybody laughed.

"What's our next step?" Tony wondered.

"Practice!" Alf laughed. Then he became serious. "I think you figured out the exact right place to put the tow. We can get about halfway up the hill with no problem before we start on it, and with a stronger motor — " everybody nodded "-- we can get even higher. If we want to. I know there are people around who know how to ski. When I was going up with the mules I heard about miners using skis, and there was this man, Snowshoe Thompson, who delivered the mail on skis. Over in Nevada someplace, a long time ago. We can use this hill to teach skiing, and we can go sledding here if we want. Now, anybody want to go down again?"

They all did, and kept sliding and falling until they were too hungry and wet to continue.

The ski tow turned out to be a big success, a favorite of many of the townspeople. Dr. Capshaw, as predicted, took charge of the publicity, taking the opportunity to speak about the sanatorium and the cabins in addition to the ski runs. With word spreading throughout Pinyon Creek, efforts began almost at once to strengthen and lengthen the ski tow. At first Charles and

Barbara were offended that their hard work hadn't been appreciated, but they soon became leaders of the tow project, stationing themselves on the hill each day of their vacation. Anyone who wanted to go skiing paid one of them a nickel a trip, the money going toward a larger motor and additional equipment.

It even attracted skiers from outside of Pinyon Creek. It seemed that people had wanted to try skiing the mountain slopes above the Owens River, but were frightened of the steep hillsides. Several miners from Nevada who had been skiing cross country between mining camps came over to teach ski construction and make suggestions for further improvements.

The early winter deposited snow in greater than usual quantities. On sunny days everybody who could find time seemed to be out in the hills practicing their new skiing skills, learning both cross country and downhill skiing. The Methodist Church men's club scraped a large pond-sized stretch of land just east of town and flooded it, making an ice skating pond perfect for even small children. Those whose jobs kept them busy in town picked up snowshoes to move from place to place.

The construction work had slowed to a crawl till the Spring thaws. Most of the workers returned home to Los Angeles, but a dozen or so stayed in Pinyon Creek. Tony had managed a few hours of work each day, primarily repairing tools and improving the bunkhouses. He and Alf spent much of their free time together, often working on the ski tow or improving their skiing techniques.

"So is it worth it, to go to college?" Tony asked idly one afternoon.

"Oh it is! Hard work, though. I've about read my eyes out, and memorize! I spend hours just reading lists to myself, memorizing names and numbers and stuff. We thought we knew a lot about the different minerals here, but we didn't even begin. I don't think I told you, but while we were up here last Fall, up in the hills by Cerro Gordo, we went out one evening after dark, and they parked the trucks facing the hillside and turned on the headlights and we looked for fluorescence, spooky blue light shining from the rocks. We're going to be studying that some more. I'm pretty sure we'll keep coming up here, too. We took bags and bags of rocks, specimens, down to identify and label."

"Have you been up to see Mr. Pettingill?"

"Yep, one of the first things I did. Did you know he fixed it so I'm staying with his cousin in Pasadena? Costs less than the dorm, and I can work for him to help with the food bill."

"He's a good man."

"Yup. He's worried about the valley. Says this aqueduct will ruin it. What do you think?"

"I can't decide. For me, it's great. You know that. I've got a good job, and I think I'm going to get a promotion maybe in Spring. I can use the survey equipment. They're teaching me a lot of stuff. But this is one big aqueduct they're building. Have you seen what we're working on?"

They saddled Banjo and Toojay ("I haven't been on a mule in so long!" "Neither have I") and rode out to the construction site. The structure being built sat in the middle of the Owens River north of Pinyon Creek. Now in winter there were patches of ice on the surface of the water, but the river still ran swiftly. It looked like a cement bridge. When finished it would offer travelers a means of crossing the river. The water now ran freely through the two giant openings.

"Later, the aqueduct water will go through this hole," Tony explained. "Then it will be diverted to the aqueduct itself which is – look – starting over here." He gestured to his right, where the river bank began to resemble a canal's walls. "Everybody in town thinks that there'll be a little less water, but not much change. Me, I can't believe that they would put so much money and men and time into something that would give them only a little water."

"Me neither. But look at it this way. There's often times when we have too much water. There isn't hardly a Spring that we don't have a flood. Seems like a decent trade, our extra water for Los Angeles, so they'll have enough drinking water. If that's all they want. I don't trust these guys. They come into the valley and act all decent and friendly, but how do we know what they have in mind? I saw the cement plant – I've seen it a couple of times now, every time I go between home and Throop. It's big. "

They turned their mules around and headed back to town.

Chapter XVI – Tuesday Table

The early snows had forced an early pause in the aqueduct construction, so as soon as the snows began to melt the crews were back at work. Tony continued to work on the intake structures, Spence and his mules spent much of their time on freight trips to and from Mojave, and the town continued to observe with interest the continuing activities.

Because of the heavy snows, Owens Lake and Mono Lake were higher than usual. The Owens River ran fast with occasional local flooding. By April, the valley floor was thick with wildflowers. Matilda Howell, keeping a scrapbook of pressed wildflowers, kept Dr. Capshaw busy making buggy rides out to capture additional examples.

Mollie and Velda watched through the window of Mollie's Place as the two rode out of town one bright morning.

"Do you think they'll get married some day?" Velda asked. "How would you feel about that, having a stepmother?"

"I can't imagine that. But I can imagine them getting married. Papa needs to take care of somebody and our family is getting too grownup for him. He wants to have somebody to talk to, to listen to all of his thoughts and encourage his plans. She does a very good job of that."

"I can see Mrs. Howell wanting to get married again," Velda said thoughtfully. "She had a good marriage but now she is alone, and she surely depends on your father for advice and help of all kinds."

"Sometimes I worry about that," Molly said. "I think papa sometimes gives advice on things where he doesn't really have all the information. Take these water rights, for example. Just because the only farming she does is raise hay, she shouldn't give away her water rights. I don't think so, anyway. What if she needs more water later?"

"This valley has more water than we know what to do with. Just look at the river of water rushing down Main Street right now. We'll have lots of muddy boots in here today!"

Mollie's Place continued to do a brisk business and was becoming known in the other towns of the valley. Sometimes people would come into Pinyon Creek for shopping with special plans for a nice lunch at Mollie's Place, or a birthday dinner would fill several tables with family members. Mollie and Velda had learned some new recipes and had found several families to supply them with chickens and eggs.

The big table at the front of the restaurant had become known as the Tuesday table because on every Tuesday, starting shortly after ten o'clock, a group of local business leaders would assemble for a long lunch. They would start with several pots of coffee and some biscuits, but by noon the table would be crowded with platters of sandwiches, tureens of soup, and plates of pie.

Discussions were sometimes agitated, always lively, occasionally quite loud.

It was an informal group, with participants attending as their duties allowed. Judge Baker would be there whenever there were no cases in court that morning, Willie Chalfant the newspaper editor was usually on hand, one of the Watterson brothers, sometimes both, would often attend. At least one of the ministers would drop by. The foreman of the construction crew, who had been Pinyon Creek's blacksmith for decades, was a regular. Dr. Capshaw, of course, was one of the first at the table each week. There was no agenda and nobody ever took minutes, but some of the bigger decisions affecting Pinyon Creek were made at that table.

"Going to be a busy Springtime," Baker remarked as they poured their coffee. "I hear the Outing Club is planning to even expand their outings. Spence mention any of that to you?"

"Yes. In fact, they are hiring several of my cabins starting the beginning of May. Too late for wildflowers but early enough to still find some snow. You can expect to see them in town any time from, say, May tenth on."

"Anybody know how the building is going on, at the intake? Any sign of a change in our water levels?"

"Seems they are coming along about as expected. Now they are working downstream more."

"Eaton up north of here has bought more cattle. He seems to think he can make a go of his ranch. Stays up here pretty often."

Chalfant, the *Town Crier* editor, had been silent. Now he spoke, with a grim face. "I've been hearing from my contacts in Los

Angeles that they have plans for this water that they haven't been telling us. It's not just drinking water they want. It's irrigation water, and they have in mind a huge area. I think we should ask more questions."

"Water's water, in my opinion." This from Lars Knudsen, a rancher from south of Pinyon Creek. "If they want to spread it on bread, that's their business. Long as they pay for it and we have enough, well then let them have it."

A general murmur erupted. Then:

"There's part of this that we keep forgetting about. Just about the time they started coming up, the Bureau of Reclamation was making its plan, and that plan called for not allowing new land to be purchased up here. Right now much of the land north of here is just lying fallow, and the plan is still in effect, as far as I know." The speaker was the Methodist minister.

"And you think – ?"

"I think I don't know. And there's more that I don't know, like what will happen to Mono Lake. And the birds on the islands up there. I'm with Chalfant. We need to keep an eye on all of this."

"But on another subject, when does the Spring baseball season start? We should have a schedule posted around town. Who do we play first? Joe, will you be pitching again this year?"

Joe the blacksmith spoke. "I'm pitching and we have a couple of other good ball players, new this year. From the construction crew and also from the Forestry Service. Nice strong men. I think our chances are good. I'll get somebody to make the schedule on some posters and we'll post them at the Fire Station and the post office as usual. And in front of the general store."

Mollie was serving their sandwiches. "And one for Mollie's Place as well, please."

"Wouldn't miss that." he grinned. "This is the center of town, as far as I'm concerned."

Barbara, at sixteen, was busy finishing her high school studies and working at Mollie's Place. She had hoped to find a summer job in the orchards near Manzanar, but, unsuccessful, agreed to work one more summer at the Outing campground where Charles would be working as well. Today she was helping her mother at the restaurant.

"I think I'll be expected to cook up there," she said. "It's a good thing I'm getting some practice here with you. There's surely a lot of different between cooking for six and cooking for thirty-six. Or a hundred and six, because I hear there's going to be that many."

"What do they do up at the camp?"

"Well, they take hikes, and sometimes they'll arrange for some mules for a longer trip. I think Charles will be working on that. Then they study the trees and the flowers. They are making an inventory of the plants and trees that grow there naturally, so they can tell in case plants come in from elsewhere. Sometimes somebody brings seeds, or even pits of fruit, or sometimes an animal will drop something they've eaten somewhere else. They say that these – invasive plants they call them – can spread quickly and overcome the natives."

"If they spread quickly, wouldn't they be good?" Velda asked sceptically. "Far as I can see, we need all the plants and plant species we can get here. Think how hard it's been to get vegetables to grow in this soil!"

"Yes, but that's down here," Barbara responded. " Up in the mountains it's a whole nother story. In fact, sometimes it's hard to get something growing because there are too many trees."

"Huh. Well. What else to they do?"

"Oh, they study the history of the area, and they have sing-alongs, and they sometimes just relax and read, and when there are little children, we organize play times and games. We generally follow the lead of the campers and try to do whatever it is that they suggest."

"So there are people there of different ages?"

Barbara got pink.

"Oh," smiled Velda. "And there are perhaps some boys there? Maybe somebody you met last year will be returning?"

"Maybe." Barbara hastened off to clear the last lunchtime tables.

When Alf came home for his Spring vacation, he and Tony tried to find time to spend together, although Tony was fully occupied with the aqueduct.

"When I'm not working, I'm sleeping," he told Alf. "Just ask Aunt Velda. Sleeping and eating. That's all I do when I'm not out on the job. And it looks like it'll continue for at least another year."

"That's a long time," Alf agreed. "I heard that this is going to be some kind of record-breaker for distance of an aqueduct. Anything to see yet? Any pipes laid?"

"If you want to see what looks like a canal, I can show you that. They'll be placing pipes here and there, and they have major plans for farther south, around Jawbone Canyon. You'll really see something when they get that going. I tell you, though, I don't think it's going to do anything good for Pinyon Creek."

"Why do you say that?"

"Well, just look around. The people who sold their water rights, say, last year, they've spent their money and now they don't have anything to show for it – maybe some new equipment, or they've paid off a debt but they'll be right back in the red. And they won't even be getting the access to the water that they used to, because more of it and more and more will be going to Los Angeles."

Tony's voice was rising. He took a deep breath and continued.

"But the worst of it all is this. Have you had a chance to look around Los Angeles?"

"No, Pasadena is almost a day trip from downtown Los Angeles. Anyway, why would I?"

"Well, I've been hearing from some of the guys who get down there. Like this guy who is hauling some special pipe for us. He is saying that north of downtown there's a whole batch of land that is for sale right now, and they say that it will be farmland when the aqueduct is finished, because there will be so much water that they will be spilling it into this land – they call it the San Fernando. Right now it is as dry and dusty as, well, Crumville or Mojave. And you know Mojave is dusty. AND they say that some of the big landowners there are the same men who have been pushing the aqueduct."

"Wow. Have you told anybody? How about Uncle Stuart?"

"That's hard. You know how he is about progress. He's just so excited about the aqueduct – all the publicity that will come from it – that he can't see any problems with it. He seems to kind of look down his nose at anybody who hasn't wanted to sell their water rights. So I haven't said anything. Maybe you could talk to your dad?"

"I'll see what I can do." They were quiet for a few minutes, then Alf looked up more cheerfully. "Let me show you some great rocks I've found. Charles showed me where they found some tungsten. I think something's going to come of this, I really do."

Chapter XVII – Banjo Gets Sick

Charles Richardson, just turned 14, was entrusted for the first time with taking a pack trip up to the Outings location above Pinyon Creek. He chose the mules he knew best, Banjo, Toojay and a relatively new mule named Fruitcake. His job was to move supplies, including a new camping stove, tent poles, tent fabrics and some basic foodstuff to the camp. He coaxed a friend from school, Peter Cummins, to help him.

"First, we'll take the string for some walks, without any gear," Charles told Peter. "That'll get you used to working with them. That's how dad taught me."

Peter soon learned how to coax the mules to do what he wanted, how to make them turn and stop on command. "Easier than horses," he commented at one point.

The two boys were as eager to try out their skills as the camp managers were to receive the supplies, so early in the morning they packed their three animals and set out for the camp. The mules were accustomed to the trail and moved along steadily. By the time they reached the fork at Little Creek Meadow, where they had planned to eat lunch, it was only mid-morning, so they pressed on, hoping to impress the Outings staff with their early arrival. After a short stop to give the mules water and a rest with sandwiches for themselves, they reached the campsite by mid-afternoon. Unpacking quickly, they picked up the list for the next trip and headed back toward home.

Once again they stopped for a rest at Little Creek Meadow. This time they let the mules wander freely. The creek was flowing rapidly and the first of the Spring grass and flowers were thick on the ground.

Charles and Peter stretched out under a tree and relaxed, proud of what they had accomplished so far. They talked about their baseball team and about the end of school and what they would do in the summer, and how they would spend the money they were earning for these trips. Suddenly Charles shot to his feet.

"Pete, look at Banjo! He's sick!"

The mule was lying on his back, his long legs thrashing in the air. He was groaning and panting. The boys rushed to his side and pulled and pushed, trying to get Banjo back on his feet. Strings of drool dropped from his mouth. Peter grabbed the lead rope and, pulling firmly, encouraged the mule to stand, while Charles took his jacket and rubbed Banjo's neck and back. The groaning was heartbreaking.

"What's happening?" Peter gasped.

Charles frantically scanned the ground around him. "Oh, Pete, I KNEW better!"

He took the lead rope from Pete and began to walk Banjo slowly.

"Look where Banjo's been eating! You can see he's just been gobbling this beautiful grass! I knew the mules shouldn't eat it. It's way too rich for them. He's got colic! Grab Toojay and Fruitcake. See if they're still ok, and tie them up so they're away from the grass! Tie them up on the trail!"

Peter ran and caught the dangling lead ropes of the two mules who were still busily drinking from the little creek and led them away from the thick light green grass. Once he had them tied up, he returned to Charles who was leading Banjo up and down, up and down near the trail. Banjo was quieter now, but tears were streaming from his eyes and his stomach muscles were jerking. The two boys removed Banjo's packs and packsaddle.

Charles was deeply frightened. "He could die, Pete! He could die right now. He could just lay down in the grass and roll over and die! My dad told me about how that's just about the worst thing you can do to a mule, let him get poisoned or eat something that is too rich, because they don't know any better. It's up to us to take care of them and I didn't!"

He stifled the beginnings of a wail in his throat. Still walking the mule, he had Pete bring a bucket of water from the creek. He offered it to Banjo who wanted no part of it. They kept walking.

"Pete, get on Toojay and ride down into Pinyon Creek and get my dad. Tell him what I did and see if he can come up and help. I'm going to keep walking Banjo right here. So I'll be here when you get back. I know you probably can't get back till tomorrow but I'll be here."

"And Banjo will be ok. I just know it," Pete answered, already moving toward Toojay.

"I hope so." Banjo was barely cooperating now. He staggered along, favoring first one foot and then another, shaking his head and making sounds that sounded like growls.

Peter threw himself onto Toojay. They rattled down the trail toward Pinyon Creek. Fruitcake, left alone by the side of the trail, shuffled his feet, pulling himself toward Charles as far as his halter would allow him.

Charles desperately tried to remember whether his father had given him any remedies for colic. He remembered another dreadful word: founder, where the mule would sink to the ground. He pulled harder on Banjo's lead, urging him to keep walking. What could he feed him? Could he feed him anything? Should he drink water? Maybe I should have gone down for Dad, left Pete here with Banjo. My dad will be so furious with me. I have to stay with Banjo. I couldn't just leave Pete here. It's beginning to get dark.

They extended their route for a little variety, now up and down the trail itself. Banjo was clearly tiring. He had stopped drooling but his head was drooping. Charles tied him to a tree, first checking to make sure there was no grass underfoot. Then he trotted over to the creek, re-filled the bucket with water and brought it back to Banjo. This time the mule took a small swallow before turning his head away.

Up in the mountains, darkness comes swiftly. As the sun dipped behind the Sierra it was getting cold. Charles put his jacket on. It smelled like Banjo and was damp in places. He took

Fruitcake's packs and saddle off and piled them near the others. He pulled his pack from the pile where they had dropped them after unpacking Banjo. He rooted around, finding one last sandwich and a bag of cookies, and ate them quickly, guiltily – I sent Pete off without food or maps or anything. He wondered whether there was a first aid kit.

The plan had been for a one-day trip, up and back. They had not had any idea that they would not be able to get home before dark. He continued to look, setting apart the saddle blankets, hunting without success for matches or lantern or cook stove. At the bottom of the pack he found a box about the size of a loaf of bread. It was marked FIRST AID. It was almost too dark to see, but he pulled it open.

Inside, he found a roll of bandages, some cream, a knife inside a protective cover, a small vial marked Aspirin, a package of needles and black thread, and a small bottle of bleach. Nothing that looked as though it would help a desperately ill mule.

Banjo was still on his feet but was leaning against his tree. His eyes were almost closed. His belly was still jerking and cramping. Charles carefully began rubbing Banjo's belly. Slowly and gently, just hard enough for the mule to feel his hands, he massaged the mule's stomach. Banjo seemed to like it. At least, Charles decided, he didn't object. After awhile they began walking again.

Through the cold night, they walked. Charles wrapped Banjo in a saddle blanket and wound another one around his shoulders. He figured that Fruitcake could make it without help. The moon was almost full, casting enough light to see the trail and the shapes of trees and rocks. He almost began to enjoy it, being outdoors all by himself.

Spence and Peter appeared around the corner of the trail just as the morning began, before sunup but after the sky began to lighten. Charles stood as tall as he could, holding Banjo's lead as his father approached.

Spence looked carefully at Banjo's eyes, opened his mouth and examined the inside of his lips, wiped the last of the drool with a rag. He lifted each foot and carefully examined each hoof. Then he motioned to Peter, who brought a sack from where it had been fastened on Toojay. Reaching into the sack, Spence removed a handful of back powder and shoved it into Banjo's mouth. The mule reflexively chewed and swallowed. Little dribbles of black ran down his muzzle.

"He's not going to die, is he?" Charles whispered.

Spence came over the gave the boy a quick hug. Pete took Banjo's lead and began to walk him again, but he tired quickly.

"No, son, it looks as though he's not as sick as he might have been. He's not out of the woods yet, though." He pulled out matches, and soon a small fire was burning. The three squatted by the fire, warming up. By now the sun was almost over the mountain ridge. Fruitcake was urgently trying to get to the rest of the group. Peter brought him and Toojay closer to Banjo.

Spence stood. "Charles, show me where Banjo got into the grass."

They could see hoof prints and the matted ground where Banjo had shifted, eating. A patch of grass had been chewed away. Spence walked around the area slowly, intent upon the ground.

"It might have been too much grass, but I don't think so. I think you were pretty quick to get him away. But there are plenty of other plants here that could have poisoned him. It was just a very unlucky coincidence. Banjo is such an eater. You know he's the first to find food, and it's hard to pull him away."

"More than Toojay or Blanket or lots of the others," Charles agreed. "Banjo has always been greedy."

"Yup, and in the Spring, like now, there are lots of smaller plants that grow along the creeks and into patches of grass. Later in the summer the mules can avoid them, but Banjo just waded right in and gulped something that wasn't god for him. You did the right thing, to walk him, because mules can't throw up so the poison has to come out the other end--"

At that moment there was a mighty roar and Banjo released a large wet, black deposit onto the ground. They all laughed, shakily.

"--But even though you did all the right things, we've all learned something here. Like, we always need to carry a sack of this, they call it activated charcoal, and we can never, never let Banjo pick out his own dinner!"

Charles leaned up against his father. Suddenly he was exhausted and cold and hungry. It was time to go home.

Now that school was over for the summer, Barbara was preparing for her own summer job. In addition to her clothes, she packed her diary and sketchpad and pencils as well as the book she was reading for the third time, Pride and Prejudice. She had worked at the camp briefly during the preceding summer, but only as extra help. She had never stayed in the mountains more than two or three nights at a time. She wondered whether any of the people she had met last summer would be returning. She wondered especially whether that tall boy named Paul would be back.

She left Mollie's Place with little regret, sorry only that her mother would have to train some new helpers, but that was a regular event these days with the growing popularity of the cafe. Her best friend, Nancy Jean, would be coming to the camp with her, which gave Barbara some pause. Nancy Jean was taller than Barbara and her hair was curlier and she was bolder at making jokes and meeting new people.

Charles and Peter gave the girls a ride up to the camp. The boys added two extra mules to the string for this trip, leaving Banjo at home to complete his recovery. The cargo this time included lumber, sacks of sugar and flour and four large bags of oranges which had been specially shipped in from Los Angeles. Barbara and Nancy perched on Toojay and Fruitcake, sharing space with the food sacks while Blanket carried most of the lumber and tools.

The camp looked almost like a little town, Barbara thought. There were several permanent buildings, including a dining hall which housed the kitchen where she would be working. A collection of tents of varying sizes circled the center of the camp. Some were quite elaborate, with awnings extending from the opening to filter the sun. A few even had carpets inside. Most were more basic because campers intended to spend most of their waking hours outdoors in the open air. A children's play yard was fenced with a sandbox and a swing strung from a tree branch. A half dozen children were hard at work making tracks in the sand for their toy trucks.

Barbara and Nancy Jean were put to work almost at once, preparing salad for the evening meal. Nancy Jean, who was not a skilled cook, volunteered for the table-setting and dish-washing brigade, while Barbara began slicing onions and chopping lettuce.

"These lettuces come from the farm just south of Pinyon Creek," she told Nancy Jean. "They always have the best produce – we use it all the time at Mollie's Place."

"I guess I thought everybody would be eating beans and bacon," Nancy Jean responded. "Like the pioneers. This seems almost like eating at home!"

By the end of the afternoon the campers began to return to the center of camp from the hikes and explorations and activities they had been engaged in during the day. They entered the dining hall and took seats at the long tables, chatting with friends about their day's events.

"We saw, I don't know, maybe twenty-five different kinds of birds, including some hawks, absolutely gorgeous."

"Did you get any photos?"

"I hope so. They are so bold, they come closer than I ever thought they would."

"We think we saw a fox. We are learning the different tracks of these smaller animals. And where they live. Like in burrows or dens."

"I made a castle!" A small child pulled at his father's sleeve.

"We found the perfect pool for swimming, or just lazing around."

Soon the conversation dwindled as the diners concentrated on their food. After dinner, many of the campers returned to their tents but several people carrying musical instruments re-entered the dining hall and set up chairs in a corner. Soon the girls and the rest of the clean-up crew could hear lively tunes, including polkas.

"Makes me want to dance," Nancy Jean called to Barbara as they carried dishes to the kitchen.

"Well, miss, may I have this dance?" it was a rather portly young man in bright blue denim.

"I'd love to, but I must finish here first,"

"Perhaps another time," he said, turning to a young camper who had appeared near the door.

"My heart is broken. My first romance has come to naught, " Nancy Jean whispered to Barbara.

Barbara tried to keep from grinning. She swept the last dishes into a carrying pan and dashed into the kitchen for a moment of gossip with her friend. Then, spotting the stern face of the kitchen manager, she returned to the dining hall.

Just entering the room was Paul, the camper she had met the previous summer.

Chapter XVIII – Camp in the Mountains

Barbara scrubbed the table top industriously, refusing to look up to see where Paul went. When her table had achieved a perfect shiny surface she looked around as though to pick her next chore. He was nowhere in sight. He had grown handsomer during the year, if that were even possible, she thought. His long legs, the way his hair fell over his forehead, the length of his fingers – she remembered him well, of course, since she had been daydreaming about him since the preceding Autumn.

She hung up her apron next to Nancy Jean's and joined her friend at the concert. They were playing familiar folk songs with the audience joining in lustily. Nancy Jean and Barbara added their voices; in some places the words were just slightly different from the ones they knew. The concert concluded with the audience forming a circle holding hands. Barbara felt a large hand reach for hers and found Paul on her left.

"Well, hi," she murmured. "Welcome back."

"Welcome back yourself," he grinned. "Want to go for a walk? It's beautiful outside, isn't it?"

"Sure."

In the time between dessert and the end of the concert the sun had passed below the mountain peaks. The gibbous moon had risen in a cloudless sky. Paul and Barbara walked down the path to a small lake. A small animal scuttled out of their path.

"It's beautiful out here at night," Paul commented. "I never get to see so many stars at home."

"Why's that?"

"Too many lights. In the city, you get light from people's windows, and stores and restaurants. It's noisy, too."

"What kinds of noise?"

"Oh, people, dogs, sometimes music. I can walk past a certain house on my way home from school, and every day I hear somebody practicing the piano. He or she is not getting much better, even after a couple of months."

They laughed.

"Sometimes I'll go out just at dusk with Jock-the-dog, and we'll walk down to the river, kind of like we're walking now, and we'll see all kinds of animals and birds and things. Deer of course, and coyotes, and wild turkeys. You probably don't get that in the city."

"No. But we do get cats and crows."

It was a comfortable amble, along the path which had grown familiar to both of them. Occasionally they passed others. The sounds of voices talking, sometimes singing, floated on the air.

"Will you be up here all summer?" Barbara asked.

"Only part of it. Till the end of July. Then I'm off to get ready for college. Stanford." Paul's voice was proud.

"Where's Stanford?"

Paul's response was slow in coming. He stopped walking and looked gravely into Barbara's face.

"Do you really mean that? Really, don't you know about Stanford? Probably it's California's best-known university."

"I don't think much about college. My brother is at Throop Institute, if that's what you mean. It's in Pasadena and he is studying geology."

"Well. Anyway. I'm going to be studying history and political science."

Barbara laughed. "So maybe sometime you'll be a famous politician. I'll be reading about you in the newspapers."

"Maybe." He smiled. "I'm kind of thinking about that. We have some politicians in our family and they're pretty interesting people."

Barbara had lost interest in the subject. "But what are you doing while you're here? What do you like best about this camp? What does your family think about camping?"

"I guess this is the best part." He pointed to the sky and the stars. "When I get back home to San Francisco I remember what the night sky looks like up here. And the smell of the pine trees. And how cold the water is in the lake!"

They walked for awhile silently.

"There are some paintings in the museum at home, about the mountains in the west – the Sierra and some others," Paul said. "When I first saw them, I thought they were just imaginary scenes, because the mountains were so huge and the people and horses in the paintings were so small. But now I see that that's really how it is."

"Tell me about the museum," Barbara answered. "What do you do there? Do you go there often? Are there other things besides paintings?"

"Haven't you ever been to San Francisco?"

"No, of course not. It's not easy to get any place from Pinyon Creek." She laughed. "And anyway, there's plenty to do here. I mean, in Pinyon Creek. At home."

"I suppose."

They had reached the shore of the lake. The water rippled softly in the moonlight. On the far shore three deer – two does and a buck – were drinking, occasionally raising a head to listen. Barbara and Paul sat on a boulder near a group of trees. Barbara identified the constellations that Alf had taught her. They began to feel the cold and turned back to the camp.

The following morning was bright and warm. After breakfast the campers spread out to different activities, some to hike and swim, others to enjoy their tents and catch up with reading and writing. The Outings staff was happily aware that they had created a successful enterprise.

Nancy Jean and Barbara hurried through the post-breakfast cleanup; they planned to practice canoe skills.

As they stepped out of the back door of the dining hall, they overheard Paul speaking with some of his friends.

"...And she never even heard of Stanford. Stanford! And she has never been to a museum, or heard a symphony concert. Poor thing! No wonder she has to work here, doing such menial jobs. I almost feel sorry for her except that she has no idea that she lives such a primitive life. I suppose it would be worse if she understood how sad her life really is."

Nancy Jean clutched Barbara's arm and pulled her back into the dining hall as Paul and his friends moved off down the hill.

Barbara's face was red and tears had welled up in her eyes. Nancy Jean led her to the sink and poured her a glass of cool water.

"Now you sit here and you drink this water and don't say a word," she commanded. "Just take a deep breath. Now drink some more water.

"I thought he liked me," Barbara murmured.

"He's just a... a... baboon," Nancy Jean responded. "He doesn't know anything. And his friends don't know anything either. Now let's go find something fun to do."

The girls decided to explore the camp buildings. Hired to work in the kitchen, they had not been interested in the other areas of camp, but Nancy Jean pointed out that there might be other, better jobs available in other areas of the organization. They left the kitchen and found their way down the hall which had store rooms on both sides.

"Gracious! Look at all of the food!" Nancy Jean exclaimed. "This must be what the boys have been bringing up, week after week after week!"

The next room held sports equipment, and the one after that contained winter snow gear, from skis to snowshoes.

The final room, larger than the rest, held a piano similar to the one at home and a variety of musical instruments, some in their cases. Barbara walked up to the piano and seated herself on the bench. She tapped a key, then another, startled by the fullness of the sound in the closed room. Nancy Jean came and sat by her. A stack of music had been left on the top of the closed lid. They riffled through the songs and suddenly Nancy Jean pulled one out.

"Look, Barbara!   Here's the music we played for the concert last month!"

It was a selection of songs from operettas which the girls had loved, arranged for four hands. They set it on the rack and started to play. Concentrating on the music, Barbara began to relax. Soon she was enjoying the challenge of the music. They found other pieces, too, some for duets, most for a single pianist. Leaving Barbara at the keyboard, Nancy Jean wandered over to a corner where she found a stack of magazines and music books. Soon she was intently reading.

Barbara was beginning to enjoy the rare experience of playing first one, than another new piece of music. A natural sight-reader, she was accustomed to accompanying singers or pinch-hitting at choir practice and had exhausted the supply of music in the Methodist church. Here was such a variety, such a combination of the difficult and easy, the harmonious and the dissonant! Here were songs with mysterious lyrics, in separate folders with covers decorated with exotic designs.

She played and played, stacking the ones she liked in a separate pile. Some of the melodies sounded familiar, but most were new to her.

Nancy Jean came over, with a music book in her hand, and placed it on the rack in front of Barbara. "Play these! They sound like they'd be fun!"

"These are Strauss waltzes – you know lots of them."

"Not those, in the front. I was looking at the ones toward the back of the book."

Barbara quickly turned the pages. "Oh my! It's Babes in Toyland – all of the songs."

They began with the well-known march, then continued to the other pieces, experimenting with singing in harmony, Nancy Jean's strong alto supporting Barbara's rather wavering soprano.

Suddenly they were stopped by a voice from the doorway.

"Whatever in the world do you think you are doing?"

Chapter XIX – The Sing-Alongs

Mrs. Griffiths, the housekeeping manager, was standing in the doorway. Next to her, an unfamiliar man in knee boots and a woman with a big notebook looked on curiously. Barbara slammed the music book closed and stood facing them. Her day was getting worse and worse.

"I'm sorry, I hope we haven't disturbed anybody," she said. "We were just looking around and found this room. And then we found the music – "

Nancy Jean joined her friend. "Maybe we weren't supposed to be here, but there weren't any signs or anything. And we'd finished our work for the morning. Oh lord, Barbara, what time is it anyway?"

Mrs. Griffiths smiled. "You're not late, if that's what you are worried about, girls. We were just walking past the music room and heard you and wondered who was making that beautiful music."

"Is this a room anybody can use?" Barbara asked. "Even us?"

"Because you're working here, you mean? It's free and available to anybody, and as long as you keep up with your work schedule..."

The man at the door moved forward. "Please let me see the music you were just playing. Did you find it here?"

"Yes, sir."

"But you and your friend have played it before, yes? And perhaps have sung it in school? Is that how you know it?"

"Yes, we sang it in chorus for the Spring Concert," Nancy Jean spoke up. "But we didn't know all the other music from the book, so that is what was so interesting."

He smiled, then turned back to Barbara.

"So I think you are a sight reader. It that true? If I give you some music, will you play it for me?"

"I'll try." She wished her mother were here. She hated to be the center of anyone's conversation. He handed her a book he had plucked from the stack, opened to a song she did not recognize. She studied the pages carefully for a few minutes, then sat back down and arranged the music on the rack. It was a straightforward piece, easy, she felt, to try at a fairly decent tempo.

"Very good. Very good." He came to the side of the piano and looked seriously at her. "Now can you play something you have studied? Something you have memorized?"

She did so, playing a favorite Chopin etude

"And finally – Judy, come help me here. Let's try a short flute piece." The woman with the clipboard grinned, set her clipboard on the piano, opened a case and drew out a flute which

187

she assembled and tested. She handed Barbara a piece of music from the case she had been carrying.

After reading it, Barbara set it open on the stand and they played together. Afterward Judy nodded and stepped back.

"How old are you – Barbara, is it? And you are working in our kitchen right now, Barbara?"

"I'm sixteen, Sir. And I'm the produce and salad girl for lunch and dinner, and cleanup after breakfast." She hoped he wasn't going to send her home. It was, after all, a very small offense, she thought.

"Suppose we change your job. Mrs. Giffiths?" The housekeeper bustled forward. "Suppose we take some of her kitchen duties and distribute them some way. Can we do that?"

Mrs. Griffiths nodded.

"Then, Barbara, would you be willing to play the piano for us, say, every day?"

"I, I, I beg your pardon, sir?"

"We had hired a pianist but he broke his leg just before he was due to come up. Otherwise this piano would be out in the dining hall right now. We need someone to play in the evenings when we want to sing along. We need someone also who can play hymns and such for our Sunday services, and we want an accompanist for our other musicians. Some of our campers would like to perform but they feel they need a piano to support them. I have some other ideas if this works out. What do you think, Judy?"

"I liked the way she plays, Fred. She was listening to me, sensitive to my setting the tempo. She's remarkably good."

Barbara had started to smile, and grinned broadly as she caught sight of Nancy Jean, who was bobbing up and down with excitement. "Well, I'll try my best, Sir. Do you think I can have time to practice as well?"

"Sit down with Mrs. Griffiths and work out a schedule that will be fair to her and to you. By all means, include practice time. And I think, considering that you will be replacing our previous pianist, we can find an extra ten dollars a month for you for this month and next. What do you think?"

"It's wonderful, just wonderful. I'll do my very best."

As Nancy Jean raced back to the kitchen full of news of this exciting development, Barbara and Mrs. Griffiths arranged the new schedule. Barbara would work the breakfast shift as before, and also the lunch preparations, but the afternoon would be free for her to use as she wished, including practicing and selecting music. Barbara had heard enough of past evening entertainments to know that there would be a demand for her to accompany group singing and accompany an assortment of guest musicians on a variety of instruments. They would probably also want to hear her play by herself but she hoped to keep that a very small part of her job. And Nancy Jean would help her decide what music to prepare; she had a good sense of the kinds of songs people liked because her father directed the choir in the Pinyon Creek Methodist Church as well as the Pinyon Creek BarberShoppers.

She flew through her lunch chores and was back at the piano almost before the lunch guests had finished eating. By the end of the afternoon, a crew had moved the piano into the far end of the dining hall, where it attracted the attention of campers assembling for dinner. Barbara stayed out of sight, nervously leafing through the music she, Nancy Jean and Judy had selected. After dinner and the evening's program, a presentation on snakes, the camp director announced a sing-along. To Barbara's surprise, he was the man she had met earlier in the day. Sometime, she decided, she would get somebody to tell her his name.

Stacking her music on the top of the piano, she pulled out the first songbook and played the opening bars of "Meet Me In St. Louis". At first the campers only listened, but Nancy Jean bravely began singing and soon the room was filled with song. By the third or fourth song, Barbara was beginning to enjoy herself. After a half hour, the director called for "By the Light of the Silvery Moon" to signal the end of the evening's sing-along.

"Good going," Judy told her. "This is sure to be a popular evening activity. We'll be keeping you busy from now on."

Chapter XX – The Movies

Barbara was busier than ever. She wanted to make sure she fulfilled her original job requirements in the kitchen, and she wanted to use every spare minute to practice the music she would be playing for the campers. The piano was much better than the one at home; this made practicing even more enjoyable.

As the sing-alongs became an expected part of the evening's entertainment, a growing number of campers sought her out to request their favorite songs. Sometimes while she was in the music room practicing someone would come in with an idea, or occasionally an entire list of songs. She was excited and anxious and only Nancy Jean could reassure her that everything was going well. Her books and drawing pad lay neglected in her room.

As several weeks passed with no problems, Barbara gradually began to relax and enjoy her new work. She wondered whether she might like to become a pianist when she finished school. But she still wanted to work with fruits and vegetables. There was simply too much to do.

One afternoon Charles and Peter arrived with a special load of equipment for the dining hall. Barbara watched interestedly as they carefully carried in several large wooden boxes which they set on the floor. Shrugging, they told her they had no idea what they contained, but it was supposed to be a wonderful surprise for the campers. Charles had bigger news – he was getting a second, part-time job with the new blacksmith, Joe Magnuson.

"Alf thinks he's hot stuff because he rode in an automobile, " he said. "I get to learn how they work."

"Alf rode in an automobile? Where? Why?"

"In Pasadena. He said in his letter. Just because somebody had one, I guess. And you know Alf, if there's anything new going on, he's right there getting into it."

"What letter? What else did he say?"

"Not much. More about the automobile. Oh, he met this girl. I think he likes her pretty much. Her name is Sara. OK, Barb, we'll see you in a couple of days."

Charles and Peter turned to go. Barbara pulled at her brother's sleeve. "What about Sara? How did he meet her? What is she like? Is he serious?"

Charles just smiled. "See you soon

The wooden boxes turned out to be containers for a large movie projector, the first Barbara had ever seen. Mr. Ferguson carefully explained that they were going to show moving pictures to the campers as part of occasional special programs. The films would be shipped to Pinyon Creek and then carried up by Charles and Peter. Each film would be about five minutes long, but the evening's programs would be a collection of five or six separate films.

"Now for your part," he continued. He explained that each film would tell a short story, and he hoped she could capture the emotions with her music. "Like doom-doom-doom when the giant is walking." He illustrated by stomping across the room, raising his legs high. Barbara considered for a moment and then produced a collection of chords.

"Like this? It's from a piece, Walking Giants, that I learned a long time ago."

"Exactly like that! And you'll want scary sounds, and happy birds singing, and things like that." It sounded like fun. She wondered what it would be like to have adults, and families, listening to birds chirping while they looked at pictures. She thought this would be a strange way to spend an evening, but if that was what they wanted...

Nancy Jean, whose family had visited Los Angeles on vacation, had seen a motion picture show. She described the films, singing some of the melodies she remembered. "It'll be easy, because each part has to be really short, because they go so fast."

The original shipment had included the first set of films, so they closed the music room door and, Mr. Ferguson operating the projector, they practiced and practiced. By the time of the performance they had accumulated more than a dozen musical motifs.

The audience loved it.

Dr. Capshaw had also received a letter from Alf. He brought it with him on his regular Sunday visit to Molly and Spence.

"I'm quite fond of my grandson, you know," he told them. "And I think he is making good progress at his college. I just wish he could do better in math. It will serve him in good stead even after he graduates. It's odd, Tony, who has no inclination to go to college, has mastered all of the math he needs for his surveying work. He seems to have a good feel for it. What's Alf going to do after he leaves college? Has he said?"

"Oh, I think he's determined to work in geology, maybe minerals," Spence responded. "Every now and then he'll send just a postcard with maybe the name of a new mineral he's learned about. I don't understand it, myself. I always stayed away from the actual mining. It seems like a dangerous and difficult line of work. But he seems to think that with all these people learning new ways to use them, he can get in there and discover – either new minerals or new uses for them. Or both."

"Takes after his grandfather," Dr. Capshaw said proudly. "He's got the same sense of curiosity I have. Mildred says so, too. Which reminds me. I hear they're having movies up at the Outings camp. Barbara say anything about that to you?"

"We only hear what Charles tells us," Molly said. "I think she is too busy – and too happy, I hope – to write. If there was anything troubling her, we'd hear right away, but so far this month there hasn't been a peep out of her. I'm sure she is storing up all her stories to tell us when she comes home."

"That's still a ways off," Spence murmured. "You can see we miss her."

"Anyway," Dr. Capshaw continued, "I think it's time we had movies in Pinyon Creek. Mildred and I were talking about it and we think we should form a committee and raise some money and start a movie theater. What do you folks think?"

Spence pushed away from the table and stood. "I think it's a great idea. Have you approached any of the businessmen about it? Let's go see who's around. Maybe we can start the ball rolling."

Molly watched, smiling. She was thinking that she was a fortunate woman. Her children were safe and well and doing things which interested them. Her cafe was successful. Her garden was flourishing, giving her more than enough produce for Mollie's Place; she was even selling some vegetables to the neighbors. The summer was, well, summer – hot and dry with endless cloudless skies, but it was bearable now that she had mastered the habit of rising early for pre-sunrise outdoor chores. Her father was settling into a courtship which, if not romantic, was certainly affectionate, and Molly was growing fond of Matilda Howell. Pinyon Creek was thriving, with aqueduct workers spending money and talking about the place to their friends. There were rumors that the railroad might still come, and even more firm rumors that the road between Mojave and Pinyon Creek might be paved. It was a good time.

Barbara couldn't decide which was more fun – accompanying the movies or playing for the sing-alongs which were still extremely popular evening events. Somehow, after a half-hour's lecture or lantern slide presentation about nature, the campers wanted to relax with a group activity before retiring. Judy Ferguson told her that she was hoping to organize a small instrumental group. Not an orchestra, because there weren't that many musicians, and not a chamber music group because how would you incorporate an accordion into a chamber music group? But some kind of group that could all play together now and then. Perhaps the most satisfying proposal was from a group of men who told her that they liked to sing as a chorus, and would she consider accompanying them. She could hardly wait. In the back of her mind she daydreamed of returning to Pinyon Creek and continuing to play for groups, and maybe they would put on a play with music.

She was working on a piece of music for thunder and rain and scary birds when she felt that someone had entered the room. She turned around and found Paul.

"Hi, Paul."

"Hello yourself, Barbara. Pretty busy, I guess."

"Yes, actually, I am."

"I haven't seen you since the day after we took that walk. I was hoping you aren't angry or anything."

"I'm not angry. I'm just very very busy." (Nancy Jean had passed the doorway, peeked in, and seeing what was happening had tiptoed in to stand by the wall).

"Well, are you too busy to come and take another walk with me?"

"Yes. I'm sorry, but I need to get this done. You have other friends, I'm sure." The next words slipped out before she could stop them. "Friends who don't live such a primitive life."

Paul stiffened. "You overheard what I said, didn't you. I'm sorry. I didn't mean anything by it. It's just that, well, we do come from different places. I had no idea that you play the piano, for example."

"You never thought about it. Tell the truth, Paul. I can do lots of other things, too. I can cook a meal for fifty people. I sew my own dresses. I can saddle and ride a horse or a mule. I can read maps, including topological charts. I can identify constellations. What about you?"

"Well. I'm going to be studying chemistry at Stanford. I'll be able to identify substances."

"You'll be studying things, but I'll bet these camps are the only times you actually get out of doors and do things."

"Not true. I'm on my school's tennis team."

"Great. Now I've got lots to do. Good bye, Paul"

He stared at her for a moment, then turned and left the room.

Barbara looked sadly at Nancy Jean. "I just blurted it all out. I didn't mean to be so nasty. He didn't deserve that."

"Well I say Good For You. You taught him a lesson, all right. And anyway, who needs somebody like Paul? He's just soft and spoiled. Like old cheese." She giggled.

Chapter XXI – The New Car

The first automobile Charles studied was really a truck, or it would have been if Fred Eaton had had his way. Eaton, formerly mayor of Los Angeles and currently a rancher north of Pinyon Creek, had bought a Ford Model T, one of the very first in California, as he liked to say. It was bright red, a touring car, elegant and spacious. Charles thought it looked a little funny with the passenger compartment perched on tiny, wobbly-looking wheels. Eaton had driven it to Pinyon Creek in order to consult with Joe Magnuson, the blacksmith, about converting it to a truck for use on the ranch.

Charles stepped quietly into the shadows of the blacksmith shop. The two men were standing together on one side of the car studying the way in which the chassis was fitted together.

Magnuson took out his big handkerchief and wiped away some streaks on the brilliant paint.

"I don't know," he said slowly. "What did you say you want to use her for?"

"Well, carrying things. Carrying some hay, maybe, or some water barrels. Or tools. Seems like as long as I've got this auto, why should I go back to mules for hauling?"

Magnuson shot a repressive look at Charles, who swallowed the words about to come from his mouth. "Mules can haul a lot heavier load than this auto can. Tell you what I think. This auto is still new for you, and you don't really understand her yet. How much have you driven her?"

"A lot. More than you've ever driven an auto. Let's see. Up here from San Pedro, back to Los Angeles, up here again. And back and forth from my ranch to here a couple of times. I think you can say I have a pretty good idea of what she can do. I'll bet this is the first car you have ever seen, Joe. I'd be careful about making judgments if I were in your shoes."

Charles moved closer, slowly, fascinated by the bright metal. He could hardly wait to see inside the engine compartment. The men ignored him.

"What I say is this," Joe Magnuson continued. "I say drive her on the roads where you can enjoy the looks you get from people. You can even practice scaring horses if that pleases you. You can show off your big machine whenever you like. But don't tear it apart and ruin it just because you didn't plan in advance what you wanted to use it for. Sooner or later somebody is going to make a truck and you'll buy that truck and then you'll have both and you'll decide that you are a brilliant planner. I'm not going to help you destroy a perfectly good – a perfectly beautiful – machine."

"Well," Eaton sputtered, slamming his hands down on the Ford's door.

"I don't like you, Eaton. I don't like how you came into the valley and grabbed your land and lied to folks around here. But I am the only person between here and Reno that's able and more or less willing to do whatever repairs you're going to need. And I am certain that I'm the only man around who's willing to shoe your horses and mules. So we'll continue to do that kind of business. But I'm surely not about to hack off the back of this lovely auto."

Eaton stepped back from the automobile and shook his head. He slammed the fist of one hand into the palm of the other. Taking short steps toward the front of the vehicle, he noticed Charles.

"Young man, you're Doc Capshaw's grandson, aren't you?"

"Yes, Sir."

"I see him just about everywhere I turn these days. A busy, busy man. Important too, I'd guess."

"Yes, Sir," Charles responded, puzzled.

"So you're the young man who has been driving your dad's mules, right?"

"Yes."

"Working for the blacksmith now, I take it."

"Yes Sir."

"You're pretty good with mules?"

Charles wondered what was going on. Joe Magnuson had returned to work at his anvil but kept glancing at Charles, who could not interpret the look.

"I've got a mule needs re-shoeing. Suppose I give you a ride up to my ranch, and you ride the mule back down here. Return him when he's ready and I'll give you a ride back to town. That suit you?"

"Oh yes, Sir!" Charles was overjoyed. He hurried to give the information to the blacksmith, who simply grunted and nodded.

The ride to the ranch was the most exciting event in Charles' life. Sitting in the front seat, he watched Mr. Eaton crank the engine, then move his feet from one pedal to another until the auto started forward. With a great noise they motored out of the blacksmith shop and onto the street, where large clouds of brown dust blew up behind them as they headed north. He saw Tony on his way to Molly's Place and gave him a big wave, enjoying the double-take Tony gave him. A horse tied to the hitching post in front of Will's Saloon shied and whinnied, to Charles' delight. All too soon they had left the town behind and were proceeding at a dignified pace up the road toward Eaton's ranch.

"What do you think?" Eaton had to shout to be heard.

"It's grand!" He knew how Alf must have felt on his ride down in Pasadena.

"I talked with Magnuson before you came. Told him I wanted you to help him work on this auto. I'm going to need more than just one man to keep it...." The wind was taking away some of the words. Charles strained to hear.

They continued up the road which was slowly gaining altitude. Within an hour they reached the dirt path leading to the ranch. Eaton pulled the car to a stop and waved at Charles, who hopped out and opened the large gate, closing it after the auto had passed through. He climbed back in, trying not to let dirt from his shoes mar the shiny floor. Eaton drove past the house to the stables and parked at the side next to the open stalls. Each stall was occupied by a mule or a horse.

They climbed back out of the motor. Charles walked slowly around it, trying to memorize every detail. He admired the tall wheels, the shiny leather awning across the top, the rich-looking padding on the seats. He wondered whether he dared ask to look at the engine.

"Want to see the engine?"

"Oh, yes, Sir."

It looked simpler than other engines Charles had seen. The big machines in the upper forests that drove the saws and powered the moving belts for the lumbering had terrified him but this engine looked domestic, tamed. Each piece, still new enough to look shiny in parts, seemed to have been machined expressly for use. No space in the engine compartment was wasted. He had no idea how any of it might work.

"This is what I have in mind," Fred Eaton said, looking solemnly at Charles. "I know there are people in town, like Joe Magnuson, who don't like me, but I'm not a bad man. I think that sometimes people are envious of those who appear more successful than they are. I'm going to be here for a long time, and I would like to have the opportunity to get to know some of my fellow ranchers, as well as some of the people in town. I'm hoping that you will help me."

"I don't know what I can do, Sir." Charles couldn't prevent himself from stroking the side of the automobile.

"I want to hire you as an occasional worker. For example, you can move my mules to town for shoeing and other care. You can also take care of the auto, starting with washing it sometime this week, depending on how your schedule works out. Then during the school year I'm hoping that you will continue to work at the blacksmith shop. I'll be bringing the auto in for things like changing the fluids, or repairing the tires – of course, we don't know what will need to be done, do we?"

He smiled. "But as you work for me, you'll get to know me and you will be able to tell people – your grandfather, for instance, and your father – that I'm not a bad sort. I pay my bills promptly, and I sell goods at a fair price. Does this sound good to you?"

"Yes, Sir."

"Then good. Here's a dollar in payment for taking Jasper down to the blacksmith and back. That suit you?"

"Yes, Sir."

Charles threw a saddle on the mule and headed back down the hill. His mind was still turning over everything that had happened during the last few hours. He had worked for the blacksmith for less than a month. A silent, large, careful man, Magnuson was not one to offer opinions or small talk, but Charles had already formed an opinion that the man respected honesty and loyalty. But here was Eaton, a man whom Magnuson did not respect, but nevertheless a man who had charmed Charles. Eaton offered excitement and glamor and a chance for Charles to earn more money. But what if the blacksmith objected to his working for Eaton?

The mule ambled down the trail, pausing from time to time to chew on some grass or take a drink of water from the stream that bordered the path. Charles watched the cattle on the hillside walking slowly through the tall grass. A couple of turkey vultures circled on a thermal current off to his right. A family of chukar bobbed across the track. Before he knew it, he was back in town.

The blacksmith noted the same fact, wryly. "Let's see. You and Eaton left in that machine of his, blasting out of town like the Indians were after you, about two o'clock. What time do you think you got up there?"

"It was about three fifteen." Charles was proud of his pocket watch, a birthday gift from his grandfather, and insisted on telling everybody the time as frequently as possible.

"Uh huh. And you spent a few minutes there, admiring the auto, gathering up the mule. You probably left when?"

"I was out the gate at three fifty."

"And right now the time is...."

"Let's see. Four – no, five o'clock on the button."

"So. Looks like this mule must really be a quarter horse. Must have galloped the whole way." Magnuson grinned. "What I'm saying, son, is that it'll take a while before the auto beats the mules. At anything. And that's not a bad situation, far as I can tell."

Charles grinned back. "You know I love the mules, about as much as my dad does. But that auto, she sure is beautiful. And exciting. And noisy!"

"Well, let's get back to work. I take it he wants new shoes on the mule."

Charles felt a great relief. He was still the blacksmith's helper; that was one thing that had not changed this afternoon.

Tony was at the house when Charles got home from work. "Look who was riding in the new automobile!" he teased.

Spence and Dr. Capshaw looked up from the stack of papers before them on the dining room table.

"So was it exciting?" Spence asked.

"Oh yes. It was great! You can feel the wind coming right at you! It looks really hard to work it, though. That's what I want to find out."

"That was Fred Eaton's auto, right?" Dr. Capshaw looked as though he had just eaten something nasty. "I'm not sure how I feel about you spending time with him."

"But he wants me to learn! He wants to help me, and he'll give me a part-time job working with his mules AND the auto. He wants to be friendly to you, too."

"Huh. We'll see about that." Dr. Capshaw shook his head and returned to the stack of papers.

"What are you all doing?" Charles asked.

"We're going to get a movie theater here in town," Tony answered. "We're going to get all the businessmen to contribute money and we'll turn that saloon that used to be Bronco's into a movie hall. Maybe we can have dances there, too. It's going to be great, if we can get the money."

"And Barbara can play the piano just like she's doing now," Charles responded.

"She's what?" chorused the men.

"Well, I saw her. They have this enormous piano and she plays the music to go with the movies they show. She really likes it."

Charles laughed, seeing the astonished faces of the men around the table.

Then Tony made them all serious again as he talked about what he had seen on the aqueduct job.

Chapter XXII – Pinyon Creek Grows

"This is so much bigger than I had ever thought," Tony said. "The equipment alone is, well, you wouldn't believe it, but listen to this: they ordered about a boxcar full of hay just to feed the mules that are hauling the pipe up to Lone Pine."

"Did they ever think about buying hay from the ranchers around here?" Wallace Capshaw growled.

"Sure, but they decided that if they started doing that, the ranchers and the farmers would raise their prices. They thought they'd get a better deal from some merchant down in Los Angeles. And the cement plant! It's like a whole city all by itself. I think we'd better get used to the fact that this aqueduct is going to make some permanent changes around here."

"Do you really think it will affect us much?" Spence asked. "It does now, of course, because of all the workers coming in, and living here and buying food and drink. But when everything is built, they'll go away again and we can get back to normal."

"They may go away, but the aqueduct will be here forever and that will make changes we don't even know about," Tony said stubbornly. "Oh well, I've got to get home. Aunt Velda sends her best, Miss Molly."

The plans for the movie theater moved along quickly, because almost everybody in Pinyon Creek was curious to see the new entertainment. The empty saloon was purchased, gutted, painted and furnished with benches and some chairs. One family donated a piano (no longer used because the children had grown) and others contributed to the cost of the projector and screen. The Odd Fellows gave enough money to cover rental and shipping of the first six films, to begin during the school Winter vacation.

Barbara agreed to play the piano for the performances held during the vacation, but had to give up the job because she was too busy with her senior year in high school to continue.

As work progressed on the movie theater, the town of Pinyon Creek continued to show improvements elsewhere as well. A dry-goods store opened, selling merchandise that residents formerly had to buy from catalogs. Everything from boots to saucepans to bolts of flannel could be seen, to the delight of shoppers both male and female. Molly's Place saw the beginnings of competition as another restaurant opened. This one was named Rocky's Steak House and was open for dinner only. Molly felt more relief than apprehension. She found the long relentless days of shopping, cooking, serving and cleaning just too much, even with help from Velda and a succession of hired girls.

Barbara returned from the Outings Camp more self-confident, Molly thought, than she had ever been. Nancy Jean bubbled over with stories, but Barbara simply smiled as her friend reviewed the excitements of Barbara's piano triumphs.

By Christmas time, Dr. Capshaw was beginning to feel restless. The hard work of establishing a movie theater was almost over; the building was attractive and comfortable, the films were arriving on schedule, and the audiences were reliable. He did think the features were too short for his taste, but decided that sooner or later the movie companies would think of improvements; businesses always found improvements, he would say. He had taken photos, maintaining a stubborn silence, of Fred Eaton and his automobile and had bitten back any envy he might have felt when he examined the red Model T at close range. How anybody could put that much paint on metal was beyond him. He decided to ask Alf how they did that. He was eager for Alf to come home from school for vacation.

But Alf did not return to Pinyon Creek that Christmas. As he wrote his parents, he had received an invitation to explore the mines of Costa Rica with Dr. Davidson and his family. Dr. Davidson, he explained, was one of his geology professors and had a very pleasant family, including his daughter Sara who would also be on the trip. In Costa Rica the men would visit several mines, identifying the different ores and observing mining techniques. It was a wonderful opportunity, Alf told them, and he could pay his expenses without asking them for money because he had been tutoring chemistry all Fall. He thought that tutoring would be good preparation for when he became a teacher himself.

"Did you know he wants to be a teacher?" Spence asked Molly.

"This is the first I've heard of it. I don't remember that he has said anything about what he would like to do."

"I was kind of hoping he'd get involved in the mining business. He wouldn't have to actually mine, but with his college degree he could be boss of the miners."

"Or he could invent something," Dr. Capshaw added. "I have some ideas I'd been meaning to talk to him about."

"Well, that'll just have to wait, I guess," Spence said. "Looks like it will be a while before we see him again."

"I wonder what Sara looks like," Barbara remarked.

"Sara who?" Charles asked, and everybody laughed. Charles, embarrassed, stalked from the room.

By Spring of 1910, more and more automobiles were seen in Pinyon Creek, although most of them belonged to tourists from Los Angeles who were enticed by stories of the beautiful scenery and the improved roads which, not yet paved, nevertheless were wide and mostly free of large rocks. Workers on the aqueduct occasionally visited for weekend rest and entertainment.

Barbara had found the kind of summer work she dreamed of. North of Pinyon Creek the apple orchards were producing record crops and farmers were expanding their plantings because of increased demand from Los Angeles. As soon as she graduated she would be working every day in one of the older orchards, helping with planting and weeding, learning about all of the aspects of apple orchard care.

Charles was in his element now, with the increased automobile traffic. He had studied the engine of Fred Eaton's auto, and he and the blacksmith had taken every opportunity to examine any car that came in for repairs – and that turned out to be many cars. The dirt road was hard on the tires, the dust settled in the engine compartment. In the winter the snow and rain worked their way into fuel lines that weren't tightly sealed. Travelers used many different kinds of fuel, from kerosene to ethanol, and were not above mixing fuel types when necessary. Joe Magnuson and Charles, with the interested support of Wallace Capshaw, determined to build a still to produce ethyl alcohol.

"We'll want to work out back of your stables," Dr. Capshaw told the blacksmith. "Just in case we have any problems, we don't want anybody or anything to get hurt."

"What are you thinking about? Fire? Explosions? Things falling over?" Magnuson responded. "We probably don't have to worry about any of that. We'll put up a shack, just to keep the sun off – and the rain in the winter – and maybe even leave one side open."

"Like a leanto," Charles offered. "Like a stall but all by itself."

"Exactly. See how much wood we've got, and let's get at it."

In just a few days the building was ready for use. The roof was a sheet of tin brought from an abandoned mine site along with several old boilers, pots and pipes. Dr. Capshaw contributed several issues of his treasured Popular Science magazines and the three of them pored over the drawings, making sketches of their own, until they felt that they understood the process.

"Now we have to get corn," Charles said one morning.

"Mildred has some she'll let us have. She keeps some for the cattle but she has much more than she needs. When I told her about our experiment she was all in favor of helping."

"How will we know if it works? We surely don't want to try it on Mr. Eaton's auto if we don't know what will happen."

Dr. Capshaw chuckled, but agreed that they should test it in an old engine formerly used at the lumbermill.

The first experiments were complete failures but after several days filled with trial and error they had enough ethanol to pour into the old engine. Nervously, they prepared for the test. Dr. Capshaw and Charles stood safely away from the engine as Joe Magnuson carefully poured the fluid. Then he pulled the igniter and bang! The engine started to run.

"Success!" Charles shouted, running down the street to find his father. Spence was properly enthusiastic when he appeared and watched a second, then a third test.

"Have Mildred save her corn for you," he told his father-in-law. "I think we just added a new industry to Pinyon Creek!"

That summer, dinner discussions were lively. Barbara excitedly told about her discoveries in the apple orchards, what she was learning about improving the crops and how to prevent pests. She was in charge of a newly planted section of the orchard and nursed her seedlings carefully. She and Molly exchanged ideas for fences and ways to prevent scorching of the tender plants under the desert sun.

Charles sprinkled automotive terms into his vocabulary to the exasperation of everybody around him. Chokes and magnetos and trembler coils, crossflow radiator design, how to start the car on a hill (impossible) – Charles would draw diagrams on his napkins unless prevented. He continued his summer job of transporting freight between Pinyon Creek and the Outings camp, and reported that this year the camp was even larger, with many more campers.

"There's part of this camp business that I don't like," he said. "There are so many people, and so many animals and so much equipment, that they're ruining the land around. Not only in the camp, but they are letting people pitch tents and corral their horses just about anywhere. The shrubs are getting eaten right down to the ground. The waterholes near the camp are getting fouled. Our mules won't even stop there. I have to water them before we get there or after we leave. And it just doesn't look as pretty as it used to."

"Maybe you're just getting older," Molly commented. "Or you've just seen it so often that it looks too familiar to you."

"No. It's getting worn out. And they are building more buildings, putting up electric lights. We took a couple of generators up there earlier and they want more. Now at night when I'm getting ready to sleep, it's like daytime."

"Now, Charles."

"No, ma, well maybe I'm exaggerating a little bit, but they have these lights on in the main building and the bigger tents. If I wanted to see the stars, I couldn't. I'm beginning to wonder why these people are coming up here, if they are going to just do the same things they do at home. Except with mosquitoes."

"Do you want to turn it over to Peter?" Spence asked.

"No! Well, maybe. I like working with Mr. Magnuson. I'm learning a lot there, too. And he is going to let me do some shoeing soon. And I can change a tire all by myself now. I like doing the trips up to the camp, though. I think I would miss that."

"You just want everything!" Barbara teased.

"Maybe I do. I do think we're going to get more and more autos coming through here. Mr. Magnuson says so, too. Mr. Eaton says so, when he comes in to town."

"Take Mr. Eaton with a grain of salt, son." Spence pushed his chair back. He gave Molly a troubled look. "I forgot to tell you, honey, some of Eaton's friends have been back in town, nosing around."

"They've been at the restaurant," Molly answered. "And they try to join into the talk at the big table, you know, where the men meet. But nobody has much time for them, so they sit awhile and finally they just wander out. It's kind of sad, really."

"Mr. Eaton says it's sad that people here don't understand how important this aqueduct is. How it's making jobs and money for people, and it's letting Los Angeles grow."

"See, that's what I mean. Look Charles, Mr. Eaton is Los Angeles born and Los Angeles bred, and he is not interested in what is good for Pinyon Creek. He just thinks about what is good for Los Angeles and the too are not the same thing."

"Well, OK. But he is really nice to talk to and he knows a lot about stuff. About politics and history and engines and science."

Spence looked at his son with a troubled face. He was too trusting for his own good, Spence thought. Something was going to hurt him.

"Tell you what, son," he said. "Next week I've got to take a string of mules to Mojave and pick up some more pipe. Why don't you tell Mr. Magnuson you need to help me, and come along. You'll see what we can do with twelve mules. I don't think you've ever seen that!"

Chapter XXIII – A Trip to Mojave

Charles and his father took a wagon for the trip to Mojave; the return trip would see them carrying supplies and tools for Magnuson and other businessmen. Charles could bring the wagon back while Spence worked with the larger mule team hauling several sections of pipe.

As they began the drive, the scenery was familiar. Their road led along the Owens River valley, with the gray, granite, spiky Sierra Nevada to their right, the layers of mountain rippling away in the distance. They knew the names of some of the peaks: Whitney, Tom, Owens. They had climbed many of the mountains partway, first hiking up the narrow twisting canyons formed by mountain streams, then scrambling along the rocks until they were exhausted. Then they would look up and see that they had only begun their ascent. Charles thought that probably nobody had climbed all the way to the top of Mount Whitney, the tallest mountain peak in the country.

For Spence and Charles the canyons had their own beauty, and each was slightly different from the others. Some canyons were primarily water courses, where a hiker could be sure of cold fresh water all along the trail. Others were dry and covered with brush that would poke your trousers and slip under your shoes. To the East was the valley floor, with the Owens river boiling along even now, in the part of the year that was the driest. At the river's edge, salt cedars and mesquite trees provided shade for cattle. The pastures were mostly brown in the late Autumn, but each field held patches of green and yellow, where wild mustard or other plants had taken root.

"I saw a bald eagle here once," Spence remarked, gesturing toward the meadow dotted with oak trees. "Only once, but I keep looking."

"What was the biggest animal you ever saw out here?"

"Well, wild animal, right? Not like cows. Probably coyotes, I've seen probably dozens of coyotes. You?"

Charles thought for a few minutes. "Yes, coyotes. Sometimes I've seen whole families."

They rode past the fishery where Spence had picked up cans of fish, and through small towns, some no more than a collection of houses. Every few hours they stopped to give the mules water and a break. In Lone Pine they stopped under a tree and took out the picnic that Molly had prepared. It was early evening and the heat was beginning to dissipate.

"We'll keep going till dark, and then find a place to rest," Spence told his son.

In the quiet air, the jingle of the harness was the only sound except for their quiet voices talking at intervals. When the road neared the river, they heard the splash of water against the rocks. Owens Lake appeared on their left, large and dark blue in the early evening light, little wavelets rippling at the shore. A flock of gulls circled, swooped and landed on the water.

"Charles, did you know there used to be a steamship on this lake? It was called the Bessie Brady and it went back and forth, delivering supplies to the mines up at Cerro Gordo, not far from where I used to work, and bringing silver ore back down. It was something to see her go. Even though she only lasted a few years, it was something to see her."

"How come she's not still there? "

"Two reasons. First, the mines are all played out, no reason to haul things back and forth. But the big reason is she burned down."

Charles was sceptical. "How can something burn down in the water?"

"She was tied up at the shore because they were painting her and putting in a new engine and getting her ready to be moved to another place. There was paint and glue and all kinds of flammable liquids on her deck and poof! Up she went. I wasn't there but they said it was a sight to see."

"I guess. We're really careful with the ethanol, dad. "

"I know you are. You're a responsible young man, and Joe is a good boss."

In Cartago they found Spence's preferred overnight stop. A half-dozen tall trees circled a flat piece of ground which looked swept clean of rocks. While Charles spread ground cloths and bedrolls, Spence unhitched the mules, strung a rope corral, and hobbled them inside. They spread hay for the animals, filled several pans of water, and settled down to sleep. Charles in his blankets looked up through the tree branches at the sky. It was full dark by now, and the sky was alive with stars.

"I keep thinking," he told his father sleepily, "that those campers are paying lots of money to sleep in the mountains and all they can see are lanterns."

As they journeyed south they descended into the Indian Wells Valley. The ground was dryer, browner, less fertile. South of Manzanar there were few farms, few pastures. The only visible signs of habitation were mines and occasional stores, or corrals empty of animals. The Owens River had ended at Owens Lake; they had passed a couple of large ponds and one small lake – maybe a reservoir, Spence remarked – but they were happy to find water at Inyokern.

Just south of Inyokern they found the first signs of aqueduct activity. Crews of men were building a road from the main road to the mountainside, where the granite had been partially blasted away. Additional crews could be seen scraping and digging, hauling boulders with the help of mules and horses. Spence gave the reins to Charles and strode over to the nearest group, which gathered around him to talk.

Suddenly Tony's head appeared on the far side of the wagon. "Where's your dad?"

"Over there. Is this where you work?" Charles was impressed by Tony's appearance: a battered fedora shielded his head from the sun and wind. Pencils stuck out of several pockets. A set of binoculars was slung around his neck. He was holding a tripod.

"Yeah. I'm taking readings for this road they're making. See that pipe?" He gestured at a section of pipe so big that Charles had simply not seen it. It was so large that a grown man could stand up in it. It was standing near the wagon, at the edge of the main road, and was braced with rocks.

"They're going to move it pretty soon, after the little road is in shape, and join it to the pipe already in place. Want to see?"

He held out a hand for Charles, who tied the reins to a nearby tree and joined Tony. The two scrambled over accumulations of small rocks and uprooted plants to reach the side of the mountain where most of the work was taking place.

"Now look over there." Tony pointed up. Charles raised his head and found a second level of work. High above, men had blasted away more of the mountain to clear room for the enormous pipe. They were assembling a complicated contraption of ropes and pulleys.

At the southern end, Charles could see the pipe emerging from the mountainside. "It looks as big as a house," he exclaimed. Tony nodded.

"Yep, it's specially built. I think it's about the biggest around pipe you'll ever see. Can you imagine that full of water?"

"I can't imagine anybody needing that much water!"

"Yeah, but don't forget, we're watering an entire city here." Tony was not smiling. Charles was beginning to get the same sinking feeling each time the aqueduct was mentioned. If everybody felt so bad, why were they all working so hard to make it happen? He wondered.

Soon Spence returned and they set off for Mojave. Now the land was flat and treeless. Last year's tumbleweeds could be seen stuck against fence wire or tangled with plants. The ground was dry and dusty. Suddenly they began descending into a canyon with walls of red stone, striped and patterned in vivid patterns.

"They call this Red Rock Canyon, son," Spence told Charles. "The old Nadeau freighters liked to stop here for water and rest. Look around and you'll see some terrific sights."

The canyon walls seemed to change from one moment to the next. In places, wind and water had eroded sandstone cliffs leaving pillars and mysterious looming shapes. In others, denser stone of many colors rippled along the sides of the road. A bird with a long tail trotted across the road ahead of them. Despite the dry sandy ground, cactus of several kinds could be seen, some as tall as young trees. One group in particular made Charles gasp. They looked like trees but with collections of spikes instead of leaves. Often several trunks appeared to grow from one spot, then branch out. No two looked the same: branches bent toward the ground or developed additional divisions. "Joshua trees. They're called Joshua trees, but I don't know why," Spence said.

Mojave was a big town, larger than Pinyon Creek. There were at least two streets lined with stores, and small side streets on both sides of their road led to collections of houses. It was a noisy place, too, with animals and automobiles making a racket. Spence stopped the wagon at a collection of stables and corrals.

"Let's get out, stretch our legs and get some lunch before you turn around and go back home," he said. "And we have to pick up supplies, too."

Charles walked down the street with wide eyes. Even the stores were larger than he had ever seen before. In the store windows he recognized some of the items he and Peter had taken to the camp, but much that was displayed was unfamiliar to him. Charles would have liked to spend days shopping, but Spence made short work of the purchases. Soon the wagon was full.

"Now for lunch. How about a steak?" That sounded very adult to Charles, who nodded in what he hoped was a sophisticated way.

They walked to the Harvey House restaurant next to the train depot. It was a large cement building stretching along the walk next to the train tracks. As they entered, Charles felt cooler almost at once; a series of large ceiling fans turned slowly. The lobby was bright and filled with colorful furniture. The tall windows allowed sunlight to fill the room. The dining room was dimmer. Electric lights were located throughout but would not be turned on until evening, to Charles' disappointment.

They ordered steaks and potatoes. While they waited, several men stopped by to greet Spence and meet his son. Several were names he'd heard his grandfather mention, though often with a growl.

"J. B., good to see you," Spence said, half standing and offering his hand. "I'd like you to meet my son, Charles. Charles, this is J. B. Lippincott from Los Angeles."

"How do you do, Sir?"

"Fine, son, fine. Spence, is this your oldest? Thought he was in school someplace."

"No, this is my third child, second son. Charles is working with me and with Joe Magnuson, the blacksmith. He thinks he's going to know all about automobiles sooner or later."

"Good idea, son, good idea. Can't know too much about automobiles. That's what will bring the tourists up to your place. Once the road is paved. What are you down here for, Spence?"

"Picking up a mule team. Going to take sixteen up to Inyokern, well, to Jawbone. We're going to haul pipe and cement as long as the weather holds this Fall."

"Good man, good man. Nice to meet you, Carl." He moved off.

"Dad, he should know I'm not Alf. Because he and Alf kind of got into a fight last winter."

"Oh? Are you sure?"

"Oh yes. I was right there. See, he didn't want people in Pinyon Creek to know he works for the aqueduct people in Los Angeles. Alf explained it to me. Because before, he was up in Pinyon Creek buying water rights. He said maybe he would be farming, like Mr. Eaton. And at the same time he was working for the government, for the Reclamation Agency. Alf said if that wasn't against the law it should be. Getting paid twice."

"So what did Alf do?"

"So Alf came up to him and said, Hello Mr. Lippincott, how is everything in Los Angeles? And Mr. Lippincott kind of said hum-hum-hum, and Alf said, I hear you're working for the Water

District now. And he said it pretty loud and we were all in front of the general store so people were kind of listening, you know?"

"And then what happened. Alf never told me any of this." Spence's eyes twinkled but his face was serious.

"Well, Mr. Lippincott kind of pushed at Alf and tried to walk on past. And Alf said, Well, Mr. Lippincott, why are you up here in Pinyon Creek again? I'd think you would have bought all the water rights you wanted the last time you were here. Does your boss in Los Angeles know you're here? And it seemed like more people kind of stopped to listen." Charles paused. "I think he didn't mention it to you because he was a little bit rude just then."

"I'll say. But I can't say I blame him. I didn't know Alf was aware of all of this."

"Tony tells him a lot. So anyway Alf doesn't get out of the way when Mr. Lippincott is walking, and so Mr. Lippincott pushes him a little bit more. And Alf says, Say Mr. Lippincott, is that the way people in Los Angeles act? Do they always shove at people like that? And Mr. Lippincott got really angry and gave Alf a BIG shove and moved on through and got into his buggy and left."

"You remember that episode pretty clearly, Charles."

"Alf never gets angry in public, dad. You know that. But he came pretty close to hitting Mr. Lippincott, I think. Afterwards he saddled Blanket and rode off for most of the afternoon."

Spence sighed. "I don't know how all of this is going to work out, Charles. I'll be honest with you. A lot of people, like your grand-dad, are sure the aqueduct will ruin the valley and destroy Pinyon Creek. I don't think it's that bad. We have so much up there, so much richness. We have the mountains and the orchards and the pastures and the hayfields, and I do believe that there will always be mining of one kind or another. I can't imagine that will all be washed away by the aqueduct."

Charles was troubled by his father's solemn words. But just then the steak was served, and another visitor stopped at the table. It was Willy Chalfant, the newspaper editor, and he had big news:

"Spence, did you hear? They're going to build a railroad from Pinyon Creek across the valley. We'll have real rail service before we know it!"

Chapter XXIV – OVI Company Begins

By the time Charles reached home, everybody in Pinyon Creek was talking about the new railroad. The tracks would run from Pinyon Creek across the Owens River to Laws, where they would meet the Southern Pacific line. For anyone wanting to take the train to San Francisco or Reno or Los Angeles, or anybody wanting to ship goods, it would save time and energy, and it probably would bring more tourists to Pinyon Creek. It was all good news.

At first, Dr. Capshaw was deeply suspicious of the plan. Anything that pleased everybody had some kind of hidden hook, he declared. There had to be somebody making absurd amounts of money, or it would do damage to Pinyon Creek's reputation, or something. But after thinking for awhile and coming up with a half dozen or more plans to make some money himself from the project, Dr. Capshaw became a booster.

Charles, having seen a train at Mojave, was overjoyed. He pictured himself as engineer, or track surveyor like Tony, or somebody who would handle signals. He and Peter spent happy hours designing signal devices that would, for example, warn of loose cattle or dogs on the tracks.

Their excitement was dampened only a little by the rumors that the train cars would be small, the tracks would be narrow gauge, and the train would be powered by gasoline or electricity. It was not going to be the huge metal monsters they had hoped for, but it was still going to be a train, with tracks.

Spence was so busy hauling pipe that he had no words to spare for any discussions about trains. He was working with large mule teams, from twelve to eighteen, with a swamper beside him. Often he was gone for a week or more at a time because his work took him farther south, closer to Mojave than he would have liked.

One evening he found himself with Tony as they sat down to dinner in the workers' dining hall. Tony had grown and was deeply tanned, with broad shoulders and lines around his eyes from squinting into the sun. He had just been promoted from surveyor to crew manager, carrying his notebook and pencil with him constantly, jotting down ideas and observations.

"Your aunt Velda is pretty proud of you," Spence told him.

Tony grinned, blushing. "She keeps writing me letters telling me that. I think she misses having me around all the time."

"I think she and Molly are both feeling a little lonely. Alf's off at college, Barbara spends just about every waking minute in some apple orchard or other, and all Charles will talk about is machines. What are your plans, Tony? Will you be continuing to work on the aqueduct?"

"Oh yes. They are great to me. They sent me to a class to learn more surveying, and there are plenty of jobs I can move to, if

I don't like the one I'm on. Did I tell you I'll be bossing my own crew?"

"You must be proud. I'm proud of you, son. Where will you be working?"

"Right here for now. Did you see the pipe they put in, up high off the ground, just after Jawbone Canyon? Well, they're going to siphon the water up from the valley floor to get it into the pipes there. Our job will be to help seat the bottom pipe and work on the testing. It's something that the engineers say is pretty advanced. "

"I understand Mr. Mulholland is a self-taught engineer," Spence said.

"Yes, that's one reason I like it here. You don't have to have a lot of degrees and certificates to do the job, as far as he's concerned. As long as you are a hard worker and responsible and don't make foolish mistakes, he'll stand behind you. And his managers do, too."

"Do you still think this aqueduct is bad for Pinyon Creek?"

"Sometimes I think it's worse than I ever thought. They talk about more and more water, and there are plans to enlarge the city itself just because they can irrigate farms and orchards, and they can sell the land to folks back east. But then I look around me. Here's this Indian Wells Valley, all brown and sandy, and hardly anything grows here. But people live here pretty happily. I've met some of them. They're prospectors, or they run cattle, or there's this guy who raises goats. People like to be out in the fresh air and the sun and not be bothered by anybody. The aqueduct won't change life here, for better or for worse. Maybe it will be the same up in Pinyon Creek, or maybe I'm just fooling myself."

"We won't know till it's done. Maybe this new railroad will make more changes than the aqueduct will. Anyway, I think Pinyon Creek has enough to handle right now. Did you know Doc Capshaw has a new business of taking photos of drivers who come up to Pinyon Creek in their autos? He takes them and their passengers sitting in the car, or standing alongside, with a sign that says how many miles they drove and how many times they had to change a tire."

They laughed.

On the way home a few days later, Spence noticed activity at Manzanar, a small farming community about four hours south of Pinyon Creek. Crews of men and horses were preparing fields. The activity stretched out farther than he could see. One crew was loading large rocks onto a horse-drawn sled for relocation to a rock pile. Another used rocks from the pile to build a rock wall near the road. A third crew scrapped the dirt flat. At one side of the first field stood a large collection of saplings in containers ready for planting. A large sign read: "OVI ORCHARDS".

Reaching home, he asked Barbara what she knew about OVI. She enthusiastically told him that it was the Owens Valley Improvement Company. They would be planting apple, pear, walnut and peach trees.

"They're bringing apple trees from Washington," she reported. "Some now, and more in the Spring. "I'm hoping to go see the orchard after the trees are planted. Tony said he'd take me down one weekend."

The Autumn of 1910 and the winter that followed showed Pinyon Creek at its best. The road from Mojave was well traveled and consequently well maintained. Pinyon Creek purchased its first municipal bulldozer. Train service to San Francisco, stopping at Laws, encouraged visitors from the North. The Outing Club enthusiastically advertised its activities, and other similar organizations organized mountain and desert activities.

The ski tow originally developed by the children became more and more popular and extensive. It now ran up past Dr. Capshaw's property into the hills, and during the winter the Pinyon Creek Skiing Club designed trails for beginners and moderately skilled skiers. Dr. Capshaw continued his photos of intrepid motorists, more and more often finding repeat customers. The apple orchard north of Pinyon Creek experienced its most successful harvest, sending several hundred barrels of apples to Laws for transport to Los Angeles.

The movie theater was a roaring success. Barbara was happy to be a substitute pianist. She continued to be bothered by the public attention, and she was sure there were others in town more skilled than she. The music was an incredibly important part of the experience, she knew. If somebody had the knowledge or the experience, or even just the desire to find the best music, that would be wonderful. But no one came forward, so movie music was the domain of Barbara and her music teacher.

One additional hotel opened in Pinyon Creek that winter, due to the weekend presence of aqueduct workers, tourists, and, now, the possibility of railroad workers, not to mention prospective land buyers who were beginning to trickle in, drawn by advertisements shown in newspapers across the country.

People who had not been able to buy farmland elsewhere were lured by the idea that they could buy a share in the Owens Valley Improvement Company and share the irrigation expenses, or buy land in the Red Apple orchard north of Pinyon Creek and receive a free share of stock in the new railroad at the same time.

"I'd like to buy some stock in the new railroad," Charles told his father. "I've got some money saved. I think this is the time to invest in it."

Spence looked up from his newspaper. "Charles, do you think you want to go to college?"

"Well, sure I do."

"What do you think you want to study?"

"I... I don't know. Something scientific. Throop Institute specializes in science."

"But what kind of work do you want to do when you've finished your schooling."

"I haven't thought about that."

"Then I suggest you think about that, rather than think about investing. Keep your money safe in Watterson's Bank."

"But..."

"At least, let's wait until we see track on the ground before anybody in this house gives them any money."

231

At Christmas time, Alf came home. It was the first time he had returned to Pinyon Creek since the end of his freshman year three years before. He brought a photograph of Sara Davidson to show his family.

"She is a beautiful girl," Molly told him.

"What does she see in you?" his father teased.

Barbara and Charles examined the photo closely. Barbara was interested in Sara's dress with its intricate rows of pleats. Charles noted that her hands had long fingers, good for working with tools or machines.

"She has good hands for working with machines," he told Alf, who chuckled and said he didn't think that would be Sara's big interest.

"But does she like sports?" Charles persisted.

"Yes, she does. She's a good skater and a swimmer and she rides horses."

"Are you going to bring her up here sometime? She could go sledding in the mountains, or something."

"I hope to bring her up sometime, but not this vacation."

Alf did not tell his family that Sara's family was spending the Christmas vacation in Paris this year, her father having decided that the young people were perhaps spending too much time together.

Alf threw himself into re-learning Pinyon Creek. He helped out at Molly's Place. He went with Charles and Peter into the forests to cut Christmas trees which they sold from the porch at Molly's Place. He allowed Charles to teach him about the internal combustion engine and was properly impressed by the ethanol still.

On Christmas Day, the Richardson and Pershing families, plus Dr. Capshaw and Mildred Howell, gathered for noonday dinner of turkey and mashed potatoes and applesauce and pie. It was a noisy, chatty gathering. The leading topics were, of course, the construction of the aqueduct and the preparation for the railroad and the growth of the apple orchards.

"All right, we'll finish the day celebrating one of the best recent improvements to Pinyon Creek," Spence announced. "They're having a special Holiday Movie night and I have bought tickets for everybody!"

The snows came late and stayed late that year. The mountains were covered more deeply in snow than anybody could remember. Alf, Tony and Charles spent every available moment before Alf's return to school practicing their skiing. They worked on improvements to the skis, argued techniques and equipment, and wore themselves out on the hillsides.

As more automobiles found their way to the valley, Charles and Joe Magnuson found they had to spend much of their free time learning the variation in construction of the engines. In addition, Joe needed to order a greater variety of parts and supplies. Even though most motorists carried either spare tires or tire patching equipment, there were always some who had forgotten, or perhaps had more accidents than expected. Charles and Joe spent the winter days when snow and ice kept travel to a minimum poring over catalogs and making orders.

Molly took Alf aside just before he left to return to Throop Institute. She gave him the shirt she had made him and a basket containing jars of applesauce and packages of cookies.

"Alf, I think you are serious about Sara."

"I think we are, mom, but I know her parents don't want her making up her mind this early. I still have two more years of school before I can get my degree. But I feel pretty sure I would like to marry her."

"Do you know where you will want to live after you graduate? What you will do?" Molly worked hard at keeping her voice level and her face impassive. What would she ever do without him nearby? These years were hard enough even when he came home on occasional vacations.

"I think I will want to work at Throop, mom. I think they will want me, and I would be a good teacher. And I'm still curious about minerals. But I think I will want to spend lots of time up here, too. I'm convinced this valley is full of minerals we haven't come close to identifying yet. I've convinced my geology teacher – he's new to Throop this year – to bring a field trip up here this Spring. The more people learn about this valley, the more they will want to preserve it when we need to."

"You're talking about the aqueduct, aren't you?"

"Well, yes. Tony and I have talked a lot about what the Los Angeles plans are, and what the possible or probable effect will be if they discover that they need more water than they thought."

"You think that will happen?"

"I'm almost sure it will. Anybody who reads the papers down there knows Los Angeles is determined to be the biggest and brightest and richest city in America. For that, they need water, because Los Angeles is in the middle of a desert."

"Then, the next time you come up, try as hard as you can to bring Sara. And bring her family too. We'll put them up here, or at a hotel in town. If Sara is going to live even part of her life here, she needs to know what it's like. She needs to see the isolation and the distance from everything she knows. But she also needs to look outdoors at night and see the stars."

Chapter XXV – Charles Meets Len

The Spring of 1911 was the most beautiful anybody in Pinyon Creek could remember. Late snows coated the Sierra Nevada with brilliant white. In late February the ice in the mountain streams began to melt. As the water rushed down, the sounds of the rapids combined with bird songs, and anybody hiking into the hills could see the bubbling water rushing over brown rocks, pushing against the sparkling snow and the occasional dark green pines. Here and there smaller bushes pushed up, attracting deer. By the time the snow melted, wildflowers spread in a thick blanket across the valley floor. They only lasted a week or so before they began to disappear, but the marvel of the tiny blossoms, some no larger than a fingernail, was an annual delight.

Barbara spent the spring of her senior year in Pinyon Creek High School enjoying parties, studying for her final tests, and trying to decide what she would do next. She was tempted to stay home and continue all of her current activities – working at Molly's Place, helping in the apple orchard, learning more gardening skills and continuing her piano lessons. She thought about trying to get a permanent job with the Outings Club. They had so many activities, including many in Owens Valley and the nearby Sierra Nevada, and they had indicated they would be happy to have her as a permanent employee. But that would take her away from Pinyon Creek, up into the forests and Yosemite Park, where they were lobbying to become a National Park. She thought she would like to stay near Pinyon Creek, in case Tony might have a chance to come visit. And she was following the activities in Manzanar, where more and more fields were being prepared and planted.

Charles and Joe Magnuson were busier than ever. Between the blacksmith business and their growing line of automotive services, they had little time to waste. Charles spent most of his school day afternoons at the blacksmith shop until called home to do his homework.

And Molly's Place continued to thrive. Velda and Molly managed a menu with several specialties now, including stew, pot roast, oven-fried chicken and several kinds of pies. The aqueduct workers, loyal since the beginning, continued to appear for meals, especially at pay day. The big table traditionally filled by local leaders had grown: it was the same table, with the same number of chairs, but it was no longer the Tuesday table. Somehow a custom of meeting after breakfast and mid-afternoon had become standard. Most men stopped by once each weekday, but there were some, like Willy Chalfant, the editor, and Brooks Long, a writer relatively new to Pinyon Creek, who spent much of their time at the table.

Long was gathering information about the politics of the aqueduct, he told Chalfant. He suspected that the long arm of Los

Angeles politics was reaching out in all directions, from the Owens Valley to the borders of San Diego.

"Brooks, you are a deeply suspicious individual," Chalfant said.

"I just have this feeling that something is going on under our noses and we should ask more questions. I lived in L.A., you know, before I came up here. In fact, as I'm sure you have figured out, that's why I came up here. There's plenty of corruption in Los Angeles politics and no reason for it to stay cooped up there."

Dr. Capshaw pulled up a chair and joined the two. "I saw Lippincott up here again," he reported. "He acted like butter wouldn't melt. What's he nosing around here for?"

"You'd think they'd have enough to do, just keeping the aqueduct building on schedule," Chalfant responded. "Have you seen the siphon at Jawbone Canyon? Damn near miraculous, seems to me. I must say that I am eager to see how the water will flow over two hundred miles to get to Los Angeles."

"And I'm eager to see how much is left up here after it all starts, " Dr. Capshaw responded. "Already the irrigation ditches take some of the river water and I'm assuming they'll continue to do so. I'm hoping the Associated Ditches have negotiated some reasonable agreement."

"Have you heard that Los Angeles is planning to irrigate the land north of the city?" Long put in. "It's not even really part of the city, but I hear from my sources that people like Mulholland and Eaton and Lippincott own tracts of land there, and they're planning to maneuver the contracts to divert some of the water to their land."

"As I say, you are a deeply suspicious man," Chalfant repeated.

"Well, I know what I know. Here they are, advertising as far away as Pennsylvania, hoping to get people to move out here and farm. Farm in a desert! I ask you! How can people be so naïve! They don't mention, of course, that Los Angeles is built right in the Sonora desert – or it would be if they hadn't jiggered the maps. All of this is so that Los Angeles will become more important than San Francisco."

"They can't really compete, now, can they? San Francisco is where the finance is, where the transport is. The trains go to San Francisco, at least if you're coming through mining country," said Stuart Pershing, joining the group for his lunch hour.

"Well, Pershing, good to see you! You don't usually have a chance to get away during the day. Looks like your practice continues to grow, judging by the people coming and going."

"It's interesting to me to watch the changes," the doctor responded, giving Dr. Capshaw an affectionate glance. "When I came here I had no idea that I'd be staying, and working harder than ever. The part of my practice that worries me the most, and it has for years, is all of the lung and skin problems that the men have who are working with soda ash."

"I agree," Dr. Capshaw noted. "They handle those caustic salts, especially when they are bagging them or transferring them from one railroad car to another, and their hands burn and they rub their faces and it all gets worse and worse. And the company doesn't do anything for them. Stuart and I have talked about face masks, gloves, fans – and the company said it all was too expensive."

"Do they have a union?" Brooks Long asked

"We don't talk much about unions up here," Chalfant replied. "It's not like it is down in L.A., where there are unions all over, and – we heard about how the Los Angeles Times building was bombed. Wasn't that a union job?"

"They're still fighting that out. I haven't seen any union activity up here. Why's that?"

"Well, we're still a small place. You work for a company here, and you and the company president end up in the same church on Sunday. Everything is personal. Maybe times will change, but so far we haven't seen the need for unions."

"But the men with the soda ash burns," Long persisted. "Why is nobody helping them? "

"Simple," said Stuart. "The men don't think the ash is making them sick. They sometimes see the burns where they've sweated while they're re-sacking the ash, but it's like when you ride too long and get chafed, or you pick up a hot pan off the stove – just something that happens. Then after years of all of this they come see me and they say, Doc, I'm having trouble breathing. And I listen to their lungs and I just know what's happening. I give them masks – I actually got the company to give me a pretty big supply, Wallace – but the men won't wear them. They say they're too hot, or not manly."

"On another subject," the minister spoke up. "Who is working out the baseball schedule for this spring?"

It was easy to let the rest of the world slip by. There was more work to do than there were men to do it. Much of the work was out-of-doors, work that would become more difficult as summer progress, but which was agreeable in the Spring. The aqueduct absorbed all the men who wanted to work, especially now that the route had been laid out and progress could be seen from day to day. Parts of the water's path was through open ditches lined with concrete, and part was through the giant pipes laid in tunnels. North of Owens Lake was the area of the great diversion, where the river's water was directed into the aqueduct channel.

One April afternoon, Charles left school and hurried over to the blacksmith's shop where Joe Magnuson was waiting for him. The Outings Club had announced a trip to see the wildflowers, and the valley was expecting a large number of tourists from Los Angeles and San Francisco. They would come by Southern Pacific train to Laws and then transfer to the caravan of buses provided by the Outings Club. They would stay at the two hotels overnight and then, early in the morning, would be driven to the selected wildflower viewing sites.

"We're ready for them," Joe announced, displaying a stack of tires and a collection of belts and leather straps. "We need to get some buckets filled with drinking water."

Charles hitched Blanket to a wagon and drove to the creek at the north side of town. The Associated Ditches had built irrigation canals along the river. Charles' favorite spot for filling water barrels was a small creek which fed one of the canals. It had a rock bottom and seemed to be always full of water. The water always tasted fresh and cold. Best of all, he could bring the wagon almost to the edge of the creek.

He unhitched Blanket to graze and pulled his big dipper – made from a saucepan with a welded handle, one of his first metalworking projects with Joe – from under the wagon bench. He crouched next to the creek and filled it. Suddenly he stopped. He could sense that he was being watched. He stiffened, then stood up slowly. He looked around him but could see nothing out of place. Near him was a large poplar tree already in leaf.

He finished filling the dipper and took the water to the bucket. He'd have to keep moving to get the job done by supper. Returning to the creek, he leaned down for a second dipperful. Again he had the sense that he was not alone. Was it an animal?

With the second dipper he walked quickly to the bucket and dumped the water in. He whirled around and caught a hint of motion in the lower limbs of the tree. Pretending he hadn't seen, he returned to the creek and made his third trip. This time on the return to the creek he stopped under the tree and looked up into the branches.

Somebody was looking back down at him.

Charles could see a brown face, straight black hair and large dark eyes, a boy about his age dressed in a plaid shirt and brown pants, perched on a large branch with his back against the tree trunk.

"Who are you?" Charles asked, just as the boy said "What are you doing here?"

The boy leaped down and stood facing Charles, feet wide apart, arms crossed.

"Who are you?" Charles repeated. The boy made no move. Charles tried harder. "I'm Charles Richardson. I'm loading up some water barrels for Mr. Magnuson, back in town."

"Oh. I'm Len. Len Reyes."

"Where do you live? I haven't seen you at school. Are you here on a visit?"

"No. We live here. He pointed north.

"You mean Bishop?" Charles asked..

"No. We live at the Fort."

"Who's we?"

"My family and my people. We live at Fort Independence."

"Oh." Charles had heard about the Fort but it wasn't a place he knew. Nobody from Pinyon Creek ever went there. He vaguely remembered learning about the Indian Wars from History class but he believed the Indians were all gone now.

"Oh." Charles picked up his dipper. "Want to help me?"

"OK."

Len climbed into the wagon. Charles filled the dipper and handed it up for Len to fill a barrel.

Soon they had established a comfortable routine. In less than a half hour the barrels were filled. Charles pulled two apples from a sack under the wagon seat and offered one to Len. They sat on the wagon tail, swinging their legs.

"Len, why were you in the tree?"

"Because you were coming. I climbed up when I saw your wagon. I didn't know whether there'd be trouble."

"But. I don't know you. Where do you go to school? Why haven't I seen you before? Fort Independence isn't so far from Pinyon Creek."

"I was in boarding school. Far away so I lived there. Farther than Los Angeles."

"Why?"

"They try to get all Indian children to go there. They are trying to make us not be Indian any more."

"But why are you here now? It's still school time."

"I kept running away so my dad said I could stay home."

He finished his apple and threw the core into the bushes. Charles sat silently trying to figure out how to make people not be what they were.

Len jumped down. Charles joined him. They lifted the tailgate into position. Charles brought Blanket back to the wagon.

"We're going to have a fandango at home tomorrow," Len said. "It's going to be wonderful.. Music and food and everything. I'd have missed it if I was still in school."

"Can I come?" Charles asked.

Len looked solemnly at him for a moment and then shook his head. "It's our fandango for us. Maybe sometime you can come. You would like it. But not this time. Next time, maybe."

Chapter XXVI – The Davidsons Visit

Returning home for dinner, Charles told his parents about meeting Len. "They're having a festival at Fort Independence. Why don't we know about it? I asked if I could come and he said not this time."

Spence and Molly looked at each other.

"They have their own festivals. We have ours. How many Indians do you see in town?" his father said.

"Why not?"

"Because they stay at Fort Independence, that's why. They have their own customs, they live their own lives. That's the way it is."

Molly added, "There are a lot of places around here that we know nothing about. You know that, Charles. You wouldn't go up to a miner and want to know how he found his claim. You don't go up into the canyons unless you have a reason. Let this alone."

Charles was silent but decided not to let it alone. For a week he found excuses to return to the creek and the big poplar tree, but Len never re-appeared. He thought about mentioning him to Peter, but decided against it.

He returned to spending his after-school hours with the blacksmith. They had acquired a Model T runabout which had been driven into a ditch by a tourist who wanted no part of the automobile after his accident. Joe bought it for five dollars and the two dissected it whenever they had spare time. During the summer months they rigged a canvas roof over the car; otherwise the metal would have been too hot to touch. Even with this shade, they quickly discovered that the best time to work was just after sunup or very late in the afternoon.

They had taken the wheels off, setting the chassis on blocks of wood, when Tony stopped by.

"What do you call that thing?" he teased.

"It's a runabout. Not that it's running anywhere right now, " said Charles. "We're going to work on the motor next. We want to learn exactly how it works."

"Great idea," Tony said. "If you two can get away for a whole day sometime, come down to where we're working and I'll show you some REAL machines."

It was mid July by then, and Joe's business had almost disappeared. No tourists wanted to visit the desert in the summer time, and the local ranchers and farmers did only the most necessary maintenance. It was easy for Charles and Joe to take the wagon to Olancha, where the aqueduct crews were busily lining the new canal with cement. Near the work site, Joe pulled the wagon to a halt. On the river bank, a giant machine was scraping the surface. Instead of wheels, it wore jointed treads which moved around two axles. The driver was seated high above the machine which was belching smoke from a long smokestack. He grinned and waved.

"He gets a lot of people stopping and staring." Tony had come up unseen, enjoying their amazement. "That's Mr. Mulholland over yonder – with the hat? They say the first time he saw this machine he said it looks just like a caterpillar."

"I think he's right," Joe said, shaking his head. "I just can't believe it. What will be next? I'll bet that machine can move more dirt in an hour than a crew with shovels could move in a day. Am I right?"

"Right and then some. Especially on a hillside or if there are lots of rocks. We just feed it some fuel and off they go."

"What about the men though? The work crews? Did they lose their jobs?"

"Not really," Tony responded. There's still a lot of work for everybody to do. Mr. Mulholland says that we're pretty much on schedule, which means there's work for everybody for at least another year. Then who knows?" He turned again to the bulldozer and waved. "Watch now."

The giant machine turned slowly and began crawling up the hillside toward the mountains. As it moved, it spilled rocks and dirt to the sides. Behind it, the ground looked smooth. Charles and Joe felt they could watch forever. Each silently envied the driver.

Tony watched as well. He was considering whether to stay with the aqueduct project or move to the new railroad project which was advertising for workers. The work would be different from what he was currently doing, and would teach him some new skills. It would also remove him from the aqueduct project, about which he was having more and more doubts. But the railroad project had not yet truly begun. And Barbara was going to be working in Manzanar, close to the aqueduct. He decided to wait and see.

With her high school diploma behind her, Barbara was eligible to work at several jobs at the Owens Valley Improvement Company plantations at Manzanar. The first of the apple trees would be planted in the Fall. She had already begun to learn how to tell one variety from another, and would be participating, like everybody else on the farms, in the planting itself. But in addition, she was helping with publicity and news releases in the press office.

If you lived in Pennsylvania or Ohio or Michigan, you would have received news of the OVI because your newspaper would be printing articles, some written by Barbara, telling about the glorious opportunities available at one of the Chaffey farms. When you bought a share of land, you would also receive a certificate entitling you to a share of water from the Chaffey irrigation system. The apple trees, imported directly from the state of Washington, guaranteed apples sure to be beautiful and juicy and flavorful. Barbara searched through files of photos, some taken by her grandfather, to find the most appealing shots to attach to her reports. She thought that maybe in addition to playing the piano and cooking and gardening, she might like to be a newspaperwoman, like Nellie Bly.

Visitors to the Owens Valley in the Summer and Fall of 1911 found a serene valley, spotted with small, self-sufficient communities, where cattle and sheep dotted the hills and farms harvested many kinds of vegetables and fruits. The growing apple orchard business began to bring a certain fame to the area. The Outing Club activities attracted intellectuals and well-to-do families of many different interests as the writings of John Muir gained in popularity.

The men sitting around the table in Molly's Place couldn't help but congratulate themselves. Their businesses were prospering and their sense of community was strong. Even the increasing noise and dust from construction projects – the aqueduct and the Red Apple Railroad – seemed to be signs of healthy growth.

"I was up at Laws the other day," Dr. Capshaw remarked to the group one morning, "and there's more and more talk of making the engines on the new railroad run by electricity. Can you beat that?"

"We should think about street lights," said Willy Chalfant.

"Bosh. Nobody is on the streets at night. No need for light. "

"People are out if they are going to the movie theater. Or a party."

"We've got plenty of other ways to use the money." There was nothing Dr. Capshaw enjoyed more than a spirited debate. "For example, we could pave Main Street. From one end of town to the other. "

One of the Watterson brothers spoke up. "We could rent that big machine they've got, that Caterpillar."

The rest of the group joined in, acknowledging that it was an excellent idea. Chalfant spoke everybody's thought: "Then we could see it in action right here."

"I saw it down by Olancha. Mulholland the engineer was there. He was standing high up on the bank, just watching. Didn't say a word as far as I could tell, except that all of his men knew he was there and he was watching."

"They're about to connect to the river pretty soon, I'm told. "

"I think it is just a test. They won't have any place to send the water till the whole thing is finished, all the way to Los Angeles."

"Have you heard anything more about the new land – San Fernando – that Mulholland and them bought? I heard they are going to use our water to irrigate it for farming and all those owners are going to make a million dollars. Using our water!"

"We should ask Lippincott what he knows."

"You can if you want to talk to him. I choose to believe he doesn't exist." That was Dr. Capshaw.

"You know, Wallace, you hold a grudge better than just about anybody." Stuart Pershing's calm voice quieted the discussion.

"Damn right – sorry Molly – darn right I do. Man is a turncoat. Came in pretending to be a state employee when he was really in the pocket of the city of Los Angeles. Now he has the gall to keep coming back trying to make friends. He's still trying to pick up water rights. He's looking to make a fortune one way or another.   And I'm not so sure his friend Eaton isn't far behind him."

He was working himself into a rage. Velda came over with a pot of coffee and a plate of cookies. "Help yourself, Doc," she invited. "These sugar cookies will restore your soul."

"You're right, Velda," he responded. "I do let my blood pressure get riled."

Just before school started in September, Alf came for a short visit, accompanied by the Davidson family. Professor Davidson and Alf took mules and disappeared into the mountains on the east side of the valley, where the busy gold and silver mines of fifty years past now lay abandoned.   They were looking for locations for a possible geology field trip.

Sara Davidson and her mother Belinda joined Molly, Barbara and Charles at the kitchen table for after-breakfast coffee and cookies. Sara was a tall girl with dark brown hair which lay in waves to her shoulders. Her mother also had brown hair which was starting to turn gray. They asked many questions about life in Pinyon Creek, interested in the contrast to the big city habits of Pasadena.

The conversation slowed. Barbara asked her mother if she and Charles could show Sara the town, and Molly agreed.

"It's probably not very exciting to you," Charles said as the three started down the street.

"I've been out in the desert camping," Sara answered, "but never up here. This country is so beautiful!"

"This isn't even the nicest time," Barbara told her. "I think the best time is in the Spring, when the wild flowers come out."

"Me, I like the winter," Charles said. "You can see the snow line from the beginning of Winter. First the mountain tops turn white, and then the snow line creeps down the mountainside. Have you ever been up in the snow?"

"No, never. Alfred has told me a little about what it's like. I would really like to be in the snow, making tracks in it, and sliding down in it. That sounds like fun!"

They walked on, looking through the windows of the dry goods store at all of the items inside, then, standing on apple crates Charles found, peering through the windows of the high school that was almost ready to open for the Fall season. They walked into the Methodist and Baptist churches, idly talking about the differences in the decorations. Stopping by the stables, they showed Sara the Richardson mules. Banjo came up to the fence and nudged Charles' arm. Charles found a carrot in his pocket.

"Banjo is just about the greediest mule I ever knew," he told Sara.

"And you've seen a lot?" she teased.

"I have. My dad drives some of the big mule teams and I can drive four, now."

At the blacksmith's, they introduced Sara to Joe Magnuson, who offered each of them a piece of toffee candy. "Man gave me a box of these yesterday. He blew two tires just on the trip from Mojave. Must have been driving like the devil," he told Charles. "Anyway, he was so relieved that I could fix both wheels, he gave me this box of candy and left his old tires as well."

They stopped at Molly's Place where Velda offered each of them a piece of pie and a glass of milk.

On the way back to the house, Sara said, "You must know everybody in town."

"Well, not really, but we've always lived here, and so have most folks."

"I've always lived in the same house in Pasadena and we don't even know the people at the end of our street."

Even though it was September, it was still hot in the afternoon, so the women and children sat on the wide porch, Sara and Barbara in the swing, Molly and Belinda in rocking chairs, Charles on the top step. They idly watched the crows pecking at the gravel. A covey of quail ran across the back yard. A jackrabbit hopped up to Molly's garden till Charles saw it and threw a stone at it.

"It is so, so quiet," Belinda murmured after a bit. "It's amazing. I think I can hear the breeze blow."

"Wait till tonight," Barbara told her. "Before you go to bed, you can come outside and see the stars completely fill the sky."

Chapter XXVII – A Visit to Pasadena

Alf and Dr. Davidson returned with notebooks filled with ideas for field trips and additional investigations. The variety of minerals available for study excited the professor, as well as the exhilarating knowledge that the Owens Valley was not well known to the larger academic community. Like a prospector himself, Dr. Davidson was strongly tempted to keep his discovery closely held until he and his Throop Institute colleagues could spend more time developing their knowledge.

His wife and daughter had more nuanced reactions to the valley, which they shared on the way home.

"It's a beautiful place," Sara told Alf and her father. "But it is a frightening place as well. I have never been in a place where I could see so far, and where there are so few people. I think I might be very lonely there."

"Pinyon Creek is a pleasant little town," Belinda added, "and, Alf, your family is generous and charming. We had such a good time visiting them. I only wish they were closer to Pasadena.

It's such a – well, Sara said it – such an isolated place, even though it is beautiful."

Alf was quiet, absorbing their reactions. He was accustomed to moving between Pinyon Creek and Pasadena but was happy in both places. He couldn't imagine being unhappy about living anywhere because there was so much to see wherever one went.

"Would you like to come back again?" he asked Sara. "I know my mom would be happy to have you stay with her. She likes the company."

"See what I mean?" Sara responded. "Your mom must feel she needs more than Pinyon Creek can provide."

Alf felt his throat tighten. He wanted to make her understand how he felt. He was surprised at the strong emotions he was feeling. Surely Sara's reactions weren't that important to him, were they?

As Fall continued into Winter, the aqueduct construction drew closer and closer to Pinyon Creek. The workers from Los Angeles who had been stationed at the southern end of the aqueduct were finishing their jobs. Some moved north with the work while others went on to different projects. In Pinyon Creek, the changes included more noise and dust from earth-moving equipment, and a new crowd of laborers spending free time and paychecks in town. Molly felt that, by and large, it was pretty much normal.

The Christmas festivities in Pinyon Creek were the best ever, in the opinion of much of the town. The school choir gave a special program of Christmas music, and the BarberShoppers produced a gala event with music and a production of Dickens' The Christmas Carol. Molly's Place offered a December special of cookies and fruitcakes for sale already wrapped to be put under a tree. Spence found a way to make antlers from wire; Barbara and Molly covered them with soft wool, and they decorated his mules from December till the middle of January. Most of his mules, that is. Banjo refused to have anything to do with the idea and rubbed them off each time they tried to put them on.

For the first time, snow in town was a transportation problem. There was never so much snow that horses or mules had difficulty, but the new automobiles slipped and skidded on even small amounts of snow and ice. Charles and Joe gathered barrels of soda ash which they spread on Main Street after each snow.

The apple trees north of Bishop seemed to weather the winter without a problem. Barbara was eager to visit Manzanar so one day Alf, home on vacation, drove her down. At the OVI farms, they found that even more land had been cleared, with some evidently being prepared for crops like asparagus and beans and tomatoes, but much ready for tree planting. Once again, forests of apple tree saplings stood ready in their buckets for the ground to thaw.

Tony was waiting for them near the gate.

"Hey, Alf! How does the college boy like being outside in the real world?"

"Believe me, there's plenty of real world at college, too. What do you think about these farms?"

"I think they are still having trouble getting enough farmers to come settle here. They're afraid of the heat and the winds. Barbara could tell you. How many letters have you sent out, Barbara? And what do you hear back?"

She was pleased to be included in the conversation. Her work had stopped in the Fall. The publicity campaign had not apparently had much success, because few people were willing or able to make the long trip from North Carolina or Pennsylvania on such a risky gamble.

"The people who want to come out here usually can't afford it," she answered. "At least as far as we could tell. It's hard to convince them that these apples will be so much better than what they grow at home. I hope I can come down here and work next Spring. I think we'll have more to show by next year."

The three walked along the bank of the dry channel where the Owens River would someday run. Tony explained to Alf the intricacies of the construction.

"Mr. Mulholland is here all the time now," he said. "He never says much, but you can tell he knows what everybody is doing and if they're doing it right."

"I understand he taught himself engineering," Alf remarked.

"Not really engineering, but he started out with irrigation works and learned from there. He has some terrific ideas about storing water and directing it to where you want it to do. The OVI, for example, it has underground water storage already. Every couple of months they release some to the owners of these parcels. If you buy a parcel, you get irrigation water. That's what's going to make this work. The Indians knew that, long before the white man came."

Barbara asked the question that had been on her mind for a long time.

"What do you boys know about the Paiutes at Fort Independence?"

It was a jump from their current topic. They looked at her curiously.

"Why? How did you hear about them?" Tony asked.

"Charles met a Paiute Indian last summer, up by the creek toward Bishop. He said something about hiding. And Charles and I never saw any Indians much in town."

"I don't know much," Alf responded. "Charles asked me, too. I couldn't tell him anything, except that I knew there were people living there, but they pretty much want to be left alone, and I never wanted to go barge in."

"One time," Tony told them, "Uncle Stuart and I were riding up there. We were looking for quail, I think, anyway hunting I forget what. We started up this one little canyon and all of a sudden this man comes out of the bushes. He's holding a rifle or a shotgun, I don't think I ever really saw what it was because we just turned around and lit out of there. Never went back."

"They've got pretty good reason to want to stay away from us," Alf said. "The white man has never been good for the Indian."

They nodded solemnly.

"But Tony, what about the Red Apple railroad," Barbara asked. "Have you heard any more about that?"

"No and I'm kind of disappointed. They started out so strong. And this Fall they continued to prepare the right-of-way for the tracks. They had to buy some more land, I know, and they were trying to raise money – just like the OVI is – and it was kind of hard work. But then it got to be cold, and snowy, and they just shut down for the winter."

"I hear from the men at Molly's Place," Barbara said, "that they are still planning to build on schedule. They are going to build a sawmill up in the White Mountains, to cut railroad ties."

"Well, that's good news anyway," Tony said with a grin. "They don't just go out and build construction buildings for the fun of it. I know how much work that is."

But in the Spring of 1912 the Red Apple Railroad remained quiet. There were no signs of track construction, no work on the sawmill, no communications from the owners. As the aqueduct neared completion, workers looked for other projects, but the railroad offered no possibilities. During that year, life in Pinyon Creek continued as it had for years, with occasional festivities to mark holidays, but there were no events memorable enough for Barbara to record in her diary. Even Willy Chalfant at the newspaper had difficulty finding stories to interest his readers.

The following years, though, saw plenty of excitement for the Richardson family.

By June, 1913, Spence and Molly realized that their businesses were successful beyond anything they had imagined. Spence's mules were popular throughout the valley and always in demand. He had added younger drivers to his team. They were capable of driving mule trains of up to ten; Spence could see no need for larger teams in general duty. While some of the mules – Blanket, Gus, Toojay – were nearing the end of their working life, the family kept them safe and healthy in their stables and the surrounding pasture.

Molly and Velda had yielded daily management of Molly's Place to a half-dozen younger women but retained the overall authority. The two of them determined the menus, tested and added new recipes from time to time, and continued to pay particular attention to special customers. The big table at the front of the restaurant was such an institution that newcomers to the town were frequently shepherded in to be introduced to the regular members. To be invited to join a discussion was always a special occasion.

One evening in late winter Spence and Molly, deep in a discussion of plans for the Spring, both said, at almost the same time, "Alf is going to graduate in June!"

It was only minutes before the discussion included plans to purchase an automobile. As Charles told them frequently during the next few weeks, "we need to have an automobile big enough for all of us to ride in, and sturdy enough to go to Pasadena and back." To his great delight, Spence took him to Mojave on the car purchase trip. Charles drove the mules back north while Spence finished purchasing the car and followed.

Soon it was early June and time to head South for Throop Institute graduation.

"Let's go! Let's go!" Charles shouted, urging his family into their new automobile, a Model T touring car with room for for Spence, Molly, Charles, Barbara and Dr. Capshaw to squeeze in. Charles, responsible for maintenance and repairs, had assembled a toolkit including some extra parts, two spare tires and a tire patch kit and stowed it under the back seat.

It was the first long drive for Barbara and Molly. Molly had seldom been as far away as Mojave and never had been to Pasadena. The drive took them two days. They spent the first night in a hotel in Mojave, everyone restless and vaguely anxious staying in unfamiliar quarters.

Fortunately, the weather cooperated. It was sunny and warm but not yet hot as they drove through farms and orchards at the edges of Los Angeles. Even though they avoided the central part of the city, they could see the skyline of buildings several stories high. With traffic all around them, the dust coated their clothing and made them sneeze. Spence gripped the wheel until his knuckles turned white, and growled whenever anybody spoke to him.

Alf had found lodgings for them in a boarding house not far from the college. He had made a careful map, knowing that his father would feel much more comfortable with precise directions to the very stopping place. They were all relieved when they pulled up in front of the boarding house and found Alf sitting on the front steps. Once settled, unpacked and washed, they were eager to explore.

Alf enjoyed being tour guide. The streets surrounding the Institute were filled with families arriving for graduation. He happily introduced his family to his friends who were also ushering parents here and there. His parents were properly impressed with the college buildings, especially the small museum which included some minerals from the Owens Valley.

The Davidsons had invited them to supper. Sara and her mother had prepared a large assortment of dishes "for the travelers who have had a long and difficult journey," according to Sara. It included some dishes unfamiliar to Molly, who hoped to get recipes to take home. Conversation was lively, covering everything from the graduation events to California politics.

The ceremony was impressive, with the class marching into the auditorium in robes and mortarboards. The speakers were entertaining, the speeches were relatively brief, and Alf received two awards. To Molly's eyes it was a perfect ceremony.

All too soon it was time to leave and head back to Owens Valley. Alf had shipped most of his possessions, which would be waiting by the time they reached home. They stopped at the Davidson home for luncheon. As they prepared to leave, he and Sara disappeared into the back garden. Returning to the auto, he held her hands for a long moment before slipping into his seat in the back. Everybody waved enthusiastically as they left the Davidson house.

Chapter XXVIII – Harvest Fair

On the fifth of November, the first water flowed through the Owens Valley aqueduct. The intake was north of Pinyon Creek, which gave the residents the first opportunity to see the effects of the diversion on their lands. Charles and Joe joined the many residents standing along the bank of the aqueduct watching as water began to enter the channel.

"Looks like they did a good job on lining the canal," Joe remarked. "Couldn't have been easy, hauling all that cement, laying it in. But it looks good."

"Tony showed me how they figured out where to put the canal," Charles answered. "They had to try to keep it as level as possible, and they wanted it to be covered as much as possible, or at least out of the direct sunlight, to lose as little as possible from evaporation."

"You can't cover anything this big," Joe objected. "See, right here it's open, just like the river is. Course, you don't see the river evaporating, either."

"That's an awful lot of water."

"Yep. Want to follow it down aways?"

"Sure. But don't we have to get back to the shop?"

"Any customers that might be at the shop are all here at the canal. This is a special day. Hop in the truck."

All along the canal, from the original intake as far as they felt they should go, Joe and Charles found people standing, watching the river start to fill the channel. They stopped the truck just north of Owens Lake. The Owens river was frothy, running fast between the cement walls. It was like a holiday, Charles thought, maybe like the first day of fishing season or just before a parade. After watching for a half hour, they turned the truck back toward Pinyon Creek.

At the southern end of the aqueduct, a large crowd of 30,000, including politicians, celebrities, public employees and the merely curious had gathered. The authorities opened the gates and Owens River poured into the San Fernando Reservoir. Project manager William Mulholland came to the microphone and made his speech: "There it is. Take it."

Charles had not given up his quest to learn more about the Paiutes. He continued to check the poplar tree near his preferred creek – an easy task because fetching water was one of his regular jobs – and he asked everyone he could think of about the Paiutes and Fort Independence. When he asked Joe Magnuson, he received his first real information. One afternoon when there was nothing that needed immediate attention, Charles asked Joe about the Indians. The older man poured them each a lemonade from a jug kept cool in a pail in the well, and they sat on the bench in front of the livery stable.

"When my granddad was a boy," Joe began, "there were two groups of Indians here in the valley, the Paiutes and the Shoshones. They didn't get along all that well together, but when they were out after the white man, they surely fought on the same side."

"I thought the Indian wars were a really long time ago," Charles said.

"Well, my granddad was a really old man by the time I was old enough to listen to his stories," Joe smiled. "The Indian wars were longer and bloodier and generally more hard on everybody than you would ever think. Sometimes a small group of Indians would raid a ranch and just kill all the cattle. Sometimes they'd kill people, too. See, while the miners pretty much left the Indians alone, not everybody was a miner, even in the old days. The farmers figured once they had bought or homesteaded their land, it was theirs. But the Indians always had the idea that all the land belonged to everybody, and they'd ride through grain fields or break down fences or take cattle."

"But why'd they fight like that?"

"The Paiutes depended on ground cover for their food. Can you imagine eating mostly pine nuts and the roots of vegetables? The Indians ate the blossoms of hyacinth plants. Unfortunately, the cattle also loved the wild hyacinth blooms. So the Paiutes not only watched the cattle stamping out their grain from the wild grasses, they also lost their main vegetable to the cows."

"So what happened? What finished the wars?"

"Lots of people would say the wars still aren't finished. But the fighting has pretty much stopped. What happened was, the Army came in. That was before my time, too. But my dad and my granddad told me about it. After enough people came and settled here, they asked for support from the Army because there were still Indian raids, so the Army sent some troops with horses and weapons, plenty of weapons. They set up in Fort Independence. "

"Then what happened?" Charles had finished his lemonade without realizing he had even swalloed once. He imagined raids and burning houses and all of the scenes he had read about in history books and novels

"It was all very confused. The Indians would come and steal animals, the settlers would shoot whoever they saw, and then they'd ask the Army to send more men. The soldiers who came often couldn't even find any Indians because they'd be hidden far away from where they made the raids. Here were those soldiers with their uniforms and their horses and their weapons, against the Indians with their bows and arrows, and I guess some horses of their own. The soldiers would ask themselves, What are we doing here? Because everybody knew the BIG War was taking place back in the East, at Gettysburg and Antietam and all. And they were stuck out here fighting Indians armed with rocks or bows and arrows. They'd go back South to Fort Tejon. Until the next time."

Joe stood, stretched, scratched a mosquito bite. Charles asked, "Then what?"

"There were some people, White people, who were trying to find a peaceful solution. Finally they had some meetings and made a treaty with the Indian Chief, Chief George."

"Of George's Creek?" Charles asked. It was one of his favorite places for cooling off in the summer.

"Maybe so. So everybody was happy. Except that there was this one Indian, named Joaquin Jim, who kept raiding cattle and shooting settlers. Even Chief George couldn't control him. Finally the soldiers caught him and shot him. I think it was before the end of the Civil War, but the soldiers were still kept here in California anyway. Plenty of other outlaws and Indians all over the place for them to hunt and capture. And kill. But you need to remember that there are lots of people in this valley like me, both Whites and Indians, that remember those stories. There's still a lot of distrust and even hate on both sides."

"That's crazy!" Charles sputtered.

"Not so crazy. The Indians still don't have anything as good as we have. They don't have the food, or the jobs that would pay for better food. Sometimes they just eat plants and pinyon berries because that's all they can find. You haven't seen their houses. If you ever do, you'll think they're something some child put together out of branches and leaves."

"But that boy I met -- that Len. He seemed friendly enough," Charles said.

"Oh, there are exceptions. But you don't see Len in town, now, do you? Maybe he doesn't want to come here, but maybe he is afraid to, and maybe he's right."

Joe stood and started packing tools and preparing to shut down for the night. Charles remained sitting on his hay bale, deep in thought. It wasn't until Joe started turning off the lights that he got up and left for home.

During the winter the area seemed to return to normal. The aqueduct workers had left for new jobs. There was no sign of progress on the Red Apple Railroad. The Outings Club opened a ski camp at their site in the mountains which brought tourists to Pinyon Creek. At Molly's Place, discussions of whether to pave the road through the town kept the occupants of the front table busy.

Throop had hired Alf as an instructor, a job which would allow him to continue his geology studies, so he came home only for short visits.

Spring of 1914 found Barbara working in the Manzanar orchards. Of the 22,000 apple trees planted by the OVI, most were doing well. They had survived the winter snows which had been of short duration. Barbara was involved in keeping records of the trees, continuing to write publicity materials, and working in the orchards whenever she got a chance. She was beginning to identify different varieties of apples without the use of her guidebooks. Most of them were familiar and beloved, like the winesaps, but others were strange: the Arkansas Black which was beautiful to look at, and the Spitzenberg, easy to pack and ship.

"I've been given a new project," she reported on one of her weekend visits. "We're going to make apple recipes and improve them and sell the food and the recipes to tourists. We think that will increase business."

"You'll need all the improvement you can get," Charles responded. "Most of the tourists aren't at all interested in stopping any place short of the mountains."

Alf and Tony had been spending time together, catching up on stories, each learning the activities and interests of the other. Whenever Alf came to Pinyon Creek, he tried to find Tony to talk with at least for awhile. In the late afternoons as the air began to cool they began to make a habit of walking along the creek behind the town, occasionally skipping rocks over the rippling surface of the water, sharing sandwiches and jugs of ice tea prepared by Molly. One evening they realized that they were spending much of their time talking about women. Alf had been promoted at his new job and had been assured of permanent employment with Paragon Mining and Minerals Company. He was ready to propose marriage to Sara Davidson.

Tony was similarly eager to be married. He discussed his plans with Alf.

"It's Barbara," he confessed. "I don't even know when I decided this. It's like we have always been together – you, me, Barbara, Charles."

"Barbara! She can't be old enough to get married!"

"Just because she's your little sister, you think she's still a child! But she is a grown woman now and has her own plans. And I don't guess you even know what they are. She wants to start a farm of her own, where she can experiment with fruits and vegetables. She has some good ideas for breeding some vegetables that can withstand the desert conditions. Ever time I see her she has some new idea or other."

"I had no idea," Alf admitted. "Seems to me she never says anything."

"Maybe that's because she's surrounded by louder voices," Tony said. "It's true that she doesn't speak up much, but I'm always surprised to hear what she has been thinking about. And she likes the ideas I have, too. About water conservation. That's what's going to make or break this valley. Your mom knew it from the very beginning when she made her own ditches from that creek into her garden."

"Well, I guess you're serious about this. What does Barbara think?"

"She doesn't exactly know yet. I haven't talked to her about marriage. For one thing, I was too busy on the aqueduct. What about Sara?

"I haven't actually asked her yet, either," Alf laughed. "I think I'm pretty terrified about what her parents would say. I think Sara would say yes. And I don't want to take the chance of somebody else getting her. She has lots of friends. And they are in her social circle, as they say. I'm just a primitive, from the hills."

"Oh don't sound so sorry for yourself. You're going places and you know it. When do you think you'll really be ready to marry?

"Soon if she'll have me."

"Well, she probably won't if she doesn't know you want to marry her."

"I know. I'm going to talk to her father soon."

"Better talk to Sara first."

"Well, yes. I think I would rather have a tooth pulled. What if she says no?"

"We both have to do this. I'm going to see Barbara next week and I plan to ask her then."

Barbara always enjoyed Tony's visits. She lived at Manzanar these days, in a small cottage shared with two other young women, and when Tony took her for a ride in his new car, or bought her dinner in Olancha or Lone Pine, it was a special treat. This day Tony seemed especially quiet and preoccupied.

"What's wrong?" she asked him as they drove toward Olancha.

"Nothing's wrong. I'm just thinking about things?"

"What kind of things? Is there something you're not telling me? Is somebody sick? What?"

He pulled the car to the side of the road and turned to face her.

"Barbara, I need to ask you a serious question." She did not answer but looked questioningly into his eyes. "Barbara, I would like to marry you. Would you consider marrying me?"

She sat silently for several moments. She could feel herself trembling.

"Tony, I never thought about this. You're so much a part of our family, it's like you're my brother or my cousin. But you're not. You're Tony who I love. Yes, of course, I would marry you."

He gave a huge sigh of relief.

"I'll talk to your father tonight. If he's home. Anyway, as soon as possible. I hope he'll say yes."

"Tony, silly, you're marrying me, not my father. If it's something I want, it will be fine with him, but I don't think we need his permission!"

He was almost giddy with happiness. "Barbara, we will have such a good life. You'll have a chance to make your garden and do your experiments. I'll take good care of you. I want to stay here in the valley. I hope you do, too."

"I couldn't imagine living anywhere else."

As they started driving, Tony chuckled. "I wonder whether Alf will be as successful when he talks to Sara."

Barbara sat up straight. "Tony Pershing! Did you talk to Alf about this? Without talking to me first? Shame on you!"

Every Autumn the Paiutes held a Harvest Fair in Bishop. Charles was determined to attend. It was far enough away from Pinyon Creek that many people, like his parents, never attended, but it was the one celebration where the Paiutes invited their white neighbors. They would have music and dancing and food to eat and drink, and items for sale.

He worked hard to instruct his parents about the educational nature of the event, and finally succeeded in getting their promise that they and the Pershings would journey up to Bishop for the fair.

They all rose before sunup and set out in Spence's wagon which they equipped with a barrel of water, picnic food, blankets, extra food for mules and humans, candles, and a barrel of sawdust in case of a muddy or flooded road plus tents and bedrolls; it was an expedition that would take one full day to travel each way, and one which seemed more appropriate for mules than for runabouts.

They enjoyed traveling in territory they had not often explored. As they went North the mountains on either side appeared less forbidding, the pastures even richer. They rode through occasional small forested patches. By lunchtime they had reached the half-way point. They stopped near Big Pine, where they watered the mules, ate a picnic lunch of cold roast chicken, vegetables and apple pie, then started out again. By the end of the day they reached their destination, already alive with the noises, smells and colors of a big fair. They found a sheltered spot toward the edge of town and set up camp.

The following morning, Charles was awake and exploring before sunup. The grounds around the Fair Ground were crowded with vehicles of all description, from the expected buggies and wagons to bicycles and even several motorcars. Vendors had set up small stands selling meat pies, apple pies, apples and other fruits, coffee and pastries. Additional stands which were being assembled held baskets, lengths of cloth, bunches of herbs and flowers and other goods Charles couldn't identify. There was a happy buzz of voices as people woke up and got ready to enter the Fair Ground.

All at once, Charles spied Len. He was standing with an older couple at a stand offering food for sale. Charles walked over as Len grinned and waved.

"Hi, there," Charles said. "I found out about your Harvest Fair and came with my family."

"I'm happy to see you," Len answered. His parents were watching, puzzled. He explained to them that he had met Charles long ago by the river one afternoon. They said a solemn Good Morning.

"I need to go back and find my parents," Charles said. "Will you be here all day? Can we come by and meet you and your parents?"

Len nodded yes, then returned to his job of setting up his parents' stall, stacking woven baskets and arranging sacks of pine nuts.

The rest of the day passed swiftly. The Pershings and Richardsons met Len's family and talked a few minutes, constrained by the Reyes' limited English. But everybody smiled, determined to overcome language barriers. Len suggested that he walk with them and show them the Fair.

For Charles it was a blur of new experiences. The medicine man walked through the crowd, waving a bunch of sage twigs which he had lit. The fragrant smoke filled the air and the aroma settled onto people's clothing. He ate new foods, examined baskets and jewelry; he and Len carried purchases back to their tent until it was full. Molly and Velda were particularly pleased with the tightly woven baskets, while Stuart and Spence bought and immediately wore wide-brimmed hats. By afternoon the games began. Charles joined the races and the ball-throwing contests, although he won none of them. He was pleased that he at least did not embarrass his new friend. The men paid close attention to the exhibits of deer and rabbit hides, and asked many questions about the obsidian scrapers displayed with them.

All too soon the sun began to set. Molly directed everybody back to their tent and wagon for the supper she had packed, supplemented with Paiute specialties.

Then it was time for dancing. The family watched, entranced, as the Indians performed their traditional dances accompanied by a small orchestra of several violins, an accordion, two trumpets and a drum. After perhaps an hour, the announcer called, "Square dance time!"

All around the audience, couples, both Indian and White, stood up and made their way to the central square, forming squares as the caller made his preparations. After two dances, Charles noticed that Molly was getting restless. She pulled Spence to his feet and they joined the group. Charles had no idea that his parents could move as lightly and gracefully as they did.

It was one of several major discoveries.

In the next weeks, Charles paid several visits to Fort Independence. He played baseball with the boys' team and practiced running with Paiute boys. He continued to visit with Len, who showed him caves and pools of water and collections of bones. The best places were the caves where the Army soldiers had camped when they first came to the Valley. It was old history now, but the caves remained, mysterious with markings on the walls and the occasional cartridge or pipe or other discarded tool. Laughing, Len offered to swap old Army cartridges for the obsidian arrowheads Charles had been collecting. It was one of the few jokes made by this serious, apparently humorless young man.

Chapter XXIX – Father Crowley

Outside the Owens Valley, World War I was raging. The residents of Pinyon Creek and their neighbors were generally oblivious to the issues. They were concentrating on their daily activities, on ranching and farming and, once again, mining. Claims had been established for minerals deemed necessary for the war effort (and therefore sure to pay well): antimony, borax, copper, dolomite, gypsum, lead, marble, pumice, silver, zinc, and tungsten. To the surprise of many, much of the prospecting was done by auto. Beef and grain were also in great demand. Although the Red Apple Railroad had never resumed construction, the Southern Pacific freight trains began increasingly frequent service to the Valley towns in order to ship meat, grand and produce. Life seemed to be better than ever.

Alf and Sara were married on June 15, 1916, a gloriously sunny day, in Pasadena at the Davidson home. Sara wore her mother's wedding dress, cream-colored satin with lace collar and cuffs and embroidered panels on the skirt which reached almost to her ankles. Molly decided that she was the most beautiful girl she had ever seen, which made it possible for her to watch her son become an adult with a happy heart. Sara had found a job teaching first grade in Pasadena, while Alf worked as a geologist for Paragon Mining and Minerals. He was concentrating on the many different kinds of salts to be found in and around Owens Lake, but he was also investigating the rumors of tungsten located in the mountains north of town. This activity allowed him to bring Sara to Pinyon Creek for a long summer vacation so that she could get to know his family and learn more about the town itself.

Tony and Barbara had a less formal but equally happy wedding in Pinyon Creek, with the ceremony at the Methodist church followed by a party afterward which filled Molly's Place with relatives and friends. Barbara wore her grandmother's wedding dress which brought Dr. Capshaw to tears. How many times he had almost left the dress behind as he and Molly moved across the country! Now it had served both his daughter and granddaughter.

The newly-weds bought property in the OVI lands. Tony worked on the irrigation system learning more about how water can be stored and measured and distributed. Barbara continued her efforts to develop peaches and pears which could withstand the salty summer winds and survive shipment of several hundred miles. It was a slow process. She had grafted the plum and peach trees in her study group with varieties offering better survivability. Now she needed to wait for them to produce fruit.

Charles was entranced by the War. He read everything he could find about the Army's vehicles, from trailers for heavy artillery to the light airplanes sometimes pictured in the newspaper. He badgered his parents to allow him to enlist.

"I'm not interested in fighting," he told them repeatedly. "I want to get my hands on these machines and see how they work."

Spence, possibly because of his own intense interest, was sympathetic to Charles' desires, but told him that he was needed in Pinyon Creek.

"The jobs for my mules have increased because people aren't using motor vehicles so much for freight these days," he told his son. "I need you to work the smaller teams. When we get caught up, we can talk about this again."

Bitterly disappointed, Charles poured out his frustrations to Len when they met at the river.

"I'd be a soldier if I could," Len responded. "But my people don't want to get too well known here. We keep to ourselves. Anyway, I don't think they'd let us fly any airplanes. We're still too young."

Their youth had one advantage: with so many young men being drafted, the Pinyon Creek Eagles baseball team was in dire need of players. Len's speed and Charles' fielding skills brought the Eagles one of their best seasons.

Charles spent time with Tony and Barbara, as well. Tony reported that he had seen more men from Los Angeles here and there in the Valley, offering sales of water rights to more and more people.

"I don't know what they think they're going to do with all of that water," he complained. "They have already flooded the land in the San Fernando Valley several times because they have no place to keep it all."

But more and more landowners, hearing about the prices being offered for parcels of their land, were accepting offers.

The mood at the big table in Molly's Place was frequently contentious. Between the War and the water rights, everybody had an opinion and no two opinions were the same.

"Ever since the aqueduct opened we've lost water from our ditches," one rancher complained."Have any of you visited the aqueduct lately? The channel is full but our own ditches are lower."

"Of course they are," another rancher replied. "It's summer. Our ditches are always lower in the summer. They're basically what you'd expect, aqueduct or no aqueduct."

"Now that they're farming down there in the San Fernando valley, they're competing with us for produce of all kinds, from apples to tomatoes. And they'll get the best of it because we have to ship ours further. "

"Yes, but ours are better quality. Can't deny that."

"People, especially people in the cities, aren't so much interested in quality as in price. They buy whatever's cheapest."

"I repeat, we'll rue the day that we ever allowed the aqueduct to be built," Dr. Capshaw stated.

"Now, Wallace, you can't say you're suffering. You aren't even farming. What's your interest anyway?"

"Mildred Howell is ranching and she is worried about water. The more I learn about water issues here the more worried I get. Just the principal of the thing, for one thing."

"Mildred has water wells, just like the rest of us. She should get along fine."

The war ended without any of Spence's family enlisting.

Joe Magnuson tore down the blacksmith shop and replaced it with a filling station. He and Charles continued to make fuel, storing it in large metal barrels, but he was investigating the possibility of contracting with Standard Oil for regular deliveries. As Charles grew more mature and competent, Joe thought more frequently of turning over operation of the filling station to him.

Charles kept looking for opportunities to learn about machines and machinery. In addition to working with Joe, he got a part-time job with the Southern Pacific railroad in Laws, just a few miles away. He worked his way to being a fireman on the locomotive.

One day the men at the big table were surprised to see the postmaster coming in, accompanying a chubby, smiling young man in rimless eyeglasses and wearing a clerical collar.

"Gents, this is Father Crowley," the postmaster said. "He's the new Catholic priest – probably the first Catholic priest this valley has ever seen."

"Well, welcome, sir." Dr. Capshaw gestured at the group. "Come and join us and let us tell you all the big lies and stories we know about the valley."

"I'll happily join you," the priest said with a broad smile. "I'm kind of a circuit rider out here. You'll see my sturdy flivver out the front door."

"Where is your church?" someone asked.

"Wherever there are Catholic families," Crowley answered, grinning. "I call myself an ecclesiastical tramp, a religious hobo. I'm setting up my route, which will take me from Death Valley all the way to Bishop, with stops in between. With any luck, I'll be able to say Mass as often as once a month here. At least, my parishioners will know there's a priest available if they need one."

"Welcome then, Mr. Crowley," Dr. Capshaw shook his hand.

"I'm Father Crowley, or Father John, Doctor," the priest said.

"I'm sorry, son, I just can't call a youngster like you Father. And I'm not a Catholic."

"Almost nobody in this area IS Catholic. But some are, and those the the people I serve. But I hope to be a part of all the community. Call me John, if you prefer."

Charmed by his ready grin and his matter-of-fact acknowledgment of the small number of Catholics, they moved over and found a seat for him.

"I hope I'll be here often," the priest told them. "But it depends on so many things."

The ministers of the Methodist and Baptist churches listened with great interest. The group began to talk about the valley, its attractions and troubles, the aqueduct and the apple orchards, the mountains.

"I understand," Crowley said, "that in this area we have both the highest and the lowest spots in the country. Death Valley and Mount Whitney – I've been to Death Valley but I must find my way to the top of Mount Whitney sometime. Have any of you been to both places? The highest and the lowest? "

No one raised a hand.

"Any Catholics here?" he asked, looking searchingly around the group. Again, no one responded. "Well, then, we'll meet as colleagues and friends if not as parishioners and priest. That's fine with me, and I hope it is with you."

The new priest was the subject of much conversation for several days, until the novelty wore off. Gradually, the town became accustomed to seeing him motoring into town, stopping first at the filling station where Charles and Joe filled the tank, inspected the tires and made small adjustments to the engine.

The next excitement was not long in coming: a string of cars and trucks drove up along the road from Mojave and stopped at Lone Pine, where they turned off onto a side road leading into the Sierra foothills.

The movies had come to town.

Chapter XXX – Landscaping the Desert

One by one, the trucks turned up at Magnuson's Shell Station, looking to fill their gas tanks and check their tires. They had already unloaded much of their equipment at their Alabama Hills headquarters, but Charles spotted some intriguing pieces of equipment still in the back of one of the trucks.

"What are those?" he asked the driver.

"Oh, blowers and light bases and floodlights and ladders and stuff."

"You folks going to be up here long?"

"Actually, we're here, probably, for several weeks now, and if it all works out we understand that we'll be coming back later. Why?"

"Oh," said Charles. "Just interested. I can recommend a really good place to eat --- my mom runs Molly's Place right up the street."

"Thanks for the recommendation," the driver told him, "but we pretty much carry our own food. I'll tell the cook, though – maybe he'll want some help."

"What kind of movies are you making?"

"Here? Westerns, of course. We made some out in Los Angeles, but the chief thought we'd have an easier job out here away from the city. Don't know whether it's worth the effort, yet."

"Will you be hiring any help?"

"That's always the big question, isn't it? I don't know yet. Keep your ears open though. Maybe something will turn up."

Tony found out about the possible work before Charles did. The film companies were looking for carpenters, mechanics and general laborers. There was nothing to interest Tony, who was deeply involved in the Southern Pacific's narrow-gauge-to-standard-gauge transfer process in Owenyo. But he told Charles about the movie jobs and Charles lost no time in applying.

The headquarters was a set of large tents in the foothills not far from the main route, just west of Lone Pine. It was perhaps two hours from Pinyon Creek, closer to an hour if you hurried. Charles decided that could be done. And if he got full-time work, maybe they'd let him camp out there. He tied his mule, Barter, to a low-hanging poplar branch and walked to the opening of the largest tent.

"Hello?" he called.

"Yes, come," a deep voice replied.

The man behind the desk was large, strong-looking and heavily bearded. In a plaid flannel shirt and jeans he looked just like the men from Pinyon Creek. He was making notes on a pad of paper. Charles could see stacks of drawings and maps on tables along the tent wall.

"I'm here looking for work. I understand you're hiring."

"What can you do? Understand, we're really not hiring much, and not for anything close to permanent. This is a kind of experiment, see whether filming out here could work. Maybe later there'll be more."

"Yes, sir. Well, I'm working at the filling station right now, I can do lots of different things, like I can weld, and I've done some building..."

"That your mule out there?"

"Yes, sir. That's Barter. I've had lots of experience with mules. My dad runs most of the mule skinning around here."

"Why did you call him Barter?" the man leaned forward.

"We got him in trade for an old wagon and six apple pies my mom made," Charles answered. "He's a good mule but kind of slow unless you keep at him."

The man smiled.

"It just happens we could use a man who can bring a couple of mules and drive them. Could you do that?"

"Yes, Sir! We'll be here first thing tomorrow."

Charles showed up the next morning riding Barter and leading Peaches ("Why'd you name... oh, he likes to eat them, right?" "Right".). Their job, it turned out, was the moving of rocks. It was hard and sweaty work. He hitched the mules to a sledge, then he and another worker loaded it full of boulders which had been declared In The Way. They hauled load after load of rocks to a dry wash and tumbled them out. Charles had his doubts about the wisdom of the whole idea, but it was work, it was something different from the filling station, the wages were good and he had a chance to see movies being made.

When Tony learned about Charles' new job, he was at first amused and then enraged.

"Where did you unload those rocks? Into a wash? Are you an idiot? How did you let them do that?"

He stormed out of the house, and the following morning appeared at the studio manager's tent, pacing up and down as he waited for the manager to arrive.

"My brother-in-law tells me that you have him dumping rocks into the wash over there," he said hotly. "Have you no idea of why there are dry washes in the desert? The desert, I may point out, is where you are at present. Not the city, the desert."

"My dear sir, I have no idea what you are talking about," the project manager huffed.

"I'll tell you, in simple terms so you can understand. Dry washes are the results of rainstorms in the desert. Rain in the mountains washes down, the water seeks the easiest path downhill, wherever there's soft sand the sand gets washed away, forming a channel, the channel becomes a river during the storm and waits for the next, where it gathers water even easier."

"And...?"

"And so, the next time it rains, which might be tomorrow – probably not – and might be six months from now, SINCE you have blocked that wash the rains will run around it, and will find new channels, which most likely will be the area you have just spent days manicuring. All your hard work will be for nothing. And more important, when we laid out the roads we knew about the major washes. We planned around them and accommodated them. Thanks to your meddling, it's about an even bet that the main road will be washed out in the next big storm."

"Charles didn't say anything."

Tony's irritation was leaving him. "Charles knows a lot about certain things – mules and machines and mining. But he doesn't know that much about the desert. He was as surprised and shocked as you were when I lit into him."

"What do you suggest we do?" The manager was still brusque but he sat back down in his chair and waved Tony to a seat across from him.

"You're planning to be here a lot, I think."

"If it works out, if it is more affordable than Los Angeles, if our actors will cooperate, if we can get the supplies and services we need – there are a lot of ifs. A boatload of ifs. But yes, I think we may end up spending weeks, maybe more, here."

"So you're wanting to make some permanent impact on the landscape. I can't imagine you hiring Charles and Barter and Peaches just for minor adjustments."

"You're right, there."

"Have you surveyed the area? Made maps of your layouts? "

"Well, no. This is the outdoors, after all. We have picked out some attractive landscapes, that's about it."

"Hire me to do your surveys and mapping. I know the area and I've got the experience you need. Here's my card."

The manager leaned back, propped his feet on his desk, pulled out his pipe and lit it, and looked closely at Tony.

"Is this your idea of a creative job application? Because I don't recall us asking for a surveyor."

Tony grinned. "No, actually I came in here preparing to yell at you till you agreed to remove the rocks, and then I planned to make a dignified exit and return to my real job."

"Where's that?"

"Southern Pacific, at Laws. I had no desire to make any changes in my life. I still don't. But I know you need help, you're still at a beginning, where change will be pretty easy. And I know I can help you. It's an interesting proposition, re-landscaping the desert for movies."

"Tony Pershing, huh? Happy to make your acquaintance – I think!" The manager stood, shook Tony's hand. "Jeb Parmentier, producer and general jack-of-all-trades. By tomorrow morning I should have a contract ready to discuss with you. But in the meantime, do you have time to come with me and decide where we really want the rocks moved? We can get Charles and his animals turned into a new direction."

When Tony told Barbara about his morning's meeting, she was unsurprised.

"I don't think I ever thought the movies would come up here," she said, "but now I think about it, it makes a lot of sense. So much of what they photograph should be outside. I got tired of seeing the same houses and the same rooms all the time. And now there's here, it's just obvious that you and Charles will be part of it."

For his part, Charles was willing to move the rocks anywhere anybody wanted. He enjoyed showing off Barter and Peaches, and demonstrating his skill as a wrangler. He joined Tony and Parmentier walking the area as Tony described possible locations and warned about potentially dangerous places. Finally they agreed upon a spot not far from the wash and easy for the mules to reach. Charles was assured of another day's work, which he happily accepted.

At Molly's Place, the gentlemen at the large table anxiously discussed the changes the aqueduct was making. The water level in Owens Lake had fallen to the point where it was almost dry. The water, originally a deep blue, had turned dark red. Where the water had disappeared, bands of white salt crusted the surface. The soda ash company, which had spent years working with chemicals to develop their products, now were faced with an entirely different problem: the salts were no longer dissolved in the water, but were separating and drying before they could be processed.

Alf, now an occasional breakfaster at the big table, brought his client, Rich Jamieson, the manager at Olean Soda Ash Company, to the group.

"We're as concerned as you are," Dr. Capshaw told Jamieson after they had introduced themselves. "We knew the water level in the lake was gradually getting lower. That's been happening, as you probably know, for decades now. We always used lake water when we needed it, and some of the ditches fed off it. But it never has been this low."

"And it's not just the lake," a rancher said. "the level in my well has been dropping. I'm worried that I'll have to drill an additional well, and I can't figure out how I could ever afford it. "

"Here's the worst thing," Willy Chalfant reported, "my sources tell me that L.A. Agents are at work again up here, buying more rights, and threatening to shut off the water if there's a drought down below."

"Well, they always claimed that," Stuart Pershing said. "they have always said that their interests are Los Angeles, not Pinyon Creek, and that's why I strongly objected to letting them have their way. What has the aqueduct done for us? Nothing, as far as I can see. It's only brought dissension and worry, and it'll only get worse."

Alf had more news. "What would you think about mining starting up again? The tungsten mine up by Mount Tom is going great guns, and they tell me that they could sell even more ore if they could only ship it faster. There are lots of other minerals we could harvest here, in case some folks need to give up farming."

"Now, that's a defeatist attitude, Alf", his grandfather said. "Give up farming? Not likely. We just need to hold Los Angeles to their agreement and make sure we get our fair share of the water, just like always. I don't think they're necessarily crooked. We just have to protect our interests."

Alf shook his head. "Lippincott is buying rights in places he hadn't looked before. I'm not part of this but I warn you all to watch out. Something's going on that isn't going to be good for Pinyon Creek."

Chapter XXXI – The Fire

Movie production started quickly. Both Charles and Tony were hired and were kept busy. Tony spent his days with Jeb, surveying the sites the manager had selected and making maps including landscape modifications that would be required. Charles had a difficult discussion with Joe Magnuson, telling him he wanted to leave the filling station for the movie location.

"I figured it was only a matter of time," Joe told him. "Always a new machine, right, Charles? Now it's moving picture cameras and gear."

"Yes, that's it. Also, they want my mules and I want to drive them. Pop says it's ok with him if it's ok with you. I figure that after they leave I can come back if you'll have me."

"We'll have to see about that. I think with all the work setting up, all that stuff you've been telling me, they intend to stay here at least during the good weather. And the good weather is going to be here for awhile yet. I'm going to have to hire another helper, Charles. You know that. When you come back – if you come back – well, we'll see what we can find."

Charles had to admit that was fair, although he felt deep regret at leaving Joe. Driving out to the production area, he felt his stomach tie itself in knots, and wondered whether he was doing the right thing.

He stopped in Lone Pine. Len had a summer job in the kitchen at the Lone Pine Hotel. As he had said, the school in Riverside trained the students to work at low-skilled jobs.

"That's all they taught us. Oh, some reading and numbers and carpentry. But they said we would be lucky to get jobs at all, so we should know how to do the cleaning and so on. I'm not going to stay long, but I'm saving some. Maybe I'll try the railroads. Or that tungsten mine."

Charles persuaded Len to take a few minutes to talk to him. Away from the watchful eyes of the hotel manager they talked about how much he hated to leave Joe but how excited he was to get work with the movie company. Just talking to him helped him to understand, he said, that he had made the right choice. Len agreed.

"With you, Charles, it is always the new adventure you want. I like that. That is the way I feel too. Do you think they will need more workers there at the movie company?"

"They won't even say how long they'll keep me. But I'll tell you first thing if I see anything."

Father Crowley was also interested in the movies, seeing it as an opportunity to tell a wider world about the wonders of the desert. One morning the early risers in Pinyon Creek heard the rattle of his car pulling up at the Richardson house as he joined Charles for the trip to Lone Pine.

"Now, all you have to do is introduce me, Charles. I've got some ideas I want to present to the management and I think they'll like them. And I want to see whether they'll have any Catholics in their employ. If they do, they should know I'm here should they need me."

"Ok, Mr. Crowley." Charles, like many others in Pinyon Creek, could not bring himself to call this smily man Father, and he was too young to adopt his grandfather's solution of "John".

Father Crowley sighed, adjusted his tall black hat, and settled himself on the wagon bench. He mouthed a short silent prayer as Charles jerked the reins and Barter and Peaches set off.

In the manager's tent, Father Crowley offered his ideas.

"First of all, I hope you will list Owens Valley, or Alabama Hills, in what I think you call the credit line – where the movie was made. We need more tourists. We always need more tourists, and I think that once they see your movies people will want to come.

"Second, I hope you'll keep track of your experiences while you're making the movies. We can write about all your crew. We have a church newspaper, the Central California Register, that gets read from here to Fresno and down to Monterey and up to Bishop and beyond. I write a column called "Sage and Tumbleweed" where I talk about things that interest me. I think we can help each other here."

Jeb leaned forward, interested. "I think you're right, Padre. Let's work on that. We can always use good publicity, just like you can. We'll be getting the actors up here soon. I'll get Charles to fetch you, so you can look on. How's that?"

Dr. Capshaw tried to contain his envy when he heard that Father Crowley had visited the movie set. "As a photographer myself, I have a technical interest," he said rather frostily at the big table one morning. "And the Padre has beat me to it. I'll just have to figure out some kind of gimmick I can use instead."

The movie production was a bright spot in an otherwise bleak landscape for Pinyon Creek. Owens Lake continued to dry up, the salt spreading across the lake bed. Farmers complained that the water level was lower in almost every ditch. In the orchards, leaves began to curl, the tips showing brown as they were burned by the desert winds while the irrigation ditches could not offer the additional water they needed. Los Angeles residents complained also. The city was growing faster than anticipated and the water department could barely satisfy the municipal need.

By late July, the cast and crews had arrived and set up their tents and trailers on the movie lots at the Alabama Hills. The actors and actresses, at first outraged at being sent so far away from Los Angeles, gradually became comfortable in the small rural valley. Townspeople from all of the little towns made efforts to please them, bringing treats in the form of cookies, pies and apples as frequent surprises. The movie crews, realizing that there was little to buy, appreciated the fact that their salaries went farther. The stunt riders loved the open range, where they could make up their own tricks in addition to those written for them. Starstruck residents were willing extras, helpers, seamstresses. Before long one movie had been finished and delivered to Los Angeles, and two more were in production.

In late August, two miners, slightly drunk, built a small bonfire just at the edge of town to cook their supper. They banked the coals, rolled out their bedrolls, and went to sleep. During the night, unusually brisk winds stirred up the embers and started them blazing. They caught on some dry grass, spread to a poplar tree and then to the roof of a shed. While townsfolk slept, the shed caught fire, and the hay stored inside began to burn. The miners, panic-stricken, rolled up their bedrolls, gathered their belongings and stowed them by the creek, then began to waken the townsfolk.

By the time men, half-dressed, had run outside, many of the buildings on the east side of Main Street were on fire. Pinyon Creek had not before seen a catastrophe of this size but they had been planning for one. A team of men formed a bucket brigade, hauling water from the nearest body of water, which was the aqueduct. Another team unrolled the hoses kept in the filling station and Lucky's saloon, the two closest buildings with plumbed faucets, and aimed them at the burning roofs. Women canvassed their neighbors, making sure everybody was outside and safe. They tended babies and small children and kept them away from the men's rushing feet.

Charles and Spence, helped by others, led the mules from the corrals where they milled about, panic-stricken, smelling the smoke. They took them out of town toward the Howell ranch and safety.

Others followed with their horses.

Joe Magnuson ran back and forth, first driving all the cars he could find out into the open desert away from the fire. Then he joined a team of four men with brooms frantically beating back flames which were approaching the filling station. The brooms, plus the water from his hose, stopped the fire just feet away from the filling station's roof.

The firefighting lasted all night, but as the sun rose it was clear that the worst was over. Several of the buildings on the east side of Main Street – the Post Office, Mike's Saloon, Pinyon Creek Dry Goods, and, saddest, the Baptist church – had been virtually destroyed. Others had received smoke and fire damage but could be repaired. The hay storage shed which had been earliest to catch fire was gone, and with it went hay intended for winter feed for the livery stable horses. Quietly, soberly, they returned to their homes to prepare for the morning's work.

The men at the large table discussed the fire in detail later that morning. There hadn't been enough water pressure for the hoses to be fully effective, they decided. The town should do what they had wanted to do for years – build a water tank on a hill outside of town, and make sure the water would be distributed fairly in town. They would tax themselves whatever they needed to make that happen. A committee was formed with orders to move swiftly: if it happened once, it could happen again, and Pinyon Creek could not afford another fire.

The Methodist minister had agreed to offer his church to the Baptist minister and his congregation, and to help them rebuild their church.

Father Crowley, arriving late to the table and just learning about the previous night's blaze, was horrified at the damage. Reassured that nobody was hurt, he was quick to offer a suggestion.

"We need to get money to build the water tank and repair the buildings," he agreed. "And that money should come from others as well as from Pinyon Creek. All of us in Owens Valley need to help each other. Let's find a way to encourage our neighbors to help."

Dr. Capshaw, still slightly suspicious of the Padre's motives, nevertheless was in agreement. "I think we could offer some entertainment, something others could pay for. And we could work on it, which will make us all feel less helpless."

"I've got a plan, Wallace," the priest told him. "I'll check it out and come see you tomorrow. We may be able to do this."

He left them quickly and drove out to the movie set where he buttonholed Jeb Parmentier. "See here, Jeb, did you hear what happened in Pinyon Creek last night?" He summarized the fire and the fire damage, then presented his proposal. "Suppose your actors and actresses put on a show up in Pinyon Creek. Doesn't have to be long or fancy. Some singing, some fancy horsemanship maybe, or maybe just a scene from a movie that the audience can see in real life. That should bring in plenty of money and make really good publicity for your studio."

"I'll talk with my boss," Jeb answered. "It's a good plan, and comes at a pretty good time. We're about to finish production of Son of the Shifting Sands, so some of the cast will have some free time. And we can always use good publicity."

Charles and Len spent much of their free time during the warm weekends out in the hills exploring and practicing sports. They frequently raced each other; Charles hoped that he could enter the foot races at the Fall Harvest Fair, but Len told him that he had a long way to go before he could be competitive.

Molly and Spence were by now accustomed to having their older children living away from Pinyon Creek, coming only for visits. Molly and Velda were no longer directly involved with Molly's Place. They sold it to the daughter of the Methodist minister, who kept the name and the menu and, they admitted, did at least as good a job as they had done.

With the opening of the Mount Whitney Fish Hatchery, Spence returned to taking occasional journeys with a string of mules to drop cans of trout into mountain lakes. In some cases, they were newly discovered lakes, while at other times he replenished the supply of trout in popular lakes where the fishing enthusiasm exceeded the source.

Much of the time, though, Spence and Molly made their own schedules, enjoying the luxury of living together in a house without children. Molly took up quilting. Spence discovered a talent for carving small wooden animals "in case we have grandchildren someday," he would smile.

Dr. Capshaw, arriving in their kitchen one September morning, told them they were the ideal pair to volunteer to manage the great Post Fire Renewal Extravaganza. With movie stars.

Chapter XXXII – The Extravaganza

When the news of the Extravaganza broke, so many people bought their tickets that there was no hope of holding it inside a building. Spence's suggestion of the rodeo grounds north of town was immediately accepted and work began. The community bands of Lone Pine, Independence and Keeler joined together to practice. They would lead the parade to the rodeo grounds on the morning of the celebration. Pinyon Creek schoolchildren prepared a short program of patriotic songs. The cast and crew from the movie studio prepared their own part of the entertainment.

"Maybe we should have charged more than a dollar for the tickets?" Molly asked. "Too late now, anyway. And it does mean that more people can afford to go."

She and Velda had gathered in Velda's kitchen to make the plans for their part of the event. They would offer stalls for people to sell goods, and they wanted to sell food and drink as well.

"It's a little early in the harvest for cider," Velda said, "but maybe we can get some. Do they keep it from one year to the next? I'll ask Barbara." She made a note.

"And barrels of water for drinking and washing and for animals to drink, too. We'll have to make sure there is enough space for the horses and mules, for the people who are coming from outside."

"And don't forget the autos and trucks as well. We'll need plenty of space. Maybe the field across the road. I hope Spence and Papa are working on that part."

Alf and Sara were preparing to return to Pasadena for their winter's work, but enthusiastically agreed to return for the event itself.

"I'll make cookies to sell," Sara contributed. "We'll bring them up when we come, the night before if we can."

Barbara had persuaded the OVI to contribute apples, pears and peaches to sell. They were mostly the seconds, the windfalls and too-large or too-small or discolored fruit which could not be packed for sale commercially. A committee of Baptist Church women volunteered to make cobblers and jams with the more unattractive fruit.

Velda's sewing club, which had clung together and had even grown over the years, hurried to create aprons, baby dresses and even one large quilt, which they would raffle off.

Everybody was infected with the excitement of the affair.

Joe Magnuson arranged for a display of Buick automobiles. "Everybody talks about Model T, but lots of people haven't ever seen a Buick and might not ever see one if we don't get any up here."

Dr. Capshaw, of course, signed up to photograph the event, and to make souvenir postcards of attendees. He found photos of

Pinyon Creek buildings he had made before the fire, and made hundreds of postcards of them to sell.

Two weeks before the Extravaganza, Spence called a meeting of the committee chairmen in Molly's Place. They closed the restaurant right after the lunch service, and pulled extra chairs around the big table. The group included the President of the Volunteer Fire Brigade and the Police Chief in charge of public safety and crowd control; the Baptist and Methodist ministers and Father Crowley, in charge of invocations, benedictions and general guidance; Dr. Capshaw, photographer; Molly and Velda, sales, crafts and food; Charles and Joe Magnuson, transportation, automotive matters and animal health, also water supply and assistance to the police. They were joined by the Outings Club President, who was passing through Pinyon Creek on his way to the mountains to check the maintenance of the cabins before winter set in. After listening to the discussion for awhile, he offered posters and maps of the mountains, to be sold or given as souvenirs.

The talk was brisk, excited, friendly. Everybody had suggestions. Most had already assembled teams of workers. "Will there be anybody to watch, or are all of us going to be backstage?" somebody asked, laughing.

Much of the repair work had been completed. The Baptist church was ready to re-open for services. The livery stable had replaced the hay, buying much of it from Mrs. Howell who had allowed so many animals to stay on her ranch in the aftermath of the fire. She was pleased and grateful for the business and provided hay bales for the rodeo portion of the program.

Early on the morning of the event, Molly, Spence and Charles went to the rodeo grounds for the final preparations. They were surprised to see Father Crowley already there. He had parked his roadster at the far end of the parking lot and was standing near the main entrance, his tall black hat bobbing up and down as he rocked on his toes.

"Morning, Padre," Spence called. "I surely didn't expect to see you here so early. I thought you were going to be in Bishop."

"I was there yesterday. I've built myself a bunk in the back of my car, and frequently sleep there. I like looking out the window at the stars, till it gets too wintry and cold. I thought I'd just come by this morning and say a little prayer for all the people who have worked so hard."

"That's very good of you," Molly said.

He helped Spence and Charles as they started setting up the stalls for the sales. Soon Alf and Sara arrived, carrying baskets of cookies.

"Sara, you must have been cooking all week!" Molly exclaimed.

"We wanted to help out, and didn't know what else we could do, since we were so far away," Sara answered, offering everybody a taste.

The Extravaganza was a roaring success, from beginning to end. At 11 o'clock, the first sounds of the band could be heard in the rodeo grounds as the flatbed truck carrying the musicians slowly moved up Main Street. Behind it, a group of movie actors in their beautifully bedecked horses walked in formation, then the school chorus, then an open car carrying starlets who waved to the growing crowds along the way.

People found their way in and took seats around the field, stopping at the stalls to examine and purchase items from potholders to jam. Many bought sandwiches, cider, or cookies to take to their seats.

The program began with trick riding by the movie stunt riders. This set the tone for the day: excitement, surprises, fun. Charles was distracted, watching for Len who had promised to come and bring her family. He watched as several Paiute families entered, and finally relaxed, seeing Len and his parents. He escorted them to the seats he had saved for them next to Alf and Sara, before reporting back to his duty as a mule wrangler.

Many people had several different roles that day. The Postmaster played in the band and later juggled several hoops. Father Crowley led the singing of some patriotic songs, accompanied by the wife of the Baptist minister on a piano which could scarcely be heard at all ("I heard it and it kept me on key," Father Crowley reassured her later). Dr. Capshaw, busily snapping away with his large camera, was part of the stage crew for the dramatic portion, a series of scenes from some of the studio's earlier movies, acted by the very actors and actresses who had made the original films.

The program lasted until well into sundown, finishing with more singing, this time accompanied by the band and the chorus. A surprise final act, supplied by the movie company, was a fireworks exhibition.

Finally the audience drifted home. Spence and Molly joined the rest of their team back at Molly's Place to count the receipts.

"The ticket sales alone came to almost a thousand dollars," Dr. Capshaw reported. "Part of that's because some folks, like Jeb Parmentier and Fred Eaton, put in extra."

"And the food sales added about six hundred fifty dollars more," Molly said, awed. "Sara's cookies alone brought in about fifty dollars." Sara and Alf, quiet in a corner, grinned and hugged each other.

Velda had added up the craft sales. "Somebody from Bishop won the quilt. The raffle came to three hundred and fifty dollars. The other sales together totaled two hundred sixty-three dollars."

Spence had been adding the numbers. "That brings the grand total to almost twenty-five hundred dollars – twenty-three thirteen in fact."

"And we have covered just about all the expenses," Molly added. "Since just about everything was donated, we can keep most of the money. Father Crowley, you have really worked a miracle here."

"It wasn't I," the priest said gently, smiling. "Can we say a short silent prayer of thanksgiving?"

Back at the large table the following morning, the group wanted to concentrate on practical matters.

"How much do we need right now?" someone asked.

"Very little," the Police Chief responded. "Most of the building repairs have been completed. The movie studio is letting us have whatever lumber they leave behind – they are really determined to be heroes to this town! – so until we get the water tower built and get ready to put in plumbing, we don't need to spend more than a couple hundred dollars, and that's just for finishing the repairs to the buildings."

Willy Chalfant spoke up. "I'm saving the entire front page of the paper for a write-up of this event. Folks throughout the valley need to know how well it turned out, and what a great show it was. And how much we all helped each other."

"Hear, hear!" from several voices.

"Wallace, can you let me have some photos?"

"You bet!"

Spence cautioned, "We need to get the money safely into the bank. And we need to decide who will be in charge of the funds. Somehow, we never got around to that before now."

Joe Magnuson spoke up. "Maybe we never really believed we'd have enough to worry about!"

They all laughed; it was so true.

By the end of the afternoon they had elected a committee to direct the water tower project, to monitor the funds, and to have the power to make deposits and withdrawals.

Spence turned to Father Crowley.

"Padre, will you be part of the committee?"

"I would love to, my son, but I've been posted back to Fresno. There will be a new priest taking over soon. So I cannot accept any responsibilities. I want to tell you, though, that I will miss this valley very, very much!"

Dr. Capshaw and Joe Magnuson were charged with the bank duties. On the following day they deposited the receipts – bills of various denominations and pounds of coins – into the Watterson Bank. Simply counting the money took them and the bank tellers several hours.

Afterward, the two retired to Mike's Saloon for a welcome beer.

"Was it worth it, Doc?"

"Every bit, Joe. What do you think? Did you see those riders? How they roped and how they jumped onto their horses? I hope my photos are half as good as my memories!"

Chapter XXXIII - Dynamite

Was it a drought? Or the unanticipated speed of the growth of Los Angeles? Or the idea that orange groves could attract real estate money to the San Fernando Valley north of the city of Los Angeles? Or simply great bad luck?

Whatever the reasons, the people of the Owens Valley began to become aware that they were not getting enough water to continue the occupations they had been following for decades. The Owens Lake dried up until it resembled the dry lakes found elsewhere in the Mojave desert. The Olean Soda Ash plant, which was forced to use more expensive methods in its evaporation process, sued the Los Angeles Water Department. They lost.

The group at the large table in Molly's Place gathered with grim faces one Tuesday morning in July to discuss recent developments.

"I don't know about any of you," Wallace Capshaw reported, "but out at Mildred's ranch her well is lower than it has ever been. And she got some kind of letter that said Los Angeles was going to reduce the amount of water she could take from her ditch. Can they do that?"

"They can and they did," a farmer from north of Pinyon Creek responded. "I don't know how my harvests are going to be this year. This is exactly the time the trees need irrigating, and I think I'm going to have trouble keeping the water flowing."

"There are more and more agents back in the valley again," Spence said worriedly. "They're continuing to press people to sell their water rights. Sometimes they are new rights but more often than not, according to what I hear, people are being pressed to sell more of the rights they already sold."

"At least we have the water tank built, on the hilltop. Pinyon Creek will have water, even if some of the ditches begin to run dry."

"And a fine thing that will be," growled the postmaster. "If the ditches run dry, then everybody who can leave the valley will leave the valley, and there won't be anybody to drink that precious Pinyon Creek water."

"A member of my congregation told me that he'd been approached again," the Baptist minister remarked. "They offered him a pretty good price for more of his water rights, but it wasn't as good as the first offer, and he decided not to accept it. Now he's worried that he'll be out both ways – no money and not enough water for his crops."

"The apple orchards up north are in trouble," Dr. Capshaw said. "It may be Los Angeles behind the failure of the new railroad. They were counting on shipping their apples by train and now it looks like there won't be any train."

"Keep your mules, Spence," somebody laughed. "We can always count on them."

"The thing is, we don't seem to have any good ideas, any of us, about what we can do about the situation. We let Los Angeles come in and walk all over us. Too greedy for that easy money, we were." The speaker was the owner of a ranch south of Pinyon Creek.

"If I can throw out an idea," Jeb Parmentier said, "You all keep talking like Pinyon Creek is only good for farming and ranching. And mining. Now one of the best parts of the valley, as far as I'm concerned, is the beauty, the natural beauty, all around us. That's a big reason we're up here making movies, you know that, and we bring in some money when we're here. Moreover, our publicity people are telling us that people from all over are asking about the desert and the mountains. They want to come see for themselves, and when they're here they'll spend money."

Molly stepped over to the table. It was probably the first time in all the years of Molly's Place that she, or any other woman, had entered the conversation. She spoke quietly.

"Well, sure, we have our scenery and we have the ski tows the children started, and we have the Outing Clubs up in the mountains and that's all good. But we live here because we have come to love the quiet and the peace of this valley. I don't think everybody wants to have tourists and stores and special events. And I surely don't want to have outsiders to deal with every day. Spence and I are happy – right, Spence? – just the way things are. I'm afraid they are going to change, but I will pretend all is well as long as I can."

"Molly, that's quite a speech," her father commented. "I agree with you, even though I guess I've been part of encouraging the tourist business. And I think I should tell Jeb that we – or at least I – think of him as a friend, not an outsider. I hate to think of trainloads of people coming out here!"

Stuart Pershing brought the conversation back to the topic at hand. "Are we truly losing more water? This is high summer, so maybe we're just anxious and expecting the worse. Does anybody know how we can get some facts?"

"I do." Tony had begun attending the conversations, now that he was married and working in the valley. "The aqueduct monitoring stations keep records. I don't know whether they are daily or weekly or what, but they record how fast the water is flowing and how full the pipes are. I'll see what I can find out."

With that, the meeting broke up. The men left, somewhat more silent than usual.

A few days later, Alf arrived unexpectedly at Tony's house in Manzanar., accompanied by Charles. Greeting his sister quickly, he pulled Tony outside. The three sat on the front steps in the hot late afternoon sun.

"There's something going on," he told them. "I'm not sure what exactly it is, and we probably don't approve of it but it sounds kind of exciting."

He had been working at the soda plant, analyzing the changes in the salts due to the drying of the lake, he told them. He had made friends with some of the managers there, and they had told him about a plan that was growing.

"They're all pretty disgusted with what's happening with the water, and how Los Angeles millionaires are making money from the water they have taken from us. They think their jobs will probably go away when the lake is fully dry, and they are hearing that other jobs in the valley will disappear also."

"They're saying the same things at the orchards," Tony said. "In fact, there's talk that some Los Angeles company may even buy up all of the Manzanar Farms, just to prevent competition with the orchards in the San Fernando valley. Maybe it's all just rumor. But I know about the water. I checked and there are measurements of water flow and the water in the ditches is lower than usual, while the water in the aqueduct is flowing at the same rate as always. So it looks like they're taking more."

"That's the kind of thing I'm talking about," Alf said. "So these men at the plant are planning some sabotage. They think that if the people in Los Angeles really knew how we feel about the way we are being treated up here, they'll force the water department to change. The guys at the plant believe that nobody would stand for the rich men in the city killing off the farms up here."

"Do you believe them?" Charles asked sceptically. "From what I hear from the folks on the movie lot, whenever there is money to be made, people's lives are not worth much."

"I don't know whether I believe them or not. But I do know I don't want to just sit around and let the valley turn into desert. So I'm thinking about joining them."

"What are they planning?"

Alf looked around, to make sure Barbara was nowhere near the front porch. He saw her walking to the back of the house, her gardening basket on her arm. He spoke quietly.

"OK, Thursday night we're going to go down south of Manzanar, you know where the aqueduct pipe leaves the tunnel by the power station?"

They nodded.

"Late Thursday night – actually, it'll be Friday morning, along about 2 a.m – there's a full moon so it will be plenty bright. I'll be coming there, with a couple of the men. We need Charles with a truck, maybe one from the garage?"

Charles nodded. "I won't tell Joe, but he won't mind. I think he's just better off not knowing."

Alf agreed. "After work Thursday, drive down to the plant. We're going to load the dynamite into the back of the truck. It will be packed for safe shipment – these guys handle dynamite all the time – and you and I will drive it over to the pipe. The guys from the plant will be following us."

"And what about me?" Tony asked.

"You're wanted to help us figure out where to place the dynamite so that the water will spill out downhill, toward the desert floor. This is a kind of first test, mostly just to see what will happen, see if it has any effect."

Charles, troubled, asked his brother, "Aren't you worried that this is illegal? Not to mention dangerous?"

"Well, of course, I'm worried. Worried as hell. But at least these guys are doing something, not just sitting around watching the valley dry up."

"What if somebody gets hurt?"

"I don't think that's going to happen. As I say, they use dynamite a lot in their work. One of the guys that'll be coming used to be a hard rock miner, so he really knows how it works. We figure, we'll put some sticks of the stuff at the right point, under the pipe – we may have to dig a hole so we'd better bring some shovels – and then hightail it out of there as soon as the fuse is lit."

"What if we get caught?" Tony asked.

"I hope we won't. But can you imagine a jury in Pinyon Creek sending us off to jail?"

The boys were not convinced, but a long history of following Alf on adventures helped persuade them.

Alf was waiting at the entrance to the soda plant Thursday evening when Charles pulled up in the truck.

"I told Mom I was going out to play poker," he said, grinning. "I expect she thinks I'm out with the movie crew, and she'll worry that I'll be spending too much money. I told her I'd sleep over there tonight."

Alf nodded. "Good plan. Sara's down in Pasadena, so I don't have to worry about her."

They caught sight of the headlights of a truck coming toward them from the plant headquarters. Alf watched carefully, then waved as he recognized the truck. Charles followed it to a small warehouse where the dynamite was waiting, each stick wrapped in burlap and nestled in cotton waste in a small carton. They carefully carried the carton to the back of the truck, in which Charles had placed a larger box half filled with sand. They secured the box to the side of the truck bed with a sturdy rope. Then Alf and Charles climbed in and started down the road, the men from the plant following. The full moon lit the entire desert, outshining the stars and making great black shadows along the sides of the road.

"I'm glad the road is so empty," Charles said softly. "I'd hate to have anybody see me. This truck is always parked in front of the garage. People will wonder."

"You'll have to take it to work with you, won't you? To keep your story straight?"

"I left a note for Joe to tell him I had it."

They chatted idly as they drove, keeping their minds away from the cargo in the truck bed.

Tony had ridden his horse up from Manzanar. They spotted it before they saw him.

"I told Barbara about wanting to exercise Rusty, and how it was a good night for a long ride to keep him in trim. She thinks I'm crazy, but then she often does." He squeezed into the front seat next to Alf and directed them to the aqueduct road.

The dirt road was filled with small rocks and gullies. The truck bounced along, even at Charles' slowest speed. They noticed that the car from the plant was keeping a good distance behind them.

Finally, after about fifteen minutes, Tony said, "Stop!"

They parked the vehicles and climbed out. He pointed to the pipe which appeared from a tunnel to their right and ran along the side of the foothill parallel to the maintenance road. It was taller than it looked from the main road, perhaps ten feet in diameter. To their left they could see it disappear into another tunnel. In front of them they saw the welds where two sections had been joined together.

"In a way, it breaks my heart to do this," Tony said quietly. "This was a beast to do. Three times we got the pipes joined and then they began to leak. Took weeks to figure out how to fix it and it put us behind schedule. And Mr. Mulholland is just nuts about keeping on schedule."

"OK, once more," Charles spoke up. "Are we absolutely sure this is the right thing to do?"

"Yes, it is." It was one of the men from the plant. "Down in Los Angeles, nobody knows or cares about the effects the aqueduct is having up here. All they know is they are getting drinking water, and water for watering their lawns, and not paying too much for it. We need to get their attention."

"Well, let's get to it." Alf climbed into the truck bed and untied the ropes. The rest stood at the tail of the truck to receive the dynamite.

Chapter XXXIV – Alabama Gates

Charles wondered how a small package like the dynamite stick could seem so heavy in his hands. Even carefully wrapped and cradled between his hands, he could almost feel it ready to explode. He glanced at Alf and Tony. Both of them had handled explosives before and seemed unworried.

They set the dynamite sticks back in the original box on the ground near the site Tony had selected. Then they dug out a shallow pit in a spot near the seam, where the ground looked easier to work. Laying the dynamite into the resulting depression, everybody moved more quickly, more accustomed to the rhythm of the job.

Finally, one of the men assembled the fuse, attaching all of the individual fuses to one master wick which ran several feet out along the ground.

"Ok, let's get ready!" he called. Charles leaped into the truck and started the engine, while the others scrambled into the back. As soon as the fuse was lit, the last man jumped aboard and the truck bounced along the rocky path back the way they had come.

They had just enough time to reach the other truck and Tony's horse and to worry that the fuse had not worked, when a gigantic explosion almost threw them off their feet. Dirt and rocks and pieces of metal flew through the air. Tony's placement had directed the explosion toward a previous rock slide where now water was pouring downhill, gathering debris as it flowed.

"Go! Go!" Alf shouted and all the men vanished as fast as possible. Reaching the main road, Charles stopped just long enough for them to see the results: here and there, tiny fires flared as the dry brush burned. The water had reached the main road south of them, seemingly gathering force as it rushed downhill. In the moonlight, it looked silvery.

The next morning, the explosion at the aqueduct was the talk of the town. Willie Chalfant was everywhere, trying to find names, details, motives for the explosion. Sheriff Brock deputized three men to serve as guards until the city could send repair crews. Tony had been called into service by the aqueduct managers to survey the area and make recommendations for repairs and future safeguards.

Alf was due to return to Pasadena. He left Pinyon Creek reluctantly, not wanting to miss a single detail. He made Charles promise to write faithfully, and, above all, to keep everything secret.

At the Alabama Hills, Charles found the movie crews discussing the same subject.

"If you ask me, it's long overdue," one wrangler commented as he and Charles stabled some horses. "Los Angeles is a big greedy monster and they'll take whatever they can get, no matter what that is."

"So you think it was some kind of revenge?" Charles asked.

"Well, of course it was, and more power to them. If I had known about it, I would have joined them. Except that dynamite scares me silly."

Charles and Tony, comparing notes that evening, decided that they had escaped detection. The experience had been an exciting one, but neither was sure that they would want to repeat it.

The following week saw representatives of the Water District back in the valley, spreading out to a variety of different projects. J. B. Lippincott was back in town, visiting stores and Molly's Place despite the cold reception he faced from most of Pinyon Creek. He was once again soliciting offers to sell water rights. This time his territory extended well away from the river, to properties along the irrigation canals. He found some willing sellers, mostly farmers who were becoming aware that their water problems were real and growing.

William Mulholland arrived in a large touring car accompanied by several engineers. After surveying the damage to the pipe he shook his head. "The man who placed the explosive knew what he was doing. I don't think this is the last sabotage we'll see."

The pipe was repaired within a week. The guards were dismissed because there was no sign of any further action. But the pressure on valley residents to sell their land and, especially, their water rights continued.

At Molly's Place, discussion centered on strategies to counter Los Angeles.

"They want to take it all. We'll never get anywhere unless we band together and make a concerted agreement," Wallace Capshaw said. "I think we should create a committee, or an alliance, and make a proposal which comes from the entire valley. We need to show them our strength."

"Good idea," Stuart Pershing agreed. "We need to name a figure – say, ten million dollars, something big enough to make them sit up and take notice – and require that they leave us a reasonable amount of water."

"I'll buy that, but we might as well realize that people are leaving the valley every day. Either they have sold their land and want to get out, or they figure they'll never make it and just leave. Or their business is failing, like John Downing at the General Store. He's selling out and going back to Michigan."

Molly and Spence listened without comment to most of the discussions. At home, preparing for bed, Molly said, "Our children are grown and gone, Spence. They have their own lives now. It's not as though we have a bond we cannot break, here. Have you thought about leaving?"

"Of course I have, Molly. Every time I see another farm being abandoned, or when I listen to Barbara talking about the problems at the orchards, or wonder whether Charles will ever settle down, I think, well, Molly and I have our own life and we could do whatever we want. Do you still think about going back to Cornwall?"

"Oh, sometimes something will remind me. But this is my home, Spence. We're lucky we don't depend on the land. I worry about the children, especially Barbara. She has her heart set on growing fruits and vegetables here. She's already seeing the signs of failure in the orchards. But I think we should stay here in the valley."

"I do, too, Molly, and that's a big relief to me. Your father is getting involved in all the politics, isn't he?"

"He couldn't stand to just stay aside and watch. You know that. He's trying to get a good price for Mrs. Howell's ranch but I'm a little afraid he's getting carried away."

"That's your father," Spence chuckled.

The consensus of the valley men was that the explosion, while it attracted momentary attention, did not change the situation. The city still wanted as much water as it could get, they said, and the rest of the state and the country just didn't care much what happened in Owens Valley. What they needed was something to give them more power to use against the city. They wanted their water back, but if they couldn't get that, then the farmers and ranchers needed enough money to get them started again somewhere else, and the town businesses needed reparations for the loss of sales and customers. Many hours were spent, at the large table and in many kitchens, discussing plans.

Molly became aware of hushed conversations quickly abandoned, of more comings and goings along the sidewalks in the evenings. Charles and Tony professed ignorance of any plans, and Spence simply refused to talk about the aqueduct at all.

One evening just as she was getting into bed, she heard car engines. She looked out the window and watched a procession of a dozen or more cars, headlights off, driving slowly but steadily south along the road out of town. It was another night of full moon. The cars were silhouetted against the hills. Molly thought the last car in line looked like the truck Charles used at the movie lot, but decided it could have been her imagination.

Spence came in from the stables just then. He had been checking on one of the mules who had an infection in his hoof.

"Did you see that?" he asked his wife.

"The cars? Do you think Charles was driving that last truck?"

"It's very probable. Just pretend you saw nothing. OK?"

"What's going on?"

Spence smiled, gave her a hug, then began to pull of his shirt. "You'll find out in the morning."

Just after sunup, the men turned the big wheels and lowered the giant gates and the aqueduct water was completely stopped. By an hour or so later, word reached Los Angeles of trouble at the aqueduct. The Inyo County sheriff, Charles Brock, had arrived on scene, having followed the aqueduct till he found the cluster of parked cars and trucks. Dozens of men, many armed with rifles or shotguns, were standing guard at the gates.

Sheriff Brock considered the situation. He examined the vehicles. Their license plates had been removed. He pulled out a notebook and began to write down the names of the men he recognized. Seeing this, others began gathering around him.

"Add my name!" they called, shouting out their names. The sheriff, shrugging, complied.

The organizers had done a good job of notifying the press of the occupation of the Alabama Gates. By afternoon, reporters and photographers from newspapers from Los Angeles to Sacramento were trickling in, delighted with the drama.

The aqueduct manager, livid with rage, demanded that the sheriff arrest everybody.

"I can't do that," Brock responded. "They're not violent. The property isn't being harmed that I can see. I kind of view this as a Free Speech protest. Or something."

The press was being invited to tour the valley and instructed in the damage already done to the fields and farms because of the diversion of water to Los Angeles. More and more journalists arrived.

By the second day, chores had been assigned, and a guard duty schedule had been adopted. Traffic on the highway into the valley slowed as drivers spotted the activity and took time for a closer observation.

On the third day, the women of Pinyon Creek, Lone Pine and other towns had organized a picnic chain, providing sandwiches, soups and stews for the men.

In Pinyon Creek, someone had made a big sign and set it at the base of the flagpole: "If I am not on the job, you can find me at the AQUEDUCT."

As always, the movie crews at the Alabama Hills participated. Western star Tom Mix brought an orchestra and entertained the assembly with western music.

Spence drove Molly and Velda down on Thursday. The back of the car was filled with baskets of sandwiches and pies and pots of soup. Molly was unsurprised to see both Charles and Tony on guard duty.

As they walked among the men, Molly heard a familiar voice.

"Hello again, my friends!"

Father Crowley had returned to the valley.

Chapter XXXV – Father Crowley Returns

Father Crowley shook hands all around, smiling and laughing as his friends welcomed him back, then withdrew with Wallace Capshaw to a quiet corner to catch up.

"What's been going on here?" he asked. "Owens Lake has disappeared – there's only a thin film of ugly moisture. I passed a couple of farms that look just about abandoned. Is it all due to the aqueduct? Hard to believe."

"Believe it, nonetheless," Wallace Capshaw said. "Farming is never an occupation to get rich in. Farming and ranching, they're almost always hand to mouth endeavors. People came here because they loved the scenery, or the land was cheap to buy, or they had family nearby. Or they came originally to prospect or work in the mines, and then just stayed on. We always managed to survive from one year to the next, and we're still surviving, most of us. But when the city came and offered a price for water rights, it was tempting. And then when things started getting tough, the city offered to actually buy the farms, and that took more people away. Now it's pretty much just us stubborn mules left here."

"And what's going on here? I was on my way to Pinyon Creek when I saw the cars and the people."

"We want to send a message to the rest of the state, and to the country, that what Los Angeles is doing isn't fair. We had reached a settlement which would provide them the water they needed, but then they broke their word and kept coming after more and more. It isn't fair that people can just buy the livelihoods of other people. And it's not that Los Angeles necessarily needs the water. They're watering lawns! In the desert! And planting gardens. Eaton and his buddies are getting rich from their manipulations. Remember J. B. Lippincott? Well, he's making a bundle from his land dealings, I'm sure of that."

Dr. Capshaw was standing now, shaking his fists. Big veins had popped out in his neck. He was redfaced and sweating.

"Sit down, sit down, my friend, and have a drink of water." Father Crowley filled a cup from a nearby bucket and handed it over.

"Yes, I'll give myself a stroke someday if I'm not careful."

Dr. Capshaw subsided. Then he spoke again. "I blame myself, you know. If I hadn't been so eager to take everybody's picture, if I hadn't been so determined to publicize the sanatorium and the ski tows and all, probably Mulholland and his pals wouldn't have found us. We'd still be here, getting along."

"And is that what you would have liked?" Father Crowley responded gently. "Seems to me that this valley cries out for tourism. Remember the Extravaganza? Just reading about it in the newspapers brought more tourists to the valley. If the farming is bad, surely people can create tourist opportunities. You know and I know how beautiful it is here. People in the cities never see the stars."

Dr. Capshaw smiled. "That's a good slogan. IF I were still interested in tourism, I'd definitely use it."

They watched the activity. The women were packing up the picnic gear to return home. The men standing guard were changing shifts. A few men stood at the roadside, papers in hand, to present the Valley story to motorists on the highway.

"So, Padre, what are you doing here? I thought you had been posted to Fresno."

"It turns out that I really love this valley," Father Crowley grinned. "My replacement here retired, and my bishop couldn't find anybody who wanted to drive all over creation to visit congregations of only seven or eight people. So I volunteered and here I am. And mighty glad to be here."

They joined Mark Watterson and Willie Chalfant and Spence in conference. Sheriff Brock had reported that the Los Angeles sheriff was coming with two carloads of armed deputies. He promised to try to persuade them to turn back, but had little hope they would do so.

"We won't let them take the aqueduct away from us," someone growled. "This time we're in it to the finish."

The newspaper reporters, whose numbers seemed to be growing by the hour, were scribbling quotes and snapping photos. Occasionally one would break free, leaving with notes and camera for a quick trip to deliver copy to his paper.

"Where's your brother, Mark?" Father Crowley asked. "You're usually in these things together."

"He's in Los Angeles, Father, trying to negotiate with the Clearing House Association. He thinks he can persuade them that they should buy the entire valley for, say, fifteen million dollars."

"Whew, that's big money!"

"It is, if we could get it. I'm not sure they'll even listen to him. We'll know when he gets up here. "

Sheriff Brock reappeared, looking anxious. "I've just been told that the sheriffs of Kern and Los Angeles Counties are sending deputies up here, fully armed, to support my struggles to get you folks to go home. I've sent Jeb Parmentier out to the highway to meet them. Jeb thinks he can talk them out of coming in, but I don't want any gunfights. If necessary, I will take their help to stop this thing."

Listening, Wallace Capshaw and Father Crowley walked to the edge of the hillside and looked out over the valley. The water pouring from the open gates had roared downhill and was now making its own path directly into Owens Lake.

"You know, it's funny," Dr. Capshaw remarked. "I see this water and I think, it's going exactly where it should go. And when I look at the aqueduct, that water is being taken far away from where it should go. This water, it will soak into our desert and filter through the underground soil and rocks and a thousand or a million years from now it will be part of a well or a river right here in the valley, not down in a part of California that was a desert and should still be a desert. Sure, we made our presence here, and probably used more of the resources than we really needed to, but we all love the valley and respect it, and you can't find a better symbol of that than the water."

"I agree," Father Crowley said. "I'll be praying for you all. Fellows," he shouted, "I'm about to leave. With your permission, I'll say a little prayer. Will you join me?"

The next day brought word that the Siege of Alabama Gates had been written up in newspapers across the country, and there were rumors that newspapers in Europe had the story as well. The men began to talk about what they should do as a next step. Some of them, worried about what was happening back home with farms and businesses, thought about how they could take a short trip back to Pinyon Creek.

In the afternoon of the fourth day, William Watterson returned with the news that the Clearing House Association had assured him they could meet a delegation for negotiations. The tired, dusty men greeted the news with cheers and made plans for a final barbecue.

By the weekend the big wheels had once again been turned and the Alabama Gates lowered. Water once again flowed through the aqueduct down to Los Angeles.

But the negotiations with Los Angeles came to nothing. The Watterson brothers complained vigorously about the lack of progress, while the Los Angeles committee maintained that they did not wish to communicate with vandals and lawbreakers. And as summer progressed, the levels of valley wells dropped and those irrigation ditches that remained grew dryer. The only flourishing

329

businesses were the tourists who visited the valley in ever larger numbers, some drawn by the dramatic stand-off at the Alabama Gates, others by stories of the great beauty of the outdoors, the contrasts between the valley floor in the desert and the spiking mountain ranges of the Sierra. Thanks to the aqueduct construction, a paved road now led throughout the valley, so that visitors from both Los Angeles and San Francisco could make a relatively easy journey.

In Pinyon Creek, several additional cafes opened and a third hotel was built. On the summer weekends it seemed as though everybody would be staying up all night. Molly and Velda, unable to stay away from Molly's Place, invested in ice cream machines and soon were locally famous.

But just when it seemed that life was settling into a pleasant routine once again, new trouble struck. One Thursday morning Willie Chalfant strode into Molly's Place and threw himself into his chair at the round table.

"The Watterson Bank has closed," he announced.

Chapter XXXVI – Ruined

The people in the restaurant were silent for only seconds. Then the room erupted in voices.

The empty chairs usually occupied by William and Mark Watterson were now obvious. The confusion of voices reached a crescendo, then Chalfant stood and held up a hand.

"The bank is closed and locked and there is a notice tacked to the door frame that says something like, we're sorry we have to close the bank. And no, I don't know any more and I have sent a reporter to Mojave because they were supposed to have been there yesterday or the day before. Charles, do you know anything?"

Sheriff Brock shook his head. "News to me. Let's hope it's just a big mistake. Those two love the valley and they have been awfully good to all of us. People say they have never foreclosed on a loan."

"They were so good when I was sick and missed a couple of loan payments. They just extended the payment schedule till I was back on my feet." The Baptist minister shook his head sadly.

"We can't do anything till we hear more," Rich Jamieson said. "I'll admit I'm concerned. Our payroll is in the bank and we'll need it by next Friday."

"Surely they won't stay closed more than a day or so. Right? What happens in a case like this?"

"I'll have to worry about the cash receipts. Fortunately," the postmaster looked around the room, "we have a large strong box with a very strong lock."

"This is like the old west," Spence remarked. "All we need are some stage coaches and some bank robbers."

"That's not funny," his father-in-law growled.

"Sorry. But we can't do anything but worry, I suppose. Willie, you'll let us know the minute you hear anything?"

But it was several days before anybody heard anything, several long days when storekeepers increasingly fretted over the cash in their lock boxes and businessmen worried about how to pay their employees. The grocer reported that people were buying ridiculous amounts of groceries – "they're buying milk and meat and fruit and it's going to spoil before they can eat it all."

Monday morning the round table was filled earlier than usual. Willie Chalfant was the last to arrive and he strode in with a grim expression and a wrinkled forehead.

"Well, it sounds bad. It sounds worse than bad. I can't believe it," he began. "Seems they were running a couple of businesses in addition to the bank – did any of you know that?"

Blank looks all around.

"And when they ran short of money they had a habit of borrowing from the bank funds. And they say they can repay the money, but my reporter says they were seen in Mojave last week taking things from their safe deposit box there."

"Why did they have a safe deposit box there when they had a bank here?" asked Spence.

"Oh innocent one," Chalfant couldn't restrain his sarcasm, "because they didn't want anybody to know about it. Or the businesses. Or the fact that Watterson Bank may in fact not have any money."

"But we've been putting money into the bank regularly. We may not have water, but we have rules. And business has been pretty good."

"The bank inspectors are due here today. We should know more soon, but I guarantee we won't hear any good news."

There was little conversation for the remainder of the meeting, as everybody thought about the possible disasters that may have just occurred.

Finally Tony spoke up. "We were going to start on construction of the new city hall this week. I suppose that's off?"

"Probably the safest course of business," Spence replied thoughtfully. "And any other projects anybody's working on, maybe we should all slow down."

It was, in fact, worse than anyone had thought. The Watterson brothers were quickly indicted for embezzlement. They claimed, according to the Crier reporter who was at the hearing, that the fights with Los Angeles had caused them to expend extra funds, for publicity and security and legal fees "and on and on and on", the reporter said dismissively. "They want to blame everybody but themselves."

"But what about our money?"

It was a refrain that only grew louder as the days and weeks passed. Mildred Howell, receiving payment for the last of her cattle, could not cash the check. The grocer could not pay for fresh stock and quickly ran out of many items. Spence had promised Alf and Sarah a check to help them buy their house in Pasadena, but had to tell them what had happened. The movie crews had relied on the bank for only part of their financial affairs, but it was obvious to all that they were hurrying to finish their current movie and return to Los Angeles.

The hardest hit were many of the farmers and ranchers who had sold their water rights or their land. The proceeds, according to the judge who had set up what appeared to be permanent residence in the school office, were probably gone forever.

"You might as well get yourselves a few head of cattle if you can," he said, "or plant something, because you're starting all over again."

Even in the shock and despair that enveloped the town, some people found good things to say about the Wattersons. They pointed out the times loans were forgiven, or payment adjustments were made. They talked about the friendliness of the two, the willing support for community projects.

"They gave me good terms when I needed to buy some new cars this season," Joe Magnuson said. "Of course, since I can't sell any cars now, that may not have been so great after all."

It was as if a dark cloud settled over the valley. Even the beginning of Autumn, which was even more glorious than usual, and the continuing tourist trade couldn't raise anyone's spirits. If your family hadn't been damaged badly, you know people whose future was in shambles. There was no point, people said, in making plans for the future, because who knew what might happen. People even started looking at friends in a more critical way. The Bank of America was given a charter and opened a branch bank in Pinyon Creek, but it just wasn't the same.

Father Crowley, back from his circuit of small Catholic settlements, couldn't jolly them into smiles. He listened carefully to all the stories, then took Wallace Capshaw aside.

"Let's go take a long walk. Are you game?"

Dr. Capshaw nodded. They took walking sticks and their wide-brimmed hats and started down the road toward the Howell ranch.

"You know, I see a lot of grief," the priest began. "And I see too much poverty. I just came from a mining camp where I think several children have tuberculosis and there's nobody to help them. Sometimes I just wonder how people stand what they stand. But somehow what's happened to Pinyon Creek makes me the saddest of all. This is such a beautiful town, and it has been such a happy town. Sure, there was the fire, and the aqueduct has been miserable for most, but you have all been close to each other, helping each other. This is a terrible reward for all the hard work that has gone into the town."

"Well, thanks for cheering me up, Padre," Wallace Capshaw said bitterly. "Barbara and Tony are about to have their first child. The Manzanar orchards are drying out, who knows where Tony will get another project if the movies leave. What a way to start a family."

"Well, Tony doesn't look too beaten down. In fact, he seems to be somewhat of a leader around here. And Charles is everywhere. I understand he's working at an airport now?"

Dr. Capshaw smiled. "Yes, he's finally found a machine that he can take apart and put back together and fly. He's a born pilot, I'd say. He's flying tourists from Los Angeles to Death Valley, now that they have that resort there. And Tony, you're right, Padre. He's a true survivor. I have to remember that when Sarah and I started out, we had no money, nothing. And we made a good life. After all, we had our Molly."

"See that's what I mean. Life in the valley will go on. Maybe the towns will be smaller. Maybe nobody will have new clothes for awhile. But the snows will still blanket the mountains, and the wildflowers will cover the desert floor, and the coyotes will howl at the full moon and terrify the sheep."

Dr. Capshaw nodded. "What you're saying Padre, is that we need to buck up this town. We need to do something to get them back on their feet. No point in grieving over the lost money. It's gone, and we'll probably never even have a new city hall! But we can pull together and survive. And I would like to see, well, most of them survive right here in the Owens Valley."

"Exactly. Now I have a small thought that I would like to share with you. You know how many hours I spend in my flivver, driving from one church to a house, to a mining camp, all over creation. There's hours and hours with nothing to occupy my mind except for the road which is usually empty. And I've been thinking. They've just about finished the road to Death Valley..."

He led Dr. Capshaw to a handy boulder and sat him down. It would be a lengthy explanation.

Chapter XXXVII – Wedding of the Waters

"You know well, Wallace, that Mount Whitney has the highest point in the United States," Father Crowley began. "And what's the lowest? Badwater, in Death Valley. And now we can get from one place to another. Or we will, once the road is actually opened."

Dr. Capshaw nodded. "Go on."

"We know that the history of settlement in the valley dates all the way to the Gold Rush."

"Much much earlier than that," the doctor objected. "Don't forget the Paiutes and Shoshones. But I agree that the Gold Rush is an important period. Go on."

"And we are most painfully aware that water is just about the most important resource in our lives right now."

"True, true," sighed the doctor.

"Here's my giant plan. We're going to produce the greatest pageant the valley has ever seen. Maybe the greatest the state has ever seen. It will make our Extravaganza look like, well, like a

Sunday School picnic. It will be a humdinger. And you and I will put it all together."

"I'm an old man, Padre." Dr. Capshaw replied. "Old and cranky and discouraged. All I want to do is sit on my front porch and watch the hawks of an afternoon. Don't go out and try to get me involved."

"You must be sick," Father Crowley answered. "Is this the same man who took his camera up into the mountains just to catch the first skiers? Is this the same man who photographs fish? This is a terrific opportunity for you – not to mention it just might encourage tourism and bring some outside money into Pinyon Creek? What were you telling me about Tony and Barbara?"

"Of course, you're right. And you're pretty persuasive, just like you always were. Actually, it sounds like fun. Maybe. How do we start?"

"The official opening of the road from Death Valley to Owens Valley is about six months away. They're always late. So I think we should plan for early June. By that time the weather should be just about ideal, and we'll have plenty of time to plan. IF we start right now."

The original committee of two quickly grew to a steering committee of twelve, bolstered by a fund-raising committee even larger. By Thanksgiving, it was necessary to divide the committees into subcommittees, just to allow everybody to take part. The Bank of America, eager to overcome the reputation of the Watterson Bank, contributed money to start the ball rolling. Willie Chalfant sent his reporters to create publicity releases and to report on committee doings. Joe Magnuson, as it happened, was descended from a member of the Donner Party and had historic souvenirs; a Lone Pine schoolteacher, Susanna Billington, was a descendant of the man who escaped from Death Valley and returned with food for the pioneers trapped in the desert. They were named honorary committee members, with Joe in charge of the vehicles subcommittee.

Throughout the winter and into the Spring, committees met and worked, making lists, writing letters, making posters, sewing pioneer costumes. The Pinyon Creek band and orchestra worked up entire programs of patriotic and western songs which would be played at the picnics and barbecues during the pageant. The Baptist and Methodist ministers met with Father Crowley to divide the religious duties between them. Schoolchildren learned special history units and practiced drawing maps and illustrations of Mount Whitney. Charles, working at the Death Valley resort as a shuttle pilot, practiced touch and go landings near Badwater.

Father Crowley, on his regular route, visited each committee, smiling and encouraging, jotting notes into his notebook.

Beginning in February, the publicity committee began to send out the notices of The Wedding of the Waters. The romantic name captured the attention of many California newspapers, and others across the country began to show interest.

In March, California Governor Clement Young indicated that he would like to participate in the Wedding of the Waters ceremony. This led to a spirited discussion about where the Governor would ride (in the Cadillac convertible provided by Joe

Magnuson's filling station) and whether it would be undignified to have a group of costumed young ladies accompany him (Yes but maybe we'll do it anyway).

By April, the official date for opening the highway from Death Valley to the Owens Valley was announced. The celebration was planned for Friday, Saturday and Sunday, June 8, 9 and 10. Now the committees snapped into action. Dr. Capshaw's notebooks were full of schedules, shopping lists, names, ideas, and maps.

By the last week of May, Father Crowley and Dr. Capshaw had to admit that the plans were coming to a fine finish. Even the Southern Pacific railroad was cooperating, lending their now-historic narrow-gauge engine and passenger cars. The hotels had filled their rooms for the weekend, with extra days for exploration – "exactly what we had in mind," Father Crowley crowed – and Joe Magnuson had cleared land near the filling station for a parking lot. The Highway Patrol had been alerted; Father Crowley distributed copies of the program to all the law enforcement agencies and railroad stations in Bakersfield and Mojave. The Boy Scouts practiced first aid and rock climbing just in case. The first barbecue would be held in Lone Pine. The pits had been dug, and all was ready. The general store ordered a year's supply of film of various sizes in case any tourists would run out (residents of Pinyon Creek were always careful to stock up ahead of any major event).

Two days before the celebration, Father Crowley came to Molly's Place to find Dr. Capshaw.

"Where do you want to be stationed, Wallace?" he asked. "Is there a special spot we should reserve for you?"

"My front porch is just fine, Padre," the doctor replied. "During the past month I have seen every vehicle, every costume, every animal involved, and I'm looking forward to sitting out on the porch with Molly and Velda, and just watching it all go by. The younger generation will be moving along with the flow, and they'll tell us all about it. I've trained young Peter Cummins to use my big camera, and he'll take as many photos as he can."

"If you say so, but as for me, I'm intent on moving along with the Governor. Maybe I can encourage him to spend some time here in the valley, take a vacation here, maybe. They tell me in Death Valley they already have a full house at Furnace Creek and Stove Pipe Wells. The campgrounds are getting full, too."

They shook hands and parted ways, each one reluctant to admit how excited he was.

Friday morning dawned sunny and cool. Groups of tourists walked along the Main Street in Pinyon Creek, pointing to the Sierra. Many had come in pioneer costume, pleasing the Pinyon Creek residents who were also dressed in gingham and fancy vests. Volunteer guides identified some of the peaks, and told them how Mount Whitney, the highest mountain in the United States, was hidden from view, tucked in behind some of the other rugged granite. Up in the mountains, at Lake Tulainyo, the highest lake in the United States, Len Reyes filled a large gourd with lake water. Then he ran down the steep mountain path to Whitney Portal, where the newly paved road began. A band of musicians from the

Paiute Reservation played as Stuart Pershing realized his heart's desire: dressed as a Pony Express rider and mounted on his horse Gallant, he accepted the gourd from Len and thundered off down the road.

Sunset always comes suddenly in the mountains and it was beginning to get dark. A procession of automobiles, previously arranged along the road, accompanied Stuart, their headlights signaling the approach of the rider and his cargo.

Reaching Pinyon Creek, the Pony Express rider handed off the gourd to none other than Hopalong Cassidy, actually Bill Boyd from the movie crew, in town for filming and delighted to be part of the action. He brought the gourd ceremonially into the bank, where it was locked in the vault for the night.

Then the first party began. Several bands stationed along the Main Street provided dance music, while visitors and residents sat together at long tables to feast on trout caught in local lakes.

The governor was served a small glass of water from the gourd and pronounced it delicious.

Early the next morning, the gourd was given to an old prospector who wandered up leading his mule. The prospector looked suspiciously like Father Crowley, but his trademark hat had been exchanged for a beat-up felt wide-brimmed affair which hid his face. The prospector ambled down the street, talking to his mule as he went.

Just at the edge of town waited a covered wagon which had stood in Pinyon Creek's livery stable ever since the height of the mining boom. Nobody remembered who had brought it into town, except that it was a family from Kansas looking for mining work.

Today it held two descendants of Gold Rush families. Joe Magnuson's great-great-grandfather had survived the terrible winter of the Donner Party, and Susannah Billington was the great-great-granddaughter of a woman rescued from Death Valley by William Manley, who walked 250 miles to bring food and help. As the covered wagon, drawn by two oxen, passed slowly down the street, volunteers passed out papers with their family stories. Susannah received the gourd from the old prospector and gave him a kiss on his cheek.

Just before the next town, the covered wagon stopped by the last of the borax wagons. The historic twenty-mule team was hitched up and waiting. Spence sat high in the seat, his swamper at his side. For Spence this too was his heart's desire, the one opportunity to drive the mules made famous by Remi Nadeau, the mules which had brought Spence to the valley. For the past three weeks he had practiced daily with the equipment, getting to know the mules, learning the jerk line, working with his partner, praying that the rickety old wagon would survive until the end of the pageant.

The wagon was so high that Susannah, leaning out of the covered wagon, could not reach the swamper's hand. Joe Magnuson steadied her as she climbed up onto the driver's bench, then stretched as high as she could, carefully passing the gourd into the swamper's hand.

Spence clicked his tongue, called "so, Bess, go mules, let's go." The lead mules leaned into their harness and they were in motion, bells jingling, harnesses rattling, sounds that had echoed across the desert floor a hundred years before. Small bags of borax crystals had been packed into the wagon. Boy Scouts tossed them to bystanders along the way.

All too soon, the wagon pulled up next to an old stage coach, the one which had delivered goods and mail to Cerro Gordo so long ago. The crowd waiting along the edge of the road watched the gourd being transferred to the hands of the driver, who then leaned down and pointed to a family in the crowd.

"Want a ride? Climb in!" he called, and, their young boys grinning in delight, they clambered in.

The younger boy received the gourd and held it carefully in his lap.

Just a mile farther, the last of the Southern Pacific narrow gauge trains stood, smoke puffing from its smokestack. The engineer blew its whistle as the stage coach approached, scaring the horses and almost causing a catastrophe as the boy almost lost his grip on the gourd.

But he successfully passed it to Governor Young, who was riding in the passenger car. The train rumbled off down the tracks of the old route, past the camps which had produced such a great harvest of silver and copper and gold. Five miles along the track, they stopped for the day. The train waited in place while the Governor, the engineer, and everybody else returned to Lone Pine for the giant parade and barbecue.

Tonight's parade included all of the people and vehicles involved in the passing of the gourd. At the end of the parade, Spence turned the mules over to his helper with some relief, and joined Molly and his father-in-law. The priest had resumed his trademark black hat, but the big brown prospector's hat could be seen on the seat of his roadster.

The barbecue was greatly appreciated and the music was lively. Couples danced in the middle of the street as bands alternated between square dance, waltzes and Mexican folk dances. Children and adults alike clambered over the wagons and the stage coach and stared respectfully at the six-foot-tall wheels of the borax wagon.

Molly and Velda had made pots of coffee and several pies, even though there was more food than the celebrants could possibly eat. "We felt we should do something, " Molly said, cutting large slices for Pershings and Richardsons. "You were out there in the middle of things. It was a wonder!"

Stuart and Spencer were exhausted, sunburned, ravenous and happy. They sat almost silent, enjoying the food and the sounds from outside. They returned to the front porch, exchanging comments with everybody who passed by.

Jeb Parmentier was rueful. "I know we should have filmed all of this. We missed a golden opportunity!"

"Everybody who was here will always remember it," Molly reassured him. "And those who weren't would never believe it!"

She cut more pie for Jeb and Father Crowley.

"You make a realistic prospector," she teased him. "Even your mule seemed to get into the mood of things."

"Where are your children?" the priest asked.

"Tony and Barbara took Len down to Death Valley for the finish. Alf and Sarah were here, but they're on their way down, too. They wouldn't miss the finish!"

346

On the final morning, cavalcades of cars drove the new road to the top of the Argus mountains. Before they could see it, they heard the train whistle as the Southern Pacific arrived. Joe Magnuson accepted the gourd from the engineer, then passed it to the Governor who sat in the back of a brand-new 1930 Cadillac convertible.

Then Joe, descendant of a family which had survived the terrible winter that trapped the Donner Party, shook hands with Susannah, descendant of a family which had survived the brutal desert summer lost in Death Valley. Together, they cut the banner across the highway and the Cadillac, now carrying the Governor, Joe, and Susannah, descended the new road into Death Valley.

On the desert playa, the crowd spotted a white passenger airplane. Charles Richardson, the pilot, accepted the gourd from the Governor, climbed into the cockpit, and, in the early afternoon, took off and circled, dipping his wings as though to acknowledge the cheers from below.

There was water in Bad Water, a still pool marking the lowest spot in the United States. Suddenly, the crowd became aware of drops of water spilling from the cockpit as the water of the glassy pond made small ripples. The water from the highest lake had entered the lowest lake and the wedding of the waters was complete.

By this time it was late afternoon. Boy Scouts from all over the Owens Valley had prepared signal fires of dried grasses and pinon pine kindling. They lit the first fire on the lowest sands when the water hit the surface of Bad Water. Then watchers saw a

347

second fire, from Dante's Peak in the hills at the edge of Death Valley. The next fire was spotted at the summit of Telescope Peak in the Panamint Valley. Boy Scouts at Cerro Gordo, the early mining center of Owens Valley, lit the next signal fire.

The people of Pinyon Creek caught sight of the Cerro Gordo signal fire and burst into applause. Finally they saw the signal fire from the top of Mount Whitney. The journey was complete.

Molly and Spence held hands. "I'm glad we're here," she said softly "I wouldn't leave the valley for anything. I know that now."

They looked over at Molly's father, in his rocking chair at the edge of the porch. Sound asleep, he snored once and muttered, "Good."